To Laurie ♡

Show Me Wonders

By Riley Nash

Riley Nash

"He smells like everything I've never had, and he feels like home…"

Copyright © 2022 by Riley Nash

All rights reserved.

The characters and events portrayed in this book, as well as the involvement of any existing institutions, agencies, publications, brands, or public figures, are entirely fictitious and have no basis in reality. Any similarity to real persons, living or dead, is coincidental and not intended by the author.

No portion of this book may be reproduced in any form without written permission from the publisher or author, except as permitted by U.S. copyright law.

The Subtle Art of Not Giving A Fuck is copyrighted 2016 by Mark Manson

ISBN-13 (e-book): 9781736082669
ISBN-13 (paperback) : 9781736082676

Cover design by Cormar Covers

To Jay
For providing an endless supply of sexy alien men,
trying to sneak them into my books,
and blessing me with your big brain feedback

Author's Note

Thank you so much for picking up *Show Me Wonders*! In this book, I wanted to bring awareness to an often misunderstood mental health condition and the reality of living with chronic disorders. The details are all drawn from real life, but please keep in mind that symptoms such as depression, anxiety, and panic attacks look different for everyone. Remember to be kind to yourself and others—there is no shame in asking for help, and offering support to a friend can make all the difference.

Content Warnings (potential spoilers)

A disaster situation (including emotional distress, claustrophobia, darkness, brief description of a vehicle accident, and brief mentions of blood and dead bodies), violence/blood, mental illness (agoraphobia, anxiety, panic, depression), mentions of attempted suicide and domestic abuse

Contents

Chapter 1	3
Chapter 2	13
Chapter 3	21
Chapter 4	31
Chapter 5	39
Chapter 6	52
Chapter 7	57
Chapter 8	66
Chapter 9	72
Chapter 10	80
Chapter 11	98
Chapter 12	108
Chapter 13	117
Chapter 14	129
Chapter 15	135

Chapter 16	146
Chapter 17	150
Chapter 18	160
Chapter 19	173
Chapter 20	184
Chapter 21	194
Chapter 22	202
Chapter 23	210
Chapter 24	222
Chapter 25	234
Chapter 26	244
Chapter 27	254
Chapter 28	269
Chapter 29	275
Chapter 30	287
Chapter 31	298
Chapter 32	303
Chapter 33	312
Chapter 34	323
About the Author	332

I

Oliver and Jackson

Don't cry.

Close your eyes and pretend I'm there, wiping the tears off your cheeks with my thumb. Pretend I kiss the tip of your nose until you smile.

I'll find you someday.

And on that day, I will show you the wonder of a world where we never have to say goodbye again.

Chapter 1

Oliver

I died this morning.

It happened so fast.

One minute, I'm riding the train to Syracuse to buy a car. I've been putting it off, but my partner, Kay, yelled at me this morning to get over myself and put my ass on the train before she locks me out of the house.

She's going to yell even louder when I come back with a used minivan instead of the Land Rover she wanted. But I'm not getting a car so she can show it off to her fucking Frappuccino-and-acrylic-manicure friends. I'm getting a car because I can't wait to be the dad who drives my daughter and her friends to dance practices and sleepovers while bumping Miley Cyrus or whatever music they listen to these days.

In a stroke of luck, I have an entire train car to myself. Late morning sun soothes the back of my neck, my seat rocking gently as I finish my third re-read of *The Subtle Art of Not Giving A Fuck*. Everyone says it works wonders, but I think I was born with way too many fucks, and I'll never get rid of them fast enough to hit zero. Obsessively scouring the book over and over for the page I must have overlooked is probably missing the point, but I can't help it.

The sunlight cuts off so abruptly it startles me, plunging us into the blue-black dusk of a tunnel. Brushing back my messy tousle of ginger hair, which desperately needs a trim, I tuck my glasses in the library reading program tote bag by my feet and rub my tired eyes.

I feel more than I hear the unspeakable thunder, like a thousand bombs going off at once. In a long, piercing shriek of metal on tearing metal, fragments of shattered glass peppering my skin like rain, my body flies forward and my face slams into the back of the seat in front of me.

It's a good thing I took my glasses off, I think very clearly and calmly. *Or else they might*

have gotten

broken.

In less than the space of my last breath, with the most pointless final thought in history, I'm gone.

And that's how I fell in love. How I lost it again. How my heart never stopped searching.

But I'm getting everything backward.

It's a long story.

First, my eyes open.

I'm not in heaven or hell or any other kind of afterlife—just absolute darkness. It presses against my skin and crawls down my throat, curling heavy in my lungs. Maybe the dead come here first, before their final destination. Maybe I'm supposed to confess everything I hoped for and never found, everything I should have done better. Everything I'm afraid to lose.

"I'mma hold a tarantula, Daddy. And a coco-roach." Megan *presses her tiny palms together and holds them out, grinning with that one gap in her front teeth where she insisted her classmate should kick her in the face because they were playing cowgirl-tames-wild-horse.*

The other girls in her preschool threw a fit when they found out the class field trip was visiting the bug and reptile museum instead of the petting zoo. Except my little wild thing, my fearless adventurer. She's talked about nothing but giant, hairy spiders and venomous snakes for weeks now.

But I didn't sign her permission slip this morning before I ran out the door. If I'm dead, they won't let her go. Her mom doesn't give a shit; she'll just throw it in the garbage. Megan will curl up in bed and sob into her dragon plushie for hours, waiting for me to come back and make it better, not understanding why I never will.

Hot tears burn my cheeks and sting the corners of my mouth; my lips taste of dirt and bitter salt and blood. I can't feel my body, but agony explodes behind my eyes whenever I move my head. The pain throbs in time to the pounding of my heart.

Oh, God.

My heart's still beating.

This is real.

And it's so fucking dark.

I can't think over the annoying noise that keeps getting louder until it fills the whole world.

It's me. I'm screaming.

I struggle and sob and scream my daughter's name until my voice gives out and I choke, gagging and retching around the dirt in my throat. No matter how hard I try, I can't force air into my lungs.

At last, my body takes pity on me and shuts itself off again.

When I wake up the second time, I feel something warm and alive moving against my cheek.

Flying *fuck* no.

Kay used to make me watch body horror movies with her; even when I hid my face in a pillow while she called me a pussy, I couldn't block out the sound effects. Now my brain goes straight to *eyeball-eating cave worm,* which is arguably worse than death, and I lash out into the darkness with a strangled shriek of terror.

My brand-new, olive green high-tops collide with a solid mass that yells almost as loudly as me, followed by the crunch of something falling into broken glass. Then…nothing. I'm hyperventilating, my breath sobbing in my chest, but I can hear it doubled. There's something in here with me. Something that breathes. *Do worms breathe?*

"P-p-please…" I'm shivering so hard I almost bite my tongue. "Please don't eat me." It's the actual dumbest thing I could say, but I'm not responsible for the words coming out of my mouth right now.

"That really fucking hurt," snarls a low, hard voice with a dangerous edge that reminds me there are other things to fear besides monsters. Something bulky scrapes across the floor, followed by a growl and the tinkle of falling glass shards. I hold my breath, my mouth coppery with the taste of blood, my chest hitching and aching.

When air brushes my cheek, I shrink back into the hard plastic of my seat. "I'm sorry. Please." I don't know what I'm begging for. I'm deeper in nightmares than I've ever gone before, and this time I can't wake up.

My exposed skin prickles in warning at the electric sense of someone else's body only inches away. I almost piss myself when rough fingers touch my shoulder, feel up my neck to the bristle of my short beard, then tighten around my jaw. Whimpering, I try to pull away. I never claimed to be tough.

"I thought you were dead." Piercing the fog in my pounding head, the voice starts to become less of a primal horror and more like me, hurting and confused and very human. He lets go of me and steps back, hissing in pain.

"What's wrong?" As my dad brain kicks in, the blind terror subsides a little. "I might have a Band-Aid in my bag." They've got cartoon firefighter dogs on them, but no one needs to know that. Fumbling around, I start the long, painful process of convincing my body that it should work properly and let me stand up. "Are you injured?"

"I wasn't until you kicked me into a pile of broken glass." There's something in the rumble of his voice that I optimistically choose to believe is humor. "But it's just a few scratches."

I've never hurt anything in my life; I have no idea how you're supposed to fix it. "I'm so sorry. As soon as we get out, we'll go right to the hospital and I'll pay all your bills." There goes my van fund. "I thought you were a worm," I explain.

After a nonplussed silence, he clears his throat. "I'm not."

"Which is good. One good thing." It's a game I play with Megan: when you're upset, think of one good thing. I play it with myself sometimes, when the reality of the life I'm trapped in starts to crush me. My one good thing is always her. Even here, even now.

Struggling to my feet, I grab the back of the seat in front of me and rest my forehead against it, trying to gulp in enough stale air to push back the tidal wave of panic looming in the distance. "I need my bag." Because somehow that will fix everything. "It has my wallet, my glasses, and my knitting." Debris crunches under my feet as I crouch down and crawl along the row of seats, feeling for the soft canvas.

"You won't find it," he declares flatly. "It could have gone anywhere."

"Help me look. Don't you have a phone?"

He huffs quietly, like that's ironic for some reason. "Don't you?"

"I forgot it on the counter next to the permission slip I was supposed to sign and the banana I was supposed to eat for breakfast. I'm not good at leaving the house, okay?"

"Stop crawling around. You'll gash your hand open." I hear him take a step closer.

"I'm serious. I can't read or knit without my glasses."

"Are you listening to yourself?" he growls, voice scraping painfully. He sounds bigger than me, angrier than me, and a hell of a lot more intimidating.

When I ignore him, a boot steps on my hand, pinning it to the cold floor. "Cut it out."

"*No*." I punch his solid calf, which accomplishes absolutely nothing. Even when I throw my whole shoulder against him, he doesn't budge an inch. I'm not some tiny twink, but the heaviest things I lift on a daily basis are a laptop and a mug of coffee.

I can hear my voice getting louder and more hysterical as the tiny amount of courage left in me fractures. "The glasses were new. Please. Kay will kill me if I lose them. And I was knitting a unicorn for my daughter's birthday, and I don't have enough gold yarn to start over, and..."

"Stop." A strong, unkind hand grabs the back of my neck, the hand of god knows who. This stranger could do anything to me in this void, with no one to hear me crying for help. Sparks flash behind my eyes as my headache flares up, and I jerk free. Scrabbling away through the filth and rocks until my back hits something solid, I pull my knees up and hug myself tightly, panting and shivering and nauseous.

He's quiet for so long I start to wonder if he just walked away. Maybe he was never here. Maybe I'm talking to imaginary friends as I bleed out alone under a pile of rubble. "How long have you been awake?" I whisper, waiting to see if he'll answer. It feels like a less scary question than *how long was I dead?*

Even though he freaks me out, I'm flooded with relief when he coughs. "Long enough to figure out that we're probably the only two survivors."

"Jesus." I press the heels of my hands into my dry eyes. "Jesus Christ. What the fuck happened? Where are we?"

The silence between our words sits impossibly heavy, absolute except for the occasional crumble of slipping rocks that sends chills up my spine.

"Still in the train tunnel." I can hear him taking cautious steps, exploring the area. "Pretty sure the mountain came down on us."

"That's impossible." The blood on my mouth seems to have come from my nose, so I do my best to wipe it away. I'm lucky my nose isn't shattered. I pull the collar of my sweater over my face and try to catch a whiff of Megan or laundry detergent or anything good and normal. "Accidents like that don't happen anymore; it's not the 1860s."

"Tell that to the million tons of rock on our heads." His footsteps stop right in front of me, and I yelp when something heavy falls into my lap. My fingers find cloth–the frayed edge where my mom's puppy chewed on the bag, the texture of the library design that Megan colored with fabric markers. I clutch it to my chest and slide my hand inside, burying my fingers in the soft yarn of Megan's unicorn.

"Thank you."

He doesn't answer, just groans softly as he lowers himself to sit next to me, his shoulder bumping mine. I almost start laughing when I catch a hint of his scent. It's the cool, edgy deodorant with wolves on the label that I sniffed at the grocery store for a long time before putting it back because I didn't think I could pull it off. It blends perfectly with what has to be his own smell, fear mixed with something earthy and wild, like rain in a lonely forest.

Neither of us speaks for a few minutes, struggling to catch our breaths. When his muscled forearm brushes mine, I can feel it slicked with sweat. His whole body's trembling a little.

"The car behind this one had an enclosed luggage area at the back. I think we should try to camp out there. It'll be warmer, and might protect us from falling rocks." Up close, I can't decide if he has a scary voice or not. Something about the low steadiness, the scratchy texture, sits comfortingly in my chest.

I imagine walking blindly into that darkness. There could be anything out there—a landslide, a pit, endless tunnels, hell itself. My hand finds the leg of the nearest train seat and squeezes it tightly. "I'm staying here. This car kept me safe, and the rescuers will know where to find me."

He makes an aggravated sound in his throat. "You just want to sit here for fuck knows how long, waiting?"

"Why not? They'll be here in less than twelve hours." *Please God or absolutely anyone else out there that might be listening.* "When you get lost hiking, you're supposed to stay in one place, not move."

"Does this look like a damn hike to you?" He scrambles to his feet. I've pissed him off again. Maybe I should care, but the pain has carved everything out of my skull except for a disoriented, stubborn urge to sit here, not moving, until the universe apologizes and puts itself right again. His shoe prods my thigh. "I'm leaving."

"Go ahead." I curl my body into a tighter ball, gripping the cold metal in my palm until it digs into my skin. "When the rescue crew comes, I'll tell them to search for you."

His clothes rustle as he crouches down in front of me, his knees bumping mine. Even without seeing him, I can *feel* his broad shoulders looming over me, his coiled, frustrated energy. "Listen to me," he murmurs, voice eerily calm. "How many life-or-death situations have you been in?"

Straightening my back, I fire off a fierce glare that's pointless in the dark. "Don't treat me like a child–"

I flinch and trail off when he leans in and rests his hands against the wall on either side of my head. His breath stirs in my hair. "Answer me."

"Zero."

"Then you have no right to make decisions here. You're nothing but a liability. You get that?" He pushes off the wall, sounding disgusted. "So you do what I tell you."

"How many have *you* been in?" For all I know, he's a fucking barista who spends his time making latte art.

He hooks a hand under my armpit and hauls me easily to my feet, pulling me after him as I struggle to keep a hold on my bag. "Let's go." His iron grip forces me one, two, three steps out into nothingness and my head starts to spin. Standing up that fast was a very bad idea. Pain pounds behind my eyes, and if I had remembered that banana this morning, I'd be puking it up right now.

"I think I'm going to faint." I can't actually tell if the words are coming out of my mouth right. When I take another step, my sense of gravity flips and my hip crashes hard into the earth. I struggle to get up on my hands and knees, disoriented and weak. Then I realize I'm alone. I can't feel his hand on my arm or hear his voice. Guess I was too much of a liability after all.

At last, I start crying for real, burying my head in my arms and sobbing as sharp bits of gravel dig into my skin. I'm not even clear-minded enough to cry for the right reasons, the part where I'm going to die horribly and never see my child again. This is just raw terror—a kid with monsters under the bed begging his mom to turn the light on.

Strong arms feel me out and slide underneath me, lifting me against a hard, warm chest. He hefts me a couple of times, trying to position me comfortably, then starts to walk in careful, shuffling steps. A massive surge of dizziness washes over me, so I rest my forehead against his shoulder, close my eyes, and stop trying to fight.

Chapter 2

JACKSON

I shouldn't fall asleep, but making it the forty feet or so to the luggage area in the next car is the most tiring thing I've ever done. It's not the dead weight after he passes out; his skinny body feels like nothing in my arms. It's this place. Where I grew up, you stayed vigilant all the time if you wanted to live. Your senses kept watch even when you slept. The blindness here has my alarm bells going off nonstop, and it's wearing me out.

The enclosed space in the car feels safe, even if it isn't. I clear the floor of rocks as best I can with one foot before laying him down and tucking his bag under his head. I don't know what to do next, so I stretch out next to him and rest my face in the crook of my elbow. When I feel myself drifting off, I throw my other arm across his body so I can't lose him. He's so useless I'm not even sure he's better than nothing, but I like hearing a voice that isn't coming from inside my own head.

Fingers twist my hair, forcing my head back. So many hands on me, vicious and hard, pinning me down. Someone pries my mouth open wide enough to take a thick, steel barrel. Even though it's way too late, I'm fighting with every muscle in my body, gagging and thrashing and squealing exactly the way they want. The metal cuts my tongue and fills my mouth with blood.

Somehow, that wasn't the worst day of my life. Neither is this. I think I'd rather die down here than be rescued and face what comes next. But look at me, still fighting to live. How about that? It's like a curse.

"Hey." A hand squeezes my shoulder. "Wake up." Normally, if someone grabbed me in my sleep, I'd have them on the ground by now, pinning their throat. But my body already knows his voice. Underneath the worn-down, raspy croak, it's soft and gentle. Like the eyes of the rabbits that the boys in the trailer park would pick off with air rifles, maiming more often than killing.

"What's wrong?" I sit up slow so we don't butt heads.

He laughs, or tries to, coughing painfully. "What *isn't* wrong?"

My eye roll is wasted on him, but it makes me feel better. "I meant why did you wake me up?" He's good at reminding me why I don't like people. Most of them are somehow stupider than me, and I barely finished middle school.

"Your breathing sounded like you were in pain." I can hear the real answer in his voice. He was scared shitless of being awake by himself.

"I'm fine. What about you? You were the one who tried to die on me."

"My head's stopped pounding, and I'm not dizzy anymore. I'm sorry, by the way." He huffs bitterly. "Everyone wants to know how they'd respond in a real emergency, right? Apparently, my answer is: be an idiot, cry, and pass out. So that's good to know."

"Hey." I bump my knuckles against his knee. "Don't get upset because you haven't almost died before."

The fabric of his jeans scuffs as he scoots a little closer. "I'm Oliver, by the way," he announces, like we're meeting at a party or in a bar. Like it matters. I turn it over in my head, *Oliver*, a posh, rich person kind of name. "I'm from Rome, New York, and I'm a writer. Well, I'm actually a copy editor, but I'm working on a novel." No one has ever tried to make casual small talk with me before, not like this. Because he can't see what I look like, my muscles and scars and ink. He can't look into my eyes and find the violence that grows all through me like thorny bindweed over cracked earth.

I realize he's waiting hopefully for me to speak. "Jackson."

When I don't elaborate, he shrugs it off. "Nice to meet you. Thank you for helping me stay alive." His voice gets sheepish. "I'm offering you a handshake."

Normally, I'd leave him hanging and walk away, but there's nowhere to go. Fumbling around in the dark, I find his long, slender fingers. "Shit," he exclaims. "Your hands are freezing." Before I know what he's doing, he traps my hands between his and rubs them together, holding them against the soft knit of his sweater and blowing until his breath warms my stiff, aching knuckles. Of course he's wearing a sweater. He's like a sweater personified.

"You really are a dad." I tug my hands away and tuck them into my armpits.

"What do you mean?" I can *feel* him staring at me. In my head, he has big blue puppy eyes.

"My mom is the only person to ever pull that kind of shit on me." I was five, coming in from the snow with no gloves. It's one of the best memories I have of her.

"Megan's turning six the day after tomorrow." Raw pain leaks into his voice, woven with a depth of love I've never even imagined. Kids where I'm from are mostly accidents that eat up what little money their parents have, where families scream and hit each other. I don't think this guy hits his kid. "She wanted a dragon-themed birthday party, so I found a guide online for making a castle cake with a Styrofoam and fondant dragon sitting on one of the towers. I was so fucking excited to see her face..." He clears his throat, voice thick with choked-back tears. "Sorry. You don't give a shit about six-year-old girls' birthday cakes."

He's right. But I can't stop thinking about it, how big the castle would be, what color he'd make the dragon. What the fuck *fondant* is. I got a chocolate birthday cake once, from my younger brother. It said *Happy Retirement* on top because he stole it from the day-after shelf at the supermarket. I never forgot that cake.

Oliver starts coughing again. I dig into my jacket pocket, searching for the crushed water bottle I saved to throw in the bin when I got off the train. Shaking it, I can hear half a mouthful of precious liquid sloshing around. "Drink this."

I wait patiently for his hands to find mine in the dark, plastic crinkling as they wrap around the bottle. They're still trembling a little.

"This is yours," he protests, sounding so worried for some reason, like I told him he should knock a kid over and run off with their backpack. He really is an idiot, but he's so damn earnest about everything. He makes the inside of my chest itch and my brain pull like a dog on a chain. "It wouldn't be fair for me to take it."

"When has anything ever been fair? I'm stuck in here with a weakling, so he gets the water."

"That's how it is now?" There's a faint smile in his voice. A moment later, I hear him swallow. I grit my teeth, trying to think about anything besides how the wet sound makes my dust-caked throat tighten and burn.

I'm not naive, but even I assumed we'd wake up to the sound of drills and heavy machinery. Instead it's silent, forgotten, like a tomb without a headstone. And I'm supposed to know what to do next. In the neighborhood church my family used to visit when they served free lunch, the pastor said something about Jesus being the only one who could get water from a stone. I'm sure as fuck not Jesus.

Oliver's hand finds my bicep. "I saved half for you." The dork sounds pleased about it.

Why are you this way?

I didn't mean to say it out loud, but he chuckles. "What way? Is basic decency not a thing where you come from?"

I just spit a mouthful of dirt onto the ground by my shoe and pour the last few drops of water down my tongue. Standing up, I take a few steps away and unzip my fly. After doing my best to un-crumple the water bottle, I feel out the opening and put the tip of my dick against it. When Oliver hears my piss spray the plastic, he goes quiet.

"Want a turn?"

His breath sounds unsteady. "We won't need to *drink pee*, Jackson. Right? They're going to get us out."

I cap the still-warm bottle and roll it across the floor to bump against his leg. "We'll look for food and water, but we might not find any."

"I don't need to pee," he lies, voice strained. "But where the hell can we find supplies underground?"

This isn't going to go over well, but he needs to toughen up sooner or later. "The other people on the train had bags with them, belongings we can search."

He groans softly, muffled by his hands over his face. "No, that's appalling. We can't."

I want to shake him. "They're fucking dead. Do you want to join them? They'll say *wow, thanks for saving that food I was never going to eat, shit-for-brains.*"

"Fuck you," he mumbles, sounding hurt but also like he knows I'm right. "That's a horrible thing to say."

"Maybe I'm a horrible person. But I'm also alive." He has no idea how many times I've looked death in the face while he was writing novels and knitting unicorns.

"Can we please wait a while longer?" His voice is smaller now, like he just realized that we're going to run out of hope around the same time we run out of water. The nightmares that lie beyond. "If we sleep a little more, I'll be stronger and we'll give rescue crews one more chance to find us."

I guess part of me doesn't want to go either, fumbling blindly through the dark, looting corpses. "Fine. A few more hours." Because apparently, I'm Disaster Survival Babysitter now. Sounds like one of the cartoon characters we watched while our parents were out getting wasted. Dora the Explorer's best friend. *Vamonos* let's go starve to death.

"Should we lay something on the ground?" Oliver asks tentatively. The temperature's already dropping to a damp, suffocating chill that seeps into my body. The guy barely weighs a thing; he's going to feel it twice as bad.

"We'll look for coats and blankets when we go scavenging, and maybe a lighter or matches to make a fire. For now, we need to conserve body heat."

He gives a little snort, like he's stifling a giggle.

"What now?"

"Sorry, it's just...the fucking romance trope. *I'm soooo cold. Here, let me hold you close. Oops, I kissed you. Let me put my dick where you can keep it warm.*"

When he's done, I leave him hanging in awkward silence for way too long. "Let it be known that I'm not the one making this weird."

The grin leaves his voice; I can picture him staring at his lap, fidgeting with his hands. "I apologize. I don't, uh, handle stress well, and to be honest I find leaving my own driveway stressful. But this isn't weird because I have a...well, I guess I have a partner. And you're not...*anyway.*"

I've never heard someone sound less sure that they're in a relationship. "I think you can be done talking now and I'll pretend this conversation didn't happen."

"Yeah. Thank you." He scoots closer, awkwardness pouring off of him in waves. "So how do we do this?"

"Just lie down."

His voice gets even quieter. "Okay."

Feeling out his profile, his shoulder and hip, I stretch out behind him on the scratchy train carpeting and hook an arm around his body, pulling his narrow shoulder blades against my chest. He's stiff at first, leaning away from me like he's scared I'll turn him gay. Maybe he'd feel better if he knew I didn't work that way, that I'm not straight or gay or bi or anything at all. That we could be naked and it still wouldn't do anything for me.

His muscles relax one by one as his breathing slows down. A few minutes later, his head drops back against my arm. He sleeps gently, just like he moves and talks. Curious, I let myself sniff his hair. He smells like things I'm only vaguely familiar with–tea and baked bread and houseplants–covered over by a more familiar sheen of sweat and fear. All this is mine to keep alive, so that his girl can have her dragon cake. It's a heavy weight.

Warmth pools between our bodies, the one comfortable sensation in this stagnant, dark pit. He's like a weighted blanket that breathes and fidgets and whimpers sometimes. My nose is freezing, so I close my eyes and tuck it into the nape of his neck.

I haven't slept for days; my body's eating itself alive with exhaustion. It's the first time in over a month I haven't had to watch my back. Maybe this is a sign, how pointless it is to keep running. Or maybe it's a gift, the one mercy I get for at least wanting to be a better person. A lonely, peaceful place to die.

Chapter 3

OLIVER

Without my phone, I have no idea what time or day it is when I crawl out from under Jackson's heavy arm and prop myself against the wall of the train car. We could have slept for thirty minutes or eight hours. Right before my eyes flew open, I heard drills and shouting, just about the cruelest dream I've ever had.

Pulling my tote bag closer, I put on my glasses out of habit and feel around for my knitting needles. The unicorn legs are too tricky to finish in the dark, so I just start row after row of mindless stitches. Maybe I can turn it into a scarf to help us stay warm. The soft click of the needles brings me back to sunny afternoons with Megan playing on the floor, or snowy evenings where I'd knit Christmas gifts while I recorded voice memos full of ideas for my book.

It's only when Jackson stirs that I realize I'm crying. Again. In apocalypse movies, survivors are only sad and pathetic for about an hour before they get all badass and start killing bandits with rusty lawnmower blades. Figures I'd be the exception. "Sorry," I mumble, wiping my eyes and holding my breath to keep down the last few sobs.

He doesn't say anything, but I hear him sit up and scoot across the floor until he's leaning against the wall next to me. The quiet stretches out as I wait for him to call me a weakling again. At last, he shifts to face me, his low voice close enough to my ear that it makes my spine tingle. "I have a question."

"Yeah?"

"How the fuck do you knit in the dark?"

A startled laugh bubbles out of me. "Oh! That's easy. I always knit while Megs and I watch *My Little Pony* and *Star Trek*, so I got used to not looking. I bet I could teach you."

"Yeah, right," he snorts. "Did my hands feel delicate to you?"

I remember wide palms, fingers that could probably crush mine if he wanted, and dry, battered knuckles. "Then I'll make you a sweater when we get out. Like mine."

"You made this?" He sounds like I told him I built the moon and hung it in the sky. His fingers explore the texture of the cable knit, rubbing the soft wool against my skin. "It feels like something you'd buy in a store where all the clothes cost a thousand dollars."

"Isn't it soft?" I know I'm gushing, but I can't stop myself. The tear-streaked dirt on my cheeks cracks as I smile. "I just about died when I picked up the yarn. But it's a good thing you can't see it; this was one of my first, so it's a giant mess. What's your favorite color?"

His hand goes still, wrapped around my shoulder, but he doesn't move it. "I don't have a favorite color."

"That's impossible."

Finally, he lets go. "I don't."

"In that case, I'll pick which color suits you best when I get a look at you. Based on your voice, I'm gonna say orange."

"You shouldn't make me a sweater."

"If we get through this, I'll make you a lifetime supply. Besides, everyone deserves something that's soft and something that smells good—those are basic human rights."

"Sure," he mumbles, standing abruptly and poking me with his shoe. "But for now, Princess, your knight in shining armor didn't come. So we're going scavenging." He sounds impatient rather than downright scornful, so I count that as a win.

I wait, shivering and trying to find my courage, while Jackson unlaces one of his shoes and knots the end of the lace around my wrist. "Now do mine."

I'm a knitter, not a sailor, so it takes me a few tries. The lace is flat; he must be wearing canvas sneakers like mine. I wonder what not-his-favorite-color he chose, but I don't ask. He tests the slack by tugging it a few times. "Now we can't get separated."

Part of me wishes we could hold hands, just to feel like I'm connected to something safe and alive. I don't want to sound pathetic, so I twine my fingers in the string and chew on my lip to keep the words in.

"Come here." He sounds different, like someone flipped a switch inside him. Calm, detached, focused. This must be the life-or-death Jackson. When I stop in front of him, he takes my shoulders and brings our foreheads so close they're almost touching. "I need you to listen to me. Yeah?"

Knowing he'll feel it, I nod. I want to see the look on his face right now, to pull strength from it.

"This might be scary, but you're going to stay calm and listen to everything I tell you. Don't think too much about what we're doing. You can freak out later if you want, but not when we're trying to be efficient and safe in a dangerous spot. Can you do that?"

Clearing my throat hurts; I'm so fucking thirsty. "Yes. Believe it or not, I am a grown adult who keeps a tiny human alive every day."

One of his hands comes up and pats the side of my face. "Good. Show me, then." He says it like a challenge, letting go and walking away into the void before I can have second thoughts. I stumble after him as best I can, trying not to trip and wondering how he's walking so fast.

"The side of this car broke open," he explains, stopping to feel for my hand and pressing it against cold, scarred metal. "So we can just walk out and along the train. I think we should try to reach the car in front of the one where I found you, see what kind of shape it's in. Keep one hand on the train and trace my path."

Walking with my eyes closed scares my body less than having them open, so I screw them tightly shut and follow the sound of his rubber soles scraping through debris. After what feels like an hour but is probably only a few minutes, he stops. I can hear his hands scraping over something as the lace around my wrist tugs lightly.

"I think this one's half crushed." He sighs. "We'll have to climb to get in. I can either leave you here or you can come with me."

"Wait." I recoil as far as the shoelace will let me. "What if we can't get back out?"

"We'll camp inside."

"With the *bodies*?" My head's starting to hurt again.

"Look, Oliver." He sounds frustrated, but less like he wishes I'd get lost and never come back. "There are a lot of things we can fight—hunger, cold. Dehydration? Not one of those things.

No water, we're dead. One hundred percent, no take-backs, dead. Think about your kid, right?"

When I'm big, Daddy, can we have a hundred pet snakes and live in a castle and be bestest friends king and queen forever?

"Okay," I whisper. "Let's go."

"It's rough, so I'm gonna help you up." He unties the shoelace between us, then wraps his hands around my waist from behind like we're going to do one of those ballet lifts. "Trust me."

"I don't know a single thing about you."

He huffs a quiet laugh. "Took you this long to realize?"

Grunting, he hoists me easily as I fumble for handholds, scrambling with no grace at all up a pile of rubble. Every time I slip he's right behind me, steady and silent, supporting my feet until we reach the top and clamber down into what has to be the inside of the car. The air feels closer here, with an unnatural smell. I shut my brain off and breathe through my mouth, concentrating on Jackson's presence next to me. His fingers find mine and squeeze.

"You're doing good. Just hang with me while I check the seats." He sounds so casual, like he's looking for a lost pair of sunglasses. I can't imagine what the hell this man has been through to make him this unconcerned around death. "Don't move from this spot. This place doesn't feel safe."

After a few minutes, his thumps and clatters turn into careful rustling. "Did you find something?"

"Do you really want to know?"

"Fuck." I shove my dirty hair off my forehead. "No."

"Hold this." He comes back to drop something heavy and synthetic in my arms–a backpack–and starts rifling through it by feel. Something clicks, followed by a sharp, clean smell. "There's a pack of wet wipes? And a hoodie. Small, but you might fit in it."

I bite the inside of my cheek until I taste blood. If I complain about wearing dead people's clothes, he'll probably leave me here. We empty the backpack of anything except the essentials, then hang it over my shoulder before moving on.

Jackson goes in front again, trying to feel out a path through the rubble blocking our way. "I think we'll have to climb up and squeeze between these boulders." He hesitates. "Can you? You could wait here, but I'm not sure I'll be able to get back the same way."

At the thought of waiting here alone for someone who's never coming back, I find his wrist and wrap it in a bruising grip. "Why do we have to go this way if it's dangerous?"

His fingers pry mine off his wrist, but he doesn't let go of them. "Because the only water in this place might be on the other side of those rocks. We don't have many other places to look."

I swallow, my throat tight. "I'll come with you."

"Good." He sounds proud of me, which is a pathetically small consolation, but better than none at all. "I'll go first this time."

Keeping a hold on my hand, he starts climbing the debris. As I do my best to follow him, something shifts abruptly under my feet and I have to bite back a cry as my ankle almost twists. Jackson steadies me, then squeezes through the gap first, the warmth of his skin leaving mine as he disappears. He struggles a little, breathing hard, and I can hear the rocks tearing at his clothes as he pushes his way through. I groan quietly, trying to keep my heart rate under control as my chest feels like it's collapsing.

"Pass me the backpack," he orders, and I toss it blindly toward his voice. "You're smaller, so you'll be fine. You don't have claustrophobia, right?"

"What a fucking time to ask." Closing my eyes again, I inch forward, the rough, unyielding swell of the boulders getting closer together until I'm forcing my way between them. Just when my mind starts to go blank and my limbs get heavy, he calls out again.

"You're not scared of anything, right? You're some kind of Super Dad. Pretend there's a dirty diaper over here or whatever the hell parents do."

I cough a terrified laugh. "Fuck you. My kid is probably better toilet trained than you are."

And by the time the last word leaves my mouth, he manages to reach me and pull me out the other side, where the air feels fresher and more open. As I stumble and fall into him, he lifts me bodily off the slippery rocks and onto flat ground, holding on to me until he's sure I won't collapse. "Look at you, Super Dad." He's probably just patronizing me, but I can hear in his voice that he's smiling.

I'm surprised to realize I am, too. "You're an asshole." My stomach turns when I catch a hint of that smell and remember where we are. "Are we going to have to do that again?"

"I hope not. This half seems more intact, so there should be windows on the sides we can climb out."

Jamming my hands in my pockets and rocking from one foot to the other to try and stay warm, I wait for him to finish the last few seats. That hoodie is sounding better and better. He collects more coats and sweatshirts, until our bag is bulging. "Thank fuck," he croaks finally. Scrambling over to me, he presses what feels like a half-full metal bottle into my hand. "Lucky you; we'll save the piss for tomorrow. Just take a little bit."

I groan as the first mouthful of warm water washes down my parched throat. It's so hard to stop, but after a couple more sips I hand it over. "Here," I pant, wiping water from my lips and sucking it off my palm while he drinks.

"God, that's good." His voice feels different after the water, still dark and a little rough, but warmer and quieter. I wonder how I sound to him.

He drops the bottle and something crinkly into my backpack. "I found, like, two peanut butter crackers. We should look for another car and see if it has more food and a lighter."

My back and belly feel scraped by the rocks, and my legs keep trying to give out. I'm not sure I can take much more of this today—groping through a pitch-dark no man's land where one wrong turn could trap you forever, surrounded by death, every step taking us further from the few square feet of ground that are starting to feel like home. "I'm not very hungry," I lie. "I ate a huge meal before I got on the train."

"Yeah, right. I just picked you up a few minutes ago." I twitch when his hands find my waist again, his thumbs pressing against my flat belly. His fingers are embarrassingly close to reaching all the way around. "You don't have any fat to burn."

I push my useless glasses up and rub my dry, aching eyes. "Can we please just eat the damn crackers and drink the water and try again later? I'm doing my best, but I need a minute."

Jackson

He's trying to sound brave, but he's done-done. I can hear it in his voice. Not the kind of done where you can push someone past their limits; the kind where he's about to break. Fear's a hell of a drug when you aren't used to it.

I squeeze his scrawny waist one more time and let go. "Yeah, let's take a break; you made it further than I thought you would. Give me a cracker."

Laughing weakly, he digs the package out of the backpack and drops a single cracker into my palm, the smell of peanut-butter hitting my nose and making my stomach growl. I throw it in my mouth whole and crunch loudly. "Fuck yes. I lived on these things growing up."

"Me too. I'd steal extras to take in my lunch and sell them to my friends in exchange for fruit roll-ups and M&Ms. The teachers called us the snack mafia."

That might be the dorkiest thing I've ever heard, like he thinks he was some kind of little gangster. He's so fucking innocent.

I felt a broken window next to the last row of seats, so I lead Oliver over to it. "Let's throw the hoodie over the sharp edge and hop out. Be careful." I don't trust that pile of rubble to take our weight again, not when one slip of those boulders would turn whoever was between them into paste.

Once we've lined the broken window with fleece, I practically throw him out and climb after him. As I swing my back leg over the edge, a vault like I've done a hundred times, the hoodie slips under my hand and sends my forearm straight into the ragged shards of glass. My vision goes white for a second as my feet hit the ground and I stagger, swallowing my gasp of pain.

"Jackson?"

It's just a cut. It has to be.

"I'm fine." I quickly grab the treacherous hoodie and press it hard between my chest and the wound to stop the bleeding. The rush of pumping blood thrums in my ears. I'm practiced at stitching myself up, but I don't think Oliver's knitting needles and yarn are going to do the trick. "Let's go."

Our footsteps echo dully as we retrace our path. I have no idea what's out there, but my gut tells me that if we leave the guiding structure of the train, we'll find nothing but death. Oliver scuttles into our enclosed space and starts laying out jackets on the floor to make a soft bed, like a mouse building a nest. "Can I sleep some more?" he asks in a small, drained voice. "It passes the time, and the thirst goes away for a bit."

The hoodie sticks to my arm when I try to pull it away, so I wrap it back up and try to pretend everything's fine. There's a deeper, stabbing pain when I move my arm that scares me. I keep flexing my fingers to make sure I still can. "Yeah, let's sleep."

It feels more natural this time; I lie down on my side with my head on the empty backpack, and he silently fits his body into the shape of mine while I make sure he doesn't touch my bloody arm. He's shaking, curled into a ball. I don't know if it's cold or shock, but he relaxes a little when I wrap my good arm around his chest. "You're okay," I say into his ear without thinking, tangled in memories of comforting my little brother when he was very small. "Everything's good."

It's always been a lie, but sometimes the truth does more harm.

As he dozes off, I catch myself rubbing the fleecy strands of his sweater again. I've never felt anything so soft in my life.

Everyone deserves something that's soft and something that smells good—those are basic human rights.

I curl my fingers into the yarn and put my nose in the short hairs behind his ear to taste his scent one more time, so unfamiliar and warm. It's how I used to imagine the houses in TV shows would smell, the ones with happy kids and family dinners. Then I force myself to pull away for good, before my skin or my breath or the things my hands have done somehow manage to taint something as pure as him.

Chapter 4

Oliver

The best nights are the ones where Kay disappears to spend the weekend with her latest affair or take a girls' trip. Megan and I camp out in the master bed with huge buckets of popcorn and watch cartoons on my laptop. She passes out next to me, her blonde hair tumbled all over the pillow and sticking up with static. If she has a bad dream, her whimpering wakes me up and I cuddle her close, making her dragon plushie kiss her cheek and nibble her nose until she giggles.

I can hear her crying, but I can't find the dragon. Rolling over, I reach for the warm body next to mine and find only damp ground. She's gone.

I jerk upright, gasping for breath and fumbling for something to hold on to, trapped in a sensation of falling.

It feels like the darkness gets heavier every time I wake up, pressing down on my chest.

The soft, scared whine comes again—it's not a dream. "Jackson?"

"Christ. Fuck." His breath catches raggedly in his throat and he groans. "Go back to sleep."

Still disoriented, I struggle to my hands and knees and crawl toward his voice. He shivers when I finally catch a handful of his flannel shirt. "What's wrong?" He smells faintly of blood, and my empty stomach churns.

"I cut my arm on the train window," he mumbles. "It won't stop hurting." Something tells me that Jackson's version of *it hurts* would have most people helpless and crying on the floor.

"Do you think there's glass buried in it?"

He blows out a slow, shaky breath.

I've had so much experience trying to do first aid on an incoherent toddler that I feel strangely calm now. "We need to get it out."

"In the dark?"

"I can help. I have smaller hands, and they're steady. All that knitting."

Rolling his head back, he lets out a wretched laugh. "You've got to be fucking kidding me."

"Hey." I kneel in front of him, imagining his scared eyes looking back. "I'm not some hardcore survivalist Rambo, but I raised a kid from birth by myself, with no idea what I was doing. I know how to step up and do what needs to be done."

"I thought you had a girlfriend."

Ignoring him, I push his shoulder. "Sit back against the wall and give me your arm."

He takes my wrist in his unhurt hand and lays his forearm across my palm. I can feel tense muscle, hair, those thick veins strong guys get in their arms—and sticky blood. When I search for the edge of the cut, he catches his breath and jerks, his knee bumping my hip.

"I'm sorry. I don't know how to make this not hurt." I hope he can't hear how fast my heart's beating.

"Just fucking hurry up," he croaks.

The one benefit to being trapped in a pitch-black death cave is that I can squeeze my eyes shut like a coward during an important medical procedure and it doesn't make any difference. I force my brain into a memory, the time Megan fell off her tricycle and came to me with gravel embedded in the scrape on her knee. That's all it is. Jackson's breathing so fast I can feel it stirring my hair. "Definitely some glass," I hum soothingly as I work, trying to distract him. "Two pieces, I think. Deep in there. After I get them out, we'll wrap this up nice and tight, and we can try again tomorrow if it doesn't—"

He groans thickly and drops his sweaty forehead against my shoulder. "Shut up and *do* it." His whole body stiffens and goes very still when I pull out the first shard.

"Almost there." I rub my ear against his tangled, chin-length hair. "Good job. The second one's deeper."

I get the last extraction over with in one quick movement and he gives a soft, gasping sob into my neck.

"I'm done. It's done." I drop the glass, grab the sleeve of one of the spare sweatshirts, and press it hard to the heavily bleeding wound. "Hold it down. You absolutely need stitches, but all we can do is tie it tight." Feeling around, I tear a few strips from the hem of the jacket and use them to wrap his forearm with as much pressure as I can manage.

"I take it back," he murmurs, a faint smile in his unsteady voice. "You're only mostly a weakling."

"I'm going to interpret that as a *thank you*." I wipe my hands off on my jeans over and over, wishing desperately for a sink and some soap. "Woah there, where are you going?"

Jackson tries to stand up, batting me away. "I'm hungry. I should look for more—oh God." He grabs my shoulder and drops back to the floor. "I don't feel so great."

"No shit." Hanging one of the spare jackets around my shoulders and hugging it close, I prop my back on the wall and stretch out. "Lie down and put your head on my leg for a bit. It's better than an empty backpack."

He growls irritably and rubs his hand over his face. "No more fucking sleeping. All there is to do here is sleep." But eventually, I feel a weight settle against my thigh.

He's right—I'm wide awake now. But I can't stand just waiting for the sounds of a rescue that isn't coming, feeling every second crawl past even as we lose all concept of time. "Jackson?"

He grunts.

"Have you ever tried a roleplaying game?"

"Uh..." He's silent for a moment. "Like when the girl dresses up as a slutty nurse and gives the guy a prostate exam? I'm good, thanks."

I cough out a dry laugh. "No, idiot. You make up a character who goes on adventures in a fantasy world. You play out what you want him to do and what enemies you want him to fight, and roll dice to see who wins." Before Kay, back when I had a life, I played every week with my friends. Sometimes I still get out the adventure guidebooks and read them to Megan like bedtime stories while she gallops my animal miniatures around the bed.

"That's the dumbest fucking thing I've ever heard," he grumbles. So much for discovering that he's a secret nerd.

"So you'd rather sit here in silence?"

"Jesus." He shifts his weight irritably. I can't imagine how much pain he's still in. "Whatever. Do it."

"First, you need a character."

Groaning, he throws his unhurt arm over his eyes. "I don't care. He's just a dude with a sword or whatever. Not some shitty fairy that farts magic."

Deciding not to push my luck by asking for a backstory, I default to the most stereotypical opening possible. "You wake up in a prison cell with no memory of how you got there. What do you do?"

Jackson sits up so fast it scares me, his face close to mine. "No."

"No?"

His voice drops to a growl. "He didn't fucking do anything. He didn't even exist until two seconds ago. You can't just put him in jail for the hell of it."

"Okay, okay. Lie down. Where do you want him to wake up?"

"This is so stupid," he grouses as he settles back against my leg.

Folding my hands behind my head, I look up at where the sky should be. "If you fell asleep and woke up right now, where would you want to be?"

"Under a naked woman?" I barely know the guy and even I can hear how forced the joke sounds, like a lie that he's told so many times it's falling apart. When I don't rise to the bait, he rolls onto his side, facing away from me, and starts playing with the shredded hem of my jeans, rolling the torn threads around his fingers. "Somewhere outside. Somewhere green."

Impulsively, I find his shoulder and work my thumb into it, massaging the tight muscles. He lets out a soft sigh and rolls his shoulder into my hand, stretching his neck. "You wake up under a summer oak tree outside the city of Garria." I pull random shit from all the different RPG books I've read and throw it together; it's not like he'll know the difference. "What do you do first?"

He snorts and slaps my sneaker. "Why is this so much fucking work? What do you mean, what do I do?"

As a father, I'm a pro at ignoring tantrums. "You tell me what your character does," I reiterate patiently, "and I tell you what happens. Did you not watch *Sesame Street*? Do you not know what an imagination is?"

"You know what?" He rolls back over to face me, and I can picture the stubborn set of his mouth. "Maybe it's hard to imagine fantasy stories when you're listening to your parents throw bottles at each other on the other side of a cardboard wall you taped together because your room is a mattress in the corner."

Everything's quiet for a minute. I stare in the direction of his voice, trying to figure out if the knot in my chest is a generic dad response to a suffering child or something to do with *him* and the lostness in his words, the way they break around the edges.

"Forget it," he says more quietly, sounding pissed at himself. "How do I know what stuff I can do?"

"You can do anything you want."

Rolling onto his stomach, he gives a pained laugh. "You're killing me." His forehead comes to rest against my knee. "Here we go: I grab the magic wand of Dickface the Wizard and cast a spell that makes everyone leave me the fuck alone. Then I go back to sleep. The End."

I grin into the dark. I've played *Dungeons & Dragons* with horny, drunk college students and hyper six-year-olds. Nothing he can do will throw me off. "Unfortunately, the wand of Dickface the Wizard is stored in the Tower of Shadows."

His fidgeting stills. "The what?"

"Twenty years ago, the villagers saw the queen of Garria wandering the forest at night, covered in blood. Everyone believed that she was transforming into the monstrous wolf that stole children from their beds under the full moon. So the king had a tall tower built with no windows and locked her inside. No one has seen her since. They say that, instead of living men, the tower is guarded by prowling shadows."

He props up on his elbow, and I can feel his eyes on me. "Why is the wand there?"

"Because Dickface and the queen were very close. There are even rumors that the royal princes are fathered not by the king, but by the wizard."

"How would they know?"

"Because they have dicks on their faces."

For the first time since I met him, he cracks up for real, his shoulders shaking as he drops his head back against my leg. It's a throaty, handsome laugh; I'm pretty sure he's attractive. Objectively.

"Okay, smart-ass, I'll bite. How do I get in the fucking tower?"

"I suppose you could sneak around the palace grounds, or ask the townspeople for advice, or get an audience with the king."

"Where's Dickface? Won't he help me?"

"You think he'll give you his wand so you can banish him?"

He scoffs. "Is there someone in town who wants Dickface gone? I'll team up with them."

I rub the back of his neck, beaming with pride. "That's a great idea."

The nameless hero chats with a blacksmith whose wife ran away with Dickface a few years ago. Jackson sounds like he's going to bail when I start doing voices for the characters, but he's a captive audience. Since we don't have dice, I make him guess numbers between one and twenty and give him results based on how close he gets. I haven't relaxed and goofed off with someone like this in so long, since my life became the four walls of a lonely house where I stay because I would give up anyone and anything if it meant keeping my daughter.

Through a string of near-perfect guesses, Jackson's character finds himself halfway through a stealth mission to infiltrate the tower, knocking out shadow guards right and left. I notice he's taking longer and longer to answer, his weight getting heavier. His face is buried against my calf, his good hand wrapped around my sneaker like human touch is the one thing keeping him sane. When he stops grunting responses and starts snoring faintly, I sit as still as I can until my ass and legs have gone numb. He needs all the rest he can get to heal.

Alone in the quiet, intrusive thoughts start clawing at the door to my mind—*I need my daughter, where is she, I'll never see her again*—so I shut Megan out of my head and focus on fleshing out the details of Jackson's nameless knight. He's not an adventurer, just a pissed-off guy with a sword who addresses the shop owners as "man" and "dude" and says "fuck" every other word. A guy who doesn't want to be here and most certainly doesn't want to be a hero.

Chapter 5

JACKSON

I have a lot of practice guessing the passage of time without seeing the sun. It's harder down here, but my gut says around sixty hours. For all that he's a dramatic little son of a bitch, Oliver's right: taking this long to dig out survivors of a high-profile disaster seems unheard of. Maybe they don't know we're here. Maybe the whole world exploded.

With nothing but half a bottle of water and some coats, we're not prepared in any way for long-term survival. Oliver won't stop shivering, and I can't think straight, my arm in agony without painkillers. I've been preparing for death every day of my life, but his frantic will to live infects me. I've never met his kid, and I never will, but I want to bring him back to her for the sake of the people I tried to protect and couldn't.

I'm starting to welcome the bad dreams now, because at least in them I'm not hungry. At least I can fight and run and hate. At least I can fucking see.

At some point in the night, I must have rolled onto my back. Oliver's still sleeping, his face resting in my armpit and his arm thrown over my stomach. I've never touched another human like this, calm and gentle, feeling their heart beat steadily against my ribs. When I stir, something hard rubs my thigh and I realize his dick is up, tenting the front of his jeans.

It happens to everyone. Even guys with girlfriends. Even me, sometimes. Now that it's pressed against my leg, I can't move without waking him up and listening to him babble apologies while I try to imagine what his blush looks like. At last he stirs, moving his hips away. His fist curls around a handful of my flannel, and his tousled, spring-scented hair brushes my neck. I'm pretty sure this is worse, that I'd rather be humped all night, because fucking means nothing while trust is something rare and real that I should never be given.

The next time I wake up, he's not there—not in front of me or behind me or anywhere in the luggage compartment. His body heat has evaporated. My mind goes blank except for the craziest, most terrifying thought, the split second where I question if he ever existed at all. "Oliver?"

When he doesn't answer, I say his name louder, then yell it, my voice cracking. Nothing. Cradling my arm to my chest, I stumble out of the train and stand there swaying weakly in the dark, listening.

He was never real. I pieced him together from the happiest, most untouchable things—parents that hug their kids, family vacations, living somewhere clean and safe.

I want to start running when I hear the rattle of tumbling stones, but that's the quickest way to break my legs. Instead, I walk as fast as I can, keeping my arm out and testing each step. "Oliver?" He doesn't answer, but I can hear panting and more falling rocks, like he's digging. "Stop it." I trip over his crouching form and almost fall. "Seriously, stop. You're going to cause a landslide."

When I touch his arm, he shrugs me off. Whatever he does next causes another shower of stones close by. Grabbing his thin shoulders, I drag him kicking and struggling away from the rocks. "The fuck is wrong with you?"

He catches me by complete surprise when he spins around and shoves me hard, shooting pain through my arm. "What's wrong with *you*?" he cries, his ragged voice sending dampened echoes around the space. "How can you be so calm about this? Do you not have anything to live for?"

I take a step closer. "Not really."

"Then get the fuck off me."

One more step, my body ready for a fight. "What the hell's gotten into you?"

His frantic words start to tremble and fracture. "It's her birthday today. Or maybe I already missed it. I can't just *sit* here. If I die knowing I didn't do everything I could to get back to her, then I don't deserve to be her dad." He throws himself back on the rocks, and this time I can hear shifting and crumbling from deeper in the mass of boulders.

I see red. Before I know what I'm doing I've picked him up and practically thrown him against the wall. When he tries to tackle me, I hit him. It's just a quick backhand, maybe five percent of my full strength, but he yelps and I regret it instantly. I've been in so many fights that I can't control my instincts when someone comes at me.

"I'm sorry." Gripping his chin, I put my forehead against his. "Can you hear me? Huh? You never walk away from me in here again. You could have killed us."

He twists helplessly underneath me. "For the rest of her life, she'll think I abandoned her with that fucking woman." A shudder racks his body, and I can feel the will to fight draining out of him. "This is all my fault," he whimpers. "I hate myself."

"You're the most extra person I've ever met." Brushing his hair roughly back from his forehead, I let go of him and step away to give him space.

He doesn't laugh; his voice sounds crushed as he slides down the wall and puts his head in his arms. "My whole life I've let people fuck me over and just apologized that I couldn't do more. I made every single choice that led me to this moment. And now here I am."

"It's called surviving." Sighing, I sit down cross-legged in front of him. "You roll over and show your belly to the people who can hurt you, so that you can build the strength to wipe them out later." That gets a weak chuckle out of him. After a long silence, I slide my shoe along the floor until it bumps the toe of his sneaker. "What fucking woman?"

His foot shifts to press harder against mine. "Seven years ago, so my early twenties I guess, I went on a couple of dates with this woman, Kay. When she found out my parents were loaded, she lied about being on birth control. She was careful to announce her pregnancy in front of them, so that they'd get all excited and pressure me to give the relationship a chance. She turns on the charm when they're around, and I think they love her more than they ever liked me."

"Shit." It sounds like a bunch of pointless rich person drama, but I can hear in his voice how much it hurts him. I'm not the only one trapped in a life they didn't choose.

"I tried to make it work for a little, but she hates being a mom and she doesn't give a shit about Megan. I can't forgive her for that. All I want to do is take my kid and go live somewhere quiet and peaceful, but she won't give up the money. She says if I ever try to leave, she'll take custody of Megan and never let me see her again."

"She's bullshitting you."

He snorts. "Would you take that risk? If I'm not there to protect my daughter, I'm scared Kay's going to find a way to abandon her in foster care." His voice trails off at the end of the sentence, and I can hear him trying to control his breathing.

"We might make it, Oliver." I scoot closer and rest my elbow on his knee. "But we're guaranteed to die if you knock the ceiling down on us."

"I know," he whispers. "I'm sorry. I just wish I could hear her voice one more time. Say happy birthday."

OLIVER

Jackson's silent for a minute, then I hear him stand up. "Come on. Let's go take a bath."

"Huh?"

He finds my elbow and helps me to my feet. "You're dirty; your hands are probably all cut up. This will help you feel better."

Bewildered, I trail after him. I'm terrified that I've gotten us permanently lost, but Jackson must have been a mountain man tracker in another life, because he takes us straight back to our safe space.

"Take off your shirt," he orders when we arrive, digging around in our backpack.

Slowly, not sure what else to do, I peel my sweater over my head. It's not so soft now, filthy and bloodied, and I'm pretty sure a stain stick won't salvage it. Jackson's clothes rustle, then the sharp, lemony scent of wet wipes fills the space.

Instead of handing me a wipe, he scruffs me with one businesslike hand and starts cleaning me himself, swiping cold, stinging circles over my chest and stomach. I hang my head and let him take over as he lifts one arm and then the other, scrubbing underneath them, then cleans thoroughly across my shoulders and back. "There." He drops one of the damp cloths into my palm. "Wipe your ass and junk, too."

Sliding the wipe into my briefs, I listen to him quickly bathing himself. "You've given a kid baths before, haven't you? I can tell."

"Sure." I hear his jeans unzip. "It's not the same as being a dad, but I took care of my siblings growing up. We were all each other had." He gives my sweater back. "Put that on. I don't want you to get cold." When I'm done, he places a bundle of soft flannel into my hands, the same shirt I've felt him wearing. "That too."

I should argue and give it back, but it's warm with body heat and every primal part of me wants to be surrounded by the smell of the only thing in this place that's keeping me safe. The sleeves hang down over my hands when I slip it on, so I focus on folding them up. "I'm sorry I fought with you."

He sighs. "I'm sorry I hit you. I mean it."

My cheekbone still hurts a little. "You needed to snap me out of it. I forgive you."

"Now let me see your hands. I bet you hurt them on the rocks."

Crouching down, he brackets my knees with his and turns my hands palm up in the air between us. This close, I can sense everything about him—his breathing, his pulse, the earthy tang of his sweat. He cups one of my hands in his bigger one and starts gently wiping them down, pausing when I hiss in pain at the sting of the wipe burning in all the tiny cuts on my skin. "Think about something else until I'm done."

The next words have been waiting on the tip of my tongue for days. "What do you look like?"

He thinks about it as he pushes apart each of my fingers and cleans between them. "I dunno. Nothing special. What about you?"

I bite my lip, trying not to smile. "I'm incredibly hot. Who's your celebrity crush? I look like that."

His quiet huff of laughter stirs my hair. "I don't have one."

"Wait, really? No one? What about ScarJo? Everyone has a crush on her, regardless of gender preference."

"Never heard of her."

I sneak one of my hands free to prod him in the ribs. "Are you kidding me?"

"I..." He trails off, then tries again. "I don't think my brain works like everyone else's. The people that everyone says are hot don't do anything for me. I think that I could want someone who had a good personality, but I've never met any good people, so what do I know?"

"Oh." That rings a bell from my gender and sexuality course in college, but I'm not sure Jackson's ready to have me start throwing five-syllable labels at him. "I didn't mean to give you a hard time."

It startles me when his fingers ruffle through my curls. "So we've established that you look like whoever ScarJo is. What color is your hair?"

"My mom calls it ginger-blond. You?"

Finishing his careful cleaning of my other hand, he squeezes my wrist but doesn't let go. "Regular blond, I guess. It gets darker every year."

"In my head, you look like a bad boy. Do you have piercings?"

"Tongue." That one simple word, the image of a steel bar in his mouth, makes my dick twitch. No guy has ever done that to me before. I shift my weight uneasily, trying to think about something else. "Any ink?"

"Uh-huh."

"Where?"

"Pretty much everywhere." I hear him scoot back to sit against the wall. "Come here. It's freezing."

I don't know if it's my idea or his or both of us at once, but he silently slides his legs apart and I crawl between them and lie down with my back against his firm chest, where I can feel his exhausted heartbeat. Just like when we're sleeping, I sink into that gentle back-and-forth of heat passing between our bodies, the most comforting thing in this nightmare place. I nudge him, smiling. "You're not getting out of telling me all about these tattoos."

He blows a breath out through pursed lips. "Two full sleeves, my chest, and my back."

"Shit. What are they?"

His shoulder jostles my head when he chuckles. "All of them?"

"What about here?" Pulling his unhurt arm away from my chest, I touch the inside of his wrist, the pulse and tendons.

"I have a chain and barbed-wire bracelet around my wrist. What?" he demands when I snicker.

"That's really emo."

"Shut the fuck up." His other hand wraps around mine and slides my fingers higher. "Then there's my brother's name, *Scout*. Above that–" he pushes my hand to the soft skin on the inside of his elbow, "–are some plain black bands." The sleeve of his t-shirt bunches up as my fingers slide underneath it. "And a deer skull wrapped up in some roses. A bunch of stereotypical shit."

"What's on your back?"

"It's blacked out." An edge creeps into his voice.

Letting go of his arm, I face forward and tuck my chilly hands into my armpits. "The whole thing? Wait, like..." I've seen TV shows where someone with gang insignias had to cover them up when they got out. I trail off, not sure how to continue.

"Yeah. Exactly like that," he says flatly. "And that's why it doesn't matter if I get out of here or not, Oliver. I'm pretty much done."

I sit up, half turning around. "You're not. No one is ever done."

"Even someone trapped in a fake relationship with a woman they hate?"

"I've always believed that someday it will get better and I'll have another chance to be happy. That's how I made it this far."

His arm hooks around my chest and pulls me back against him. "That, my friend, is some nauseating bullshit."

I jab my elbow into his ribs. "Your face is nauseating bullshit."

"You wouldn't know. Your mom is nauseating bullshit."

"What are we, twelve?"

He shoves me, our laughter mixing together and rising to the ceiling of our prison, filling the dead space.

"I take it back," he says when we get quiet again, serious in an intense, lonely way I've never heard before. His hand finds my shoulder, squeezing it, and this time his thumb traces along the collar of my sweater, barely brushing my skin. "You're gonna get out of here, leave that woman, and have a beautiful life with your kid. Good things happen to people like you."

My confused heart starts thumping, running out of my control, and I know he can feel it. "What about you? Where will you go?"

So slowly, his thumb caresses the swell of bone at the top of my spine. "I don't know," he murmurs. "Somewhere that doesn't smell like you."

A soft, involuntary sound falls from my mouth when he presses his nose behind my ear, his breath warming the back of my neck. I'm lightheaded from breathing too fast, my chest shuddering. He huffs, like he's frustrated, and wraps his hand carefully around the front of my throat. We stay that way for a long time, neither of us saying anything.

"I'm not gay," he whispers, spreading his fingers so that his thumb tips up my chin and his little finger slips under the edge of my sweater.

"Neither am I," I breathe.

He buries his face in my neck, pain and confusion laced in his voice. "Then why do you make me feel this way?"

At last, I yank away and spin around. We're so close I can feel the heat pouring off his skin, and the racing of our pulses becomes one, indistinguishable, aching and afraid. His hand cups my neck gently, his thumb resting in the hollow of my throat, and when his grip tightens I don't know if it's to push me away or pull me closer. I don't think he knows, either.

Our noses brush, and he groans in his throat and pulls back, body wound as tight as a piano wire. If a world outside still exists, this is such a bad idea. I'm not so sure it does anymore, not for us.

I've never wanted to kiss another man. But if this is what wanting to kiss someone feels like, I don't think I've ever felt it in my life. He starts to say my name at the same time I say his, and then his lips are on mine, soft and chapped and warm, swallowing my moan. He takes my face in his big hands and kisses me again, tenderly, with no tongue yet. "Shh," he breathes when I try to push forward, holding me still and planting slower and slower kisses on my mouth. It feels like the dirtiest, purest thing I've ever done.

"Shit," he whispers as I break free and climb up to straddle his lap, lacing my fingers through his hair. He opens up for me this time, the wet, sweet-tasting warmth and the steel piercing teasing in and out of my mouth. Our tongues wrestle, messy and searching, while he grips the back of my neck with one hand and pushes the other under my sweater to trace the shape of my ribcage. When I can't breathe anymore, I let my head fall back as he pants against my shoulder.

Jackson rumbles in his chest as he noses at the spot where my clavicle disappears under my collar, then nips it softly. "Can you take off your shirt?"

Adrenaline has me yanking my sweater and flannel over my head without thinking. When my brain catches up I stiffen like a prey animal, my pulse thundering as chilly air caresses my bare skin and hardens my nipples. I don't understand what my body's doing with this man, what it wants, what my *heart* wants. I do know that he's going to be disappointed with what he finds when he touches my slim, unmuscled torso. The darkness makes everything seem even more raw and vulnerable, stripped bare and breathless, waiting.

But I can still feel the sweet-salt pressure of his lips against mine, the scrape of his stubble that's getting longer every day. This isn't some one-night stand. It's Jackson—who always gives me the first sip of water, who stormed the Tower of Shadows with me, who knows secrets I've never told anyone else.

Dropping my sweater on the ground, I spread my arms, even though he can't see. "Ta-da. Remember, I look like ScarJo."

His hands wrap heavy and warm around my middle, his thumb playing with my belly button. "Does she have a waist like a Victorian lady?"

"I do *not*—" I break off with a shiver when one of his broad palms slides up to rest firm against the center of my chest. There's an ownership in it I've never felt from a woman. Both of us hold our breaths, our foreheads brushing together as his fingers explore my skin one wondrous inch at a time. He lets out a rush of air when he finds a nipple, stiff with cold and want, circling it with his thumb until I lean in and seal my mouth with his to keep myself from making a pathetic sound.

His other hand grips my chin gently, turning my face to the side as he noses at my jaw. "No. I want to learn what noises you make." Even though his movements are calm, his voice isn't entirely steady.

"This isn't fair," I murmur petulantly, and I feel him smile. "Let me touch you, too." His t-shirt rustles as he drags it off, and the air around me warms when our body heat collides. "Can I?"

He hums quietly into my hair. Feeling a little dizzy, a little drunk on the mystery of him, I reach out and fill my hand with skin and solid muscle, dusted with hair. I've never touched something bigger and more unyielding than myself, a body that isn't made of soft, bouncy curves. I trace the shape of his shoulder, down to the wiry bush under his arms, then his bicep that flexes as he moves. When I dare to lean in and press my lips to the swell of his pec, he sucks in a breath.

"You work out," I say, resting my forehead against his neck, because *you're hot* is too confusing for me to put into words just now.

"I haven't had much else to do."

"I'm sorry that I'm not...like you."

Groaning, he pulls our bodies together, my heart stopping at the shock of his skin against mine, and trails his fingers down my spine. "Who made you so bright?" He kisses the tip of my shoulder, then sucks on it, and my half-hard cock aches.

I laugh weakly. "What's that supposed to mean?" But I don't want him to answer. I don't want to hear words I can't come back from. So I find his lips again and push my tongue into his mouth as his hands roam my body, intent and reverent. I beg for his piercing, and he lets me play with it.

I've never been tasted like this, never been held, never felt such a slow unraveling of everything I thought I knew. I want him like a person wants the nameless feeling that lingers in the memory of their dreams, something taken from them too long ago to remember. And I have no idea what that means.

Chapter 6

JACKSON

    I learned what sex was by lying awake, listening to the couple in the next trailer scream and throw shit half the night, then shake the place with hate-filled animal fucking until dawn. It's illiterate high schoolers rutting in cars, coked-up thugs assaulting prostitutes, my dad jerking off to porn in the middle of our trailer in broad daylight. It's all cocks and tits and pussies and animal hunger that will make people do anything. I've never wanted it, not like that. Neither has my body. I've jerked off before, when I wake up hard, but it's just a physical ache that seems very different from the reasons people go around fucking each other.

    Now I'm hard with need for the first time in my life. It's not because I like his body—I mean, I do, I think. I can't stop touching it. It's because I want to crawl into his chest and live in the warmth and goodness that pours out of him. I want to lick every inch of his skin to make sure it all tastes of light, just like I knew it would.

Oliver stirs in my arms when my hand dips lower down the flawless curve of his back, his breath teasing against my neck as he makes soft sounds I'd never be able to hear if we weren't somewhere so silent, with only the noise of skin moving against skin. One of his palms rests lightly against my chest, while the other grips my shoulder like he's afraid of falling.

I'm not thinking clearly; I just know there's more of him and I need to feel it all. My hand pushes under the waistband of his jeans, into the back of his briefs, to palm a swell of soft, warm flesh that does something to me no other body in the world ever has. "Fuck," he whimpers, licking shy, needy kisses up the side of my neck, his whole body tense and melting at the same time.

My finger gets a mind of its own, straying down into his crack, and we both jump when it brushes his hole. Oliver curses hoarsely. I yank my hand away, resting it on his arm. "Sorry. I didn't mean to."

For a long, uncertain moment he doesn't move or say anything. Then he leans in and rests his forehead against my temple. "Please do it again," he whispers. All the blood in my body rushes to my groin, leaving me lightheaded.

Carefully, trying not to mess this up, I slip my fingers back into his underwear, between his tight ass cheeks, searching for the spot that makes him spark like a live wire. "Does it feel good?"

He nods, breathing fast, and I hear him unzip his jeans. Heat crawls and aches across my skin. "No one's ever touched me there."

"Me neither. I've never done…anything," I admit, wondering just how much of a freak that makes me—a thirty-one-year-old man who has never even gotten hard for someone before.

"Whatever you're doing, please don't stop," he pleads raggedly, rocking against my hand. He smells like raw arousal.

"Are you jerking off?" I can't think straight at the soft slap of his hand working himself.

"Yeah," he whines, shivering. I have no idea what I'm doing, but my cock wants more of this, all of it, forever, so I press harder with my finger at his hole, circle it. His panting collapses into quiet begging sounds as his hand speeds up. "Jackson, fuck, please, I—"

I lace the fingers of my free hand firmly in the soft, messy strands of his hair—ginger-blond, whatever that means, like autumn leaves—and pull our mouths together, swallowing down the most gorgeous sound I've ever heard as he jolts and something warm splatters my chest.

He pries himself off me, trembling. I can hear him fumbling to do up his jeans. "Jesus, Jackson, I'm so sorry. I just *came* on you. Let me get a wet wipe." He sounds mortified but still helplessly turned on.

I'm so hard it hurts, not a figure of speech but actual, wretched pain, throbbing and crushed in my pants. "Oliver," I moan. There should be more words, but I can't find any. I don't have words for something I've never wanted before.

"What?" He must hear it in my breathing, because he hesitates, then rests his hand on my thigh. His slim, gentle fingers slide gingerly higher until his knuckles bump my bulge. "Can I touch you?" he murmurs.

I tip my head back and close my eyes. "You can do anything you want to me."

When he presses the heel of his hand against my erection I gasp and twitch my hips, rutting into his palm. He makes another needy sound and rubs me harder. "You can hold me, if you want."

I want. My hands spread across his chest, stroke down his sides, tug his jeans a little lower so I can trace the shape of his hips. Finally, he gives a small growl of frustration and works open my fly, dragging my pants down until he can push his hand up the leg of my boxers. I don't think either of us are prepared—me to have another hand on my cock for the first time or him to realize he's holding another man's cock—and we both freeze up for a moment. Then I can't fucking take it anymore and I thrust weakly into his fingers, the living heat of them against my cock. "Please."

He groans and tightens his grip around me, makes a tight, slick hole for me to work into. I let go and chase the overwhelming feeling, while he gives in and scatters messy kisses across my chest. Because together, we're fearless. I spill into his hand with a quiet sob and he shudders, pressing his nose against my ear, breathing my name as he empties me out.

We just stay where we are for a long time, as our gasping slows down and the cold starts to creep across our skin. When he finally moves, he laces the fingers of his clean hand between mine, then presses his soft cheek with its bristle of beard against the back of my hand. "What just happened?" he whispers.

"I don't know." I run a finger all the way down from the hollow of his throat to his belly button to the top of his jeans. His skin feels so fragile compared to mine, with sweet little curves everywhere. I still don't fully understand what makes someone lust after another person's body. But I love his because it holds the person I want so badly, keeps him safe and gives him life. Lets me touch him. "What have you done to me, Oliver?"

Turning my hand over, he kisses the inside of my wrist, then again, then runs his tongue along my pulse. "I was going to ask you the same thing." He leans hungrily into my touch as I stroke his hair. We've become only this, hands and hot skin and two souls pressed together in the darkest night.

I feel something wet trickling down the back of my hand before Oliver sniffles, then lets out a muffled sob. He starts crying harder and harder, until he's choking on his own breath. "I just found you," he wails into my chest as I lie down and pull him against me, wrapping all my limbs around him. "I don't want to die."

"You won't." I rest my nose in his hair and think about dying and living and keeping him and losing him and how I don't get a choice in any of it. Because I'm just a dog, and dogs don't get to pick their fate.

"How do you know?" he whimpers.

I kiss his shoulder, knowing that one way or another it will be one of the last times. "Because I'm God down here, and I say that you won't."

"You're not."

"How do you know? I could be. If you're my celebrity crush, then I'm God."

He turns his face and kisses me, deep and messy with tears.

Maybe I'm an idiot, going half my life without wanting anyone, then falling so hard and so fast for a person I barely know. But he smells like everything I've never had, and he feels like home, and he makes sense out of the broken parts of me I've been carrying around for thirty fucked-up years. I don't know what else I could possibly do. Until I remember that forgetting is how I've stayed alive this long, and I'm never going to be able to forget this.

Chapter 7

OLIVER

My face feels stiff with dried tears when I wake up, and my hand smells like cum—my own and someone else's. When I swirl my tongue around my dry mouth, it still tastes of Jackson, his body and tongue and that steel barbell.

Rolling over, I feel out Jackson where he's lying on his stomach. I rest my face against his shoulder and push my hand under his shirt so I can rub his broad, muscled back.

After a few minutes, he hums groggily and lifts his head. "Hi."

"Hey." I hesitate, not sure where we've left things, my hand going still. Then he leans in like he can't help it and kisses me gently, brushing the tips of our tongues together.

His stomach gurgles loudly, and he groans. I try to sit up, then collapse back again and close my eyes. I'm drowsy, even though I just woke up, and I'm having trouble putting words in the right order to make complete thoughts. "I don't feel great, Jackson."

"Me neither." He rests his steady palm on my chest.

With a stab of panic, I remember news stories I've read about cave rescues. "What if there's no airflow and we're running out of oxygen?" Every breath starts to feel like a struggle, but I don't know if it's all in my head.

"It doesn't matter." He sits up, groaning. "There's nothing we can do about it. I'm going to look for more supplies today. You should stay here."

My fingers find his, slide between them and grip tight.

"You know I'll find my way back." I hear him pick up the mostly empty water bottle and shake it. "Let's go halves on this." A sloshing sound, a few gulps, and he presses it into my hand. "Your turn. Finish it up."

I stare down at the dark where my hand is. "Did you actually drink anything just now?"

He scoffs gently. "Of course."

"I don't believe you."

His fingers squeeze the back of my neck. "Stop being difficult. I'll be right back, okay?"

"Jackson—" But he's already gone, leaving behind silence. In the end, I can't stop myself from drinking all the water. Then I sit with my head in my arms and wait, trying not to breathe too much. Eventually, when he doesn't come back, I dig out my knitting. My hands ache, tired after just a few rows, and I keep fucking up stitches. I throw the needles down when something clatters and footsteps enter our camp. "Are you okay?"

He drops down next to me and pulls me closer, burying his face in my hair. His clothes feel damp with sweat, and his exhausted muscles shiver. "I didn't find anything," he croaks finally. "There aren't any more train cars. There's nowhere else to look." His body leans heavy on mine, like he used the last of his strength.

I bump his chest with my shoulder, hating myself for not saving him a mouthful of water. "Guess it's time to break out the piss, huh?"

Instead of laughing, he hugs me tighter and cradles my head in his battered hand. "I'm sorry."

And that's when the true fear finally breaks through and takes root in the center of my chest, because if he doesn't see a way out, I'm pretty sure we're fucked.

I've broken down enough times in the past few days, so I try to be the tough one today and think of a distraction. "Let's do something else. Anything."

He goes silent for a minute, and I know exactly where his mind has wandered. There aren't many options to choose from. Nuzzling my ear, he clears his throat painfully. "I wouldn't know where to start." But I can feel curiosity in his body, hear it in the way he's breathing. We can chase this as far as we want, explore each other in any way we can think of, because we have nothing else left.

"Blowjobs are a thing," I offer after a moment's thought.

He coughs a tired laugh. "So I've heard. I'm not sure my dick feels safe being your first." But his breath gets ragged when I sit up and turn so we're sitting face to face again, inches apart.

"I could just use my tongue, and go really, really slow."

I hear him groan softly, then the zipper of his jeans, and warmth floods my body. My fingers long to wrap around him again, but I keep them to myself and kiss him instead, tentatively at first, then greedily. I want to know if his whole body tastes as smoky-sweet as his mouth.

"You make my cock so wet," he murmurs, sounding confused as he pulls down his jeans, "but I haven't come."

"It's called precum." My heart is beating so hard it pulses in my vision as I slide between his legs and press my nose against the heat of his thigh, the taste of more forbidden things, the raw desire not to mess this up.

"I've seen drops before, when I jerked off, but nothing like this."

"In my experience, when I'm really turned on, it can get messy. Let me try something."

"*Fuck*." He almost knees me in the face when I find his heavy balls and massage them. I can feel wetness trickling down his shaft onto my hand.

"You smell amazing." It's indescribable, earthy but clean and all man, all him. I cup his shaft so I know where it is and kiss the base. As soon as my tongue brushes it, I shiver. "Oh, you taste good too. Fuck." I lick, then again, forgetting that I'm supposed to be doing anything more than just lapping him up.

His fingers slip into my hair and grip almost tight enough to hurt. "Don't stop."

I don't trust my teeth around his dick any more than he does, so I just run my tongue up his length, then try to suck on the V-shape under the base of his head. I'm not cut, so I don't know exactly what spots feel best. I try them all, everywhere I can think of, listening for the ones that make him jerk and whine. He's leaking like crazy now, and I make a game of trying to keep up, until I can't take it anymore. I push up on my elbows to wrap my lips around the head and bury my tongue in his slit.

Letting out a string of incoherent profanity, he scruffs me and pulls me off by the back of my sweater as he starts to come. Instead of saving my mouth, he manages to land a warm spatter all across my cheek.

"God," he gasps, shaking. "I'm sorry. I didn't–"

I climb up and rub my face against his like an animal, smearing wet cum and the taste of it between our mouths as I kiss him. "See?" I breathe, grinning like a fool. "You taste really good."

He chuckles, still breathless, then traps me under his arm so he can wipe my face off properly with the hem of my sweater as I struggle to escape.

JACKSON

Our wrestling turns into stripping off Oliver's shirt, my hands all over his slim body as I kiss his throat and his panting chest. I think both of us know where this is headed, but we're scared, unsure how to get there. When I reach for his jeans, he squirms away. "Wait, pause."

I hold my hands up, even though he can't see. "I'm sorry." I don't know the rules of sex and I already broke them somehow.

"No, you're okay." He finds my hands, tangles our fingers together. "I don't want to stop; I just have a weird rule. Please don't touch my dick or go near it. Is that alright? I'm sorry."

"Don't apologize." Relieved, I angle my head enough to bring our mouths together. I can't stop, like his smiles and stupid stories and his courage are all there in the faint salt tang of his lips.

Pulling my shirt over my head, he palms my pecs like he's been waiting all night to do that again. His voice goes shy. "So do you want to try...my ass?" Like it's an ice cream flavor.

I get a deafening *yes* from my body, eager to claim a part of him no one else has ever touched, but it feels overwhelmingly complicated. "Wouldn't we need condoms and lube?"

"We can use precum as lube, I think. As far as condoms—" He runs his fingers tenderly along my jaw. "You said you were a virgin?"

I snort. He makes me sound like a denim-skirt-wearing teenager at church camp. "Mhmm."

"The last person I fucked was Kay, a long time ago, and I got tested afterward because she was cheating. So I'm clean, if you trust me."

"We're going to starve to death long before the STDs get us."

He slaps my unhurt arm. "You're awful." Then he hesitates, sounding more subdued. "So, uh, where do you want me?"

He doesn't know what he's doing either. But he wants me to be the first person in a long time, maybe ever, to make him feel this good.

Because he's mine.

He's not.

Fuck it.

"Grab one of the coats to kneel on."

He gets on his knees with his back to me, then rests his arms on the ground so that his ass is up. I trace the beautiful arch to his back, the damp, hot skin, and the racing of his heart. "Goddamn, Oliver." He makes a startled, lewd sound in his throat when my thumb finds his hole and I can hear him start to jerk off. "Have you been getting all excited imagining this?" I'm rewarded with a soft whimper.

Since he won't notice, I touch my own ass and taint, searching for the things that make my erection ache, so I can do them to him. I don't go near his cock, but he lets me rub my fingers up behind his balls. "Are you hard again?" he whimpers after a while, squirming.

To my surprise, I am—stiff and even more sensitive this time. I think it's the sounds he's making, because the part of him I know best is his voice. "Yeah."

"Show me." He's begging, stroking himself faster, so I slide my cock into his ass crack and rut against him. "Oh God, that feels so good. Can we try now?"

Ignoring the nerves, I jerk myself a couple of times, smearing precum all over my shaft, and press my head to his hole. It's impossibly tight, resisting me, so I stroke his back. "Can you open up more?"

"I'm not sure," he groans. "With girls it kind of opens as you go, as long as everything's wet and they're ready."

I apply more pressure with my hips, roll them a little. Suddenly, the resistance gives and I find myself most of the way inside him, his walls clamped down on me.

A scream tears from his throat. "God fucking damn it," he gasps, breath sobbing.

"Fuck." My dick doesn't want to leave, but I start to pull out. Oliver grabs at my leg. "No! Don't. I–" But he can't finish. "I what?"

"Shit," he wails quietly. "It hurts."

I squeeze his hip hard enough to get his attention. "Tell me what you want, Oliver. With words."

He's silent for a moment. "I don't know. I don't want you to pull out yet." He inhales shakily. "I like it when you...when you tell me what to do...like that."

Letting all my breath out at once, I try not to laugh. I know fuck-all about sex. But taking care of someone that needs me—that's different. Dangerous, but different. "Alright." Hugging his back to my chest, I ease him down with my dick still in his ass until we're lying together, my body curled around his. "Tell me how your ass feels right now. Besides hurting." While he talks, I reach around and swipe the traces of tears off his cheeks with my thumb.

"Uhh...full?"

Snorting, I bite the back of his neck lightly. "I thought you liked telling stories. You can do better."

"It's like..." He sounds embarrassed. "It's like you forced me open, then stuffed something big in there so I couldn't close up again. It's kind of hot." His wound-up body starts to relax a little, and the iron grip on my cock eases. "I always kind of wondered what it would feel like to be a woman, to have a guy fuck your hole, you know. If it felt amazing. That makes me sound really weird."

"Shh." I stick two fingers in his mouth and he latches on them instantly. "If I don't like what you say, then you're done talking." He moans softly, sucking harder.

It blows my mind. I have the power to make him feel amazing, any way I want. Then he gets harder, which makes me harder, and it becomes a perfect cycle that only works with him, like my body's been waiting this whole time for the day I ran into Oliver.

He starts moving his hips, rubbing down on me, so I pull my fingers out of his mouth and wipe them off on his chest. "What about now?" I lick the back of his neck, dragging the piercing along his skin as his body grips and tugs on my cock.

Arching his back, he twists his head around to find my mouth. "When you move inside me it brushes that spot, I think, the one I've read about. It makes me feel like my whole body is melting."

Brushing his hair away from his ear, I kiss it. "Do you want me to fuck you now?"

"Slowly."

I work my hips against his ass steadily, carefully, playing more than fucking. He writhes when I start touching him in all my favorite places—on his chest, his hips, his thighs, and his body pulls me in even deeper.

Oliver keens softly, his body jolting as I speed up, and then he starts to moan in the same pulsing rhythm that a man's cum leaves his cock. His ass clenches around me over and over; it feels amazing, but I don't care about coming again, not when I could be focused on him.

"Good job," I murmur against his neck. "You're perfect."

"What about you?"

I ease out as gently as I can and pull his pants up around his thighs so he doesn't get chilled. My cock rests half-hard and satisfied against my hip. "I already came. I'm happy." And even though it doesn't make any sense, I mean those last two words more than I have in a very long time.

Chapter 8

Oliver

"If you don't want to come again, then tell me what you want to do." He's so gentle and complicated, curled up against me, and I have a strange feeling that no one has ever asked him what he wanted before.

"Can we...can we play more of that game?"

I shoot up onto my elbows. "Wait, really?"

"Don't you dare say a word about it."

We clean up with more wet wipes; I'm so thirsty I keep wanting to stick one in my mouth and suck the moisture out. I settle against the wall with Jackson's flannel wrapped around me and he wordlessly rests his head in my lap. It might be hours or days that we play, me describing the inside of the tower as I untangle and comb out his hair with my fingers. His weight and the pattern of his breathing all remind me of the evenings where Megan falls asleep on me in front of the fireplace, quiet and right and true, like he has always belonged there with us.

Eventually, the nameless adventurer reaches the top of the tower. "You walk into a moonlit room," I describe eagerly. "Under the window, there's a large stone chest carved with elaborate designs that look suspiciously like dicks."

"Fuck yeah." He fidgets, bouncing his leg excitedly. "I open the chest and grab the wand."

"You just throw it open?"

"Sure. Why not?"

"When you open the lid, all you see are rows of sharp teeth. The chest is a mimic."

"A *what*?"

"A monster that disguises itself as treasure chests. You'll need to make a reflex save to see if it bites your arm off." I'm a bastard, but it's all worth it for the way Jackson bolts upright, his voice hoarse with indignation.

"You *shit*. What is your fucking problem?"

"I'm not the one who didn't check for traps."

He tackles me and I try to kick him off, but I'm laughing too hard. "I hate this fucking dumbass game."

Time starts to slide and warp as we lie there together in the heavy dark. Sometimes we're asleep and sometimes we're awake, but I have no idea how long has passed. Neither of us has the energy to make ourselves get up when there's nothing left to do. I guess we should be drinking the piss, but even that doesn't feel like it matters anymore.

I just close my eyes and rest my head on Jackson's chest while he rubs my neck and toys with my hair. I think it's my imagination, but it feels like his breathing gets slower as the hours unspool like yarn dropped on the floor.

"Jackson?" My throat's wrecked, my voice weak, but he still seems to be able to understand me. "Are you sure we're not going to die?"

His fingers go still on my neck, and he doesn't say anything. Reaching up, I take his hand and hold it between mine, rest my face against it. "If this is it, what's your biggest regret?"

He barely thinks about it at all. "Being born."

My grip on him tightens. "That's awful."

"Do you want me to lie to you?"

"So you meant it when you said you had no reason to get out of here."

Again, he doesn't answer.

"What about..." I'm frantically casting around, trying to put together all the elusive pieces into something real. "What about me? Or us. If we... We could be friends," I finish lamely.

His fingers trail down my spine. "I don't think people like us are friends in real life." When I start to protest, he gently pushes his knuckles against my mouth. "Shh. What's the first thing you'll do if we make it?"

"Buy a bearded dragon."

I can sense his frown. "What?"

"Megan's wanted one for a year now. She's young, but she even did extra chores to show she could be responsible. Kay said no because she doesn't think little girls should like reptiles. I caved and agreed not to get one." I breathe out a slow breath, concentrating on not thinking about how cold I am. "I think I'm going to start standing up to Kay."

"She'll crack. Bullies are vicious, but they're weak."

I don't even react to the sound at first. I've heard it in dreams so many times my brain filters it out like static. The faint rumble of machinery goes on for almost a full minute before Jackson's hand tightens on my back. "Oliver." He shakes me gently. "Listen."

"Holy shit." I scramble to my knees, my heart pounding. "Jesus Christ." Ignoring a wave of dizziness that almost knocks me over, I scramble recklessly through the dark in the direction of the sound, to the far side of the tunnel from where I tried to dig out. From here, I can catch distant, muffled voices over the low hum of drilling. I press my hands against the rough stone, like I can shove it out of the way. "Hello? We're here!" I'm yelling as loudly as I can, but it's more of a strangled croak.

Every sore muscle in my body melts when I hear a male voice call back through the wall. "I hear you. We're working on breaking in without collapsing the tunnel. Can you tell me the names of any survivors?"

Jackson finally catches up, standing close behind me. "I'm Oliver Shaw," I call back, pausing to cough. "I'm with Jackson, uh—"

There's a long pause before he murmurs, "Moreno."

"Oliver Shaw and Jackson Moreno. No other survivors."

"Do either of you need urgent medical attention?"

"We're hungry and dehydrated, and one of us has a large cut on his arm. But that's all."

The voice disappears for a few minutes, then speaks again. "Hang tight, guys, and stay back from the wall. We'll be through soon."

I'm not crying, but I can feel tears wet on my cheeks as I turn to Jackson. "We did it. Fuck, we *made* it." Reaching up, I take his stubbled cheeks in my hands. "Thanks to you. You kept us alive." Silently, he turns his face into my palm and nuzzles it as I start babbling. "Jackson, listen. I don't know... I could try to leave Kay, for real this time. And if I did, maybe then..."

"Stop," he hums, brushing my hair out of my eyes. There's a sad smile in his voice. "Focus on keeping your little girl, yeah? That's all that matters."

"But—"

"But nothing. Sometimes we don't get a 'but.'"

The sound of rocks breaking and crumbling escalates behind me.

"Oliver?" he whispers.

"Yeah?"

"Can you just hold on to me, until they come through?" His voice wobbles. All I know of this man are his body and his words, and both of them seem wrong.

"Of course." Not sure what to do, I hug him around the waist and slip my hand up the back of his shirt to soothe his skin. He loops his powerful arms around me and pulls my face into his chest, where I can't breathe. His heart is racing.

"I can't wait to see what you look like," I say into his shirt. "And introduce you to Megan. She's a firebrand; I think you'll like her."

Sighing, he tightens his grip.

"Are you still there?" The voice sounds much closer now, like talking through a wall. The grind of machinery has been replaced by the clatter of hand tools.

"We're here!" I try to move closer, but Jackson won't let go. We stay like that, fused together in the dark, until with a final crack everything falls apart into voices and radios and hands on us and *light*. My eyes feel like they're burning and melting out of their sockets, so I squeeze them shut.

Forever after, I tell myself that I never let go of Jackson, that the rescuers pulled us apart. But some part of me knows it's not true. All I remember is sitting on the floor surrounded by paramedics, blinking painfully when they throw away my glasses and slide heavy-duty shades onto my face. I can't see Jackson beyond the ring of first responders all talking to me at once.

"Where's Megan?" I croak. "I want to see my daughter. I don't need all this."

Someone sets down a plastic stretcher next to me and I start to struggle. "Your family's been contacted," a woman says in my ear. "They'll meet you in the hospital." My next words are cut off as they strap an oxygen mask to my face and grab my arms and legs, lifting me onto the stretcher. I whimper, eyes watering, as a paramedic tries to get an IV started in my dehydrated veins.

"Keep your eyes shut," someone orders as I'm lifted into the air and carried out of the tunnel. Sun warms my skin, and a faint breeze caresses the sweat on my arms. I have no idea where Jackson went, but I tell myself they're keeping him safe.

They must have put something into my IV, because I feel like I'm floating away. When a wave of darkness pulls me under, it's a relief, like welcoming back a friend.

JACKSON

He let go of me.
I'm standing here with my hands empty.
But it's okay.
I've been preparing myself for this since he grinned and touched my hand and said he wanted to make me a sweater.

Chapter 9

OLIVER

For the first time in almost a week, I open my eyes to daylight. It's terrifying. The air tastes like bleach and clean linens instead of musty earth, and I can't figure out who or what or where I am. There's no weight of a warm body against my back, no arm around my waist or leg thrown over mine.

"Jackson?" I struggle to sit up, looking from white walls and beeping equipment to a window with the blinds half-drawn. Everything's so loud, so much open space, and my eyes burn from trying to take in too much detail at once. I clear my throat and say his name again, louder, trying to untangle my legs from blankets and swing them off the bed.

Stabbing pain in my arm makes me cry out and freeze, shivering and disoriented. There's a needle taped in the crook of my elbow, attached to a bag of fluid on a stand. I want it gone; I dig my fingers into the skin around it, but I'm not brave enough to rip it out. A thin, papery hospital gown rides up around my thighs as I move, making me feel naked.

My head snaps up as the door to my room slides open. My stomach turns at the sight of Kay's bleached hair and designer purse, the way her overlined lips twist into a frown. Her cool, hazel eyes study me up and down, taking in the absolute mess I'm sure I look right now. "You really made it."

"Sorry to disappoint."

She smiles thinly. Before she can answer, my parents almost trample her. I stare at the layers of smudgy, tear-streaked makeup around my mom's eyes, then the paleness of Dad's normally ruddy cheeks. With how much we've drifted apart since Kay came between us, it warms my chest to see that they do still love me, even when they forget to say it. "Oh, Oliver," Mom sobs. Before she can run to me, a tiny body squirms past her.

Megan rockets across the room, shrieking, "Daddy!" All the tattered pieces of my soul come back together when she throws her soft arms around me and buries her face in my stomach. "Hey, kiddo." Trying to convince myself that I won't wake up any moment and find her gone, I stroke her hair tenderly. It's tangled, her clothes full of wrinkles, because Kay doesn't deserve the title of mother in any way, shape, or form. "I missed you."

"I missed you thiiiiiis much," she announces, stretching her hands out as far as they'll go without removing her face from the folds of my hospital gown.

"Wow, that's a lot. What about Scorch?" I wiggle the black dragon plushie clenched in her small fist. "Did he miss me too?"

"He wants a kiss." Straightening up, she shoves him in my face, dancing him around until I deliver the required smooch on his snout.

"What about a Megan kiss?" My arms give out when I try to lift her into my lap, but she scrambles up on the bed next to me and presses her lips to my cheek. "Where'd you go, Daddy?"

Tears are burning behind my eyes, but they won't come out. All my emotions feel muted, delayed, confused. I can't get my head around anything that's happening.

"Megan, sweet pea, let's go get a drink." Dad holds out his hand, rescuing me from the fact that I'm just staring at my little girl, unable to come up with an answer.

Mom wraps me in her arms, her plump body comforting, but I stare over her shoulder at Kay. "Where's Jackson? The guy who was with me." I have the sickening, darkly humorous realization that I could search the whole place for him and not find him, because I don't know what he looks like. When Mom and Kay exchange a *look*, my heart stutters to a stop. "He made it, right? He was in better shape than I was."

"I'll leave you two for a moment," Mom demurs quietly, kissing me again and shutting the door behind her on the way out. She probably thinks we're going to leap into each other's arms, make out, and gush about how much we missed each other.

Kay drops into a chair next to the bed, tugging her tight skirt down. "You were pretty close with him?"

"What the fuck? Of course I was. He saved my life." When she raises a sculpted eyebrow, I want to shake the answers out of her. But if I let her see the things that matter to me, she uses them as leverage. "Where the hell is he?"

Instead of answering, she taps through a few pages on her phone, then tosses it on the bed by my hip. "Meet your new best friend."

Between my shaking hands and foggy brain, I have to concentrate on making out the news article on the screen—*Jackson Moreno, one of the two tunnel collapse victims rescued this morning, has been arrested for breach of parole after receiving medical attention.*

All the breath leaves my lungs in a rush. I can hear his voice, pressed to my ear. *Hold on to me until they come.*

"I don't understand." I stare helplessly at Kay. "Why?"

She sits back, smirking like we're on a dramatic episode of reality TV, and waves her hand at the phone. "Keep going. I can't wait to see your face when you realize how lucky you are to be alive right now."

I scroll down, skipping randomly until one sentence brings me stumbling to a halt. *Convicted for firing eleven shots into his victim at point blank range and released on parole last year, Moreno fled from officers during an altercation several months ago and has evaded arrest until being trapped in this week's dramatic tunnel collapse.* There's no photo of him, just an image of police cars waiting outside the hospital we must be in right now.

"You were trapped in there with a murderer." Kay sounds enthralled. "Was he super charming? Did he have a cover story with a wife and kids and some fancy job? Did he get in your head?"

His simplicity, his intensity. His sadness. How all the tension in his body uncoiled whenever I talked to him or made him laugh.

"It says he was charged with manslaughter, not murder." I throw the phone back at her.

"Oh, excuse me," she snaps, rolling her eyes. "I forgot that killing fellow human beings in cold blood has different levels of acceptability. He really did get to you, didn't he?"

This is the part where I tell her I'm leaving her, that I'll never lie down and take her shit again, just like I promised Jackson. But he's not here, and my tongue won't form the words. I just hang my head, my fists curled against my thighs, and wait for my old life to come back and swallow me whole.

"Surprise! Welcome home!"

I stumble to a halt in the doorway when I see my living room decorated and full of people, but there's no space for me to retreat. They're all acquaintances of Kay or my parents, because I don't have friends of my own. And here I am, utterly exhausted in an old t-shirt and sweatpants, holding a plastic bag of possessions from the hospital.

"I just pulled something together, darling," Mom whispers, squeezing my arm. "To make you feel special."

I could have done with feeling very ordinary right now, but she looks so concerned that I just smile and thank her. Over the next two hours, I learn what dissociation feels like as I watch my body get passed from hug to hug, eat hors d'oeuvres that I can't taste—the first normal food I've had in seven days—and laugh at the party games on the TV. I can't remember the last time someone threw a party for me, when this house wasn't lonely as hell. Some part of me feels pathetically grateful to these people for showing up, even if I don't know any of them.

The festivities are still going strong when I take Megan upstairs for bed. She seems to sense that I'm too weak to carry her, so she follows along with her hand tucked in mine. The light in her little bedroom is tinted the soothing green of her dinosaur lamp. I sit down on the thick rug, unable to stop touching and marveling at its softness, and read out a chapter from one of her favorite stories, *The BFG*.

When I close the book, she's lying on her side, staring at me with big, blue eyes exactly like mine. "Daddy?"

"Yeah?" I tuck Scorch in her arms and pull up the blanket to her chin.

"Why are you sad to come back?"

My throat hurts and my head aches and the salmon I had downstairs is turning my stomach inside out. Scooting up to the edge of the bed, I rest my chin on the mattress and study her face. "I'm not sad that I came back, Megs. The whole time I was gone, I just wanted to see you."

She reaches out and tugs on the edge of my unruly beard, which I haven't gotten a chance to trim yet. "You're sad, though."

I close my eyes. *Daddy met a new friend, and he misses him very much.* Instead, I lie like a coward. "I promise I'm not sad. Go to sleep, okay? I'll be right down the hall like always."

Kay and I only pretend to share the master bedroom when my parents are staying over, so I walk past it to the guest room where I've lived for four years. Mom must have gotten to it—the furniture's dusted and tucked away, the bed made up with those stiff, tightly-tucked linens you put on beds no one ever uses. It smells like Lysol. I can still hear drunk laughter downstairs.

Crossing to the window, I check on my plants. They're all green and healthy, the soil damp thanks to Mom's thorough stress-cleaning. Pulling open the closet, I kneel on the carpet and start pulling out my stuff, piling it around me. My laptop, my books, a crocheted blanket I've had my whole life, my yarn stash. I bury my hands in the fluffy, colorful skeins, digging around to find the muted rust color I imagined might suit Jackson. I just sit there for a while, legs crossed, looking at everything and running my hands over it all again and again.

Eventually, I cross to sit gingerly on the edge of the bed. My foot bumps the plastic bag of possessions the hospital handed me as I checked out. It crinkles softly as I reach down and feel around inside, pushing shit aside until my fingers find a flannel texture. Pulling out Jackson's shirt, I spread it on my knees and study it for the first time. My fingers smooth across faded brown-on-white plaid, laced with hints of navy blue. It's more tattered than I realized, with a fraying collar and holes along the cuffs; he's worn it half to death. I'll stitch it up the best I can before I give it back to him.

For the two nights I spent in the hospital, the nurses never turned out all the lights. I think they were trying to be kind. They changed shifts often enough that none of them noticed I never slept. I just stared at the ceiling all night through red, blurry eyes. Now I'm so tired I can't see straight. Padding around the room, I switch off the lamps and close the curtains. Even then, I can clearly see the outlines of my dresser and chair, so I kick the rug up over the slit of light coming under the door.

Propping a pillow against the wall, I curl up with my back pressed to it, pretending it's the same.

And I try.

I try to let go, to find the Oliver who slept here a thousand nights dreaming about pointless things, who welcomed every morning and sang Kelly Clarkson while he brushed his teeth. But he died in a sunny train car, reading a self-help book he didn't understand, and he's been replaced by a stranger I can't recognize or grasp.

There's only one person who knows this Oliver, who can explain him to me, and he's fuck knows where, in some jail cell. Alone.

Scrambling out of bed, I push the rug out of the way and hurry back to Megan's room, shutting the door quietly behind me. She's dead to the world, her mouth hanging open and her arms flung out. Her bed is one of those red plastic race cars, too tiny for any adult, but I fold all my limbs as tightly as I can, careful not to wake her as I wedge myself between her small body and the wall.

Gathering Jackson's flannel in my fists, I bury my face deep in the folds and let it be truly dark for the first time, let it be perfectly still. Fill my senses with the mixed tang of sweat and deodorant and smoke and *him*, until I can't hear the music drifting up through the floor.

One more memory finds me as I drift off, one that I didn't know existed—the moment each night after Jackson thought I was asleep, when he'd warm his cold nose in the nape of my neck. The tears that have been stuck behind my eyes for days finally release, soaking into the flannel, just a few muffled, hiccupping sobs in the silence.

Without him, I'm lost. And without me, wherever he is, he's cold.

Chapter 10

Three weeks

Jackson,

Hi, it's me.
What a stupid fucking way to start a letter. Sorry. Anyway, I tried to visit you, but they told me you won't see anyone. Can you ask them to let me in? I haven't read a single article or searched for any pictures, because I want to look you in the eyes for the first time and hear your side of the story. I promise I'm not mad at you.
I've been spending all my time with Megan, of course. She can sense that I'm a soft touch right now, because she's really pushing for that bearded dragon.

It's just one lizard, but something tells me that it's the gateway drug to having our whole house stuffed with reptile tanks.
How are you doing? Are you sleeping alright? I haven't been able to get much rest unless I'm in Megan's bed. My chiropractor bills will be astronomical.
I have a lot of things I want to talk to you about, but I'll save them to tell you in person. Standing up to Kay didn't go so well, because I'm not as brave as you think I am. I want to get your advice. Or maybe just one of your "what the fuck is your problem" pep talks. Write back and tell me a good time to visit, and I'll be there.

Oliver

Two months

Jackson,

I double-checked, and they said you got my letter. Maybe it's hard for you to believe me, with all the shit everyone's saying, but I'm not listening to them. I'm still waiting to hear it from you. I don't understand, but I don't think you're a murderer. Or if you are, there's a reason.
Someone put me in touch with this lawyer from the West Coast, Gray Freeman. If I could get some compensation for what happened, maybe I could afford to take Megan and move somewhere else. And we could try and stop an accident like this from happening again.
Mr. Freeman said a lawsuit would take the better part of a year, at least. I'm still so tired; I'm not sure I have the strength to see it through. But I don't want to let everyone down, so I'll try. He told me that if you're only sentenced for breach of parole, you might get out soon and we could take on this lawsuit together.
There's something happening to me, Jackson. I'm scared of everything, so much worse than before, and I keep having panic attacks. If I can see a therapist without Kay knowing about it, I might try.
Let's set up a meeting, okay? Please.

Oliver

Four months

Jackson,

I'm still saving a list of things to talk about in person, but I needed to get this out. I took Gray to lunch and had a long talk with him; he thinks that once I establish paternity I have a good chance of gaining full custody of Megan, even if Kay tries to stop me. He told me to start documenting and saving all the proof that I'm her primary caregiver—school reports, doctor records, receipts for her clothes. It's fucking terrifying. I had another panic attack when I made the folder and hid it in my room. But I'm going to try, for Megan's sake.
Jackson. I don't understand. Do you not want to talk to me? There's all this shit in the news—"innocent copy editor trapped in hell with a murderer"—and I can't do enough damage control to make it stop. Especially now that I barely leave the house. I just want to understand what happened. I need to hear your fucking voice. Please. I know you're reading this.

Oliver

P.S. Megan got her lizard. He's named Mr. Thundertail Scalypants, because I made the mistake of letting her do the honors. Megan insists that whoever I'm writing a letter to needs to see him, so I'm including a photo.

Eight months

Jackson,

I've thought about you every single day. Does that make me pathetic? Probably. I've still managed to avoid seeing a picture of you or reading articles about your case, in case you change your mind about meeting me. If you don't, I guess I'd rather not know anything about you anyway.
So the lawsuit got fucked. There was a small settlement, but that's it. The opposition said they'd reopen your criminal case to give you a longer sentence, and I backed off.
That means you'll be out in a few months. Will you please tell me when and where and let me pick you up? I'll send Megan to stay with my parents and we can go somewhere, the mountains or something, and talk it all out.

Oliver

P.S. Megan's preschool had a play last month; she was supposed to be a bear. I made her a costume and everything. Her part was to roar at the other kids, but she legit jumped on one and bit his arm. They

dragged us all to the doctor to make sure she didn't have fucking tetanus. The other parents were so mad, but I kept having to step out because I couldn't stop laughing.
I have a picture of her set aside to show you. I had to update it this week, because the first one was getting old.

A year and a half

Jackson,

I'm so sorry. I begged Gray to help you, but he couldn't. I'm sure you don't believe me or care, but I'd wait for you, until you got out. Three years isn't that long—I guess that's a shitty thing to say to you right now, but you know what I mean. If you ever tell me where you are or when you're getting out, I'll be there to pick you up, no matter what.
If you want some other news to distract you, I'm officially leaving Kay. My parents freaked out and cut me off, because they think that will change my mind. They just want us to go back to being some precious, happy little family again. I'll make the money work somehow. Gray helped behind the scenes to make sure I got custody, but you were right—Kay didn't even fight for it. I can't believe I let her trap me for so long with empty threats. We've moved into a little apartment for now, but I don't know where we'll end up.
I guess I've made peace with the fact that you don't want to see me again. If you ever felt like writing and explaining what happened, it would give me some closure. But I think this will be my last letter, if I don't hear from you. I'm sorry I misinterpreted what happened, and that I've basically been stalking and harassing you.
Thanks for everything you did.

Oliver

Oliver,

~~*I'm sorry*~~
~~*I wish I could hear your*~~
~~*smell you*~~
~~*I wish*~~

Fuck this shit

Three years

Jackson,

Surprise, it's me.
I'm really drunk. Sorry for the spelling mistakes. Big shocker, I'm falling apart already, after only a year on my own. Freelance copy editing ain't paying many bills, so I got an office job, then BOOM, fired because of panic attacks and absences. An old family friend got me connected with a new job as a big favor, guess what happens? Now I'm stocking groceries. I'll do anything to keep us going, but I'm scared. I only work on my novel every once in a while, when I'm drunk, which is how we got here.
Megan has a snake now, too. A ball python named Mars. She plays and cuddles with him more than most kids would with a puppy. I'm attaching a picture because drunk me thinks it's hilarious that you know what my fucking pet reptiles look like, but not me or my daughter. Enjoy.
Sometimes I jerk off to the memory of your smell, but it's just something I make up. I can't remember what you smelled or sounded like anymore. My dreams remember, but they won't tell me. I'm gonna have to start dating eventually, because I've heard "but Megan needs a mom" so many times I want to tattoo it on my forehead so people will shut up about it. Maybe I'll send you a family photo when I find The One. You can hang it on your fucking fridge.

Fuck you, Jackson.
Fuck you for walking away without giving me a choice.
I hate you.

Oliver

Four years

Jackson,

It's been ages, so I think you got out at some point. Congrats. I don't suppose the prison forwards mail, so you'll probably never see this.
We're moving. The lawyer, Gray, heard that I was struggling and suggested we come out to where he and his partner live. I guess it's cheap and friendly, with more laid-back jobs. He even has kids close to Megan's age, so she'll have some friends. It won't take us far, but that stupid settlement money should keep us afloat until I find work and give us enough for a down payment on a little house. I'm not telling you where we're going, because I can't live with the tiny chance that you might show up someday.
Megan graduated elementary school, and I embarrassed her by crying. You want to hear something really fucked up? Her sense of humor, the way she talks, sometimes it reminds me of you and I forget for a minute that you and I didn't make her together. That's how hard I fell for you. I've dated a couple people, but they all fizzled out. I never got back to normal after the tunnel, and now I have a whole train load (get it? ha) of baggage that no one wants to touch. I don't blame them.
Here's the pathetic thing. I've fretted for an entire year about "I hate you" being the last words you ever hear from me. And that's why I'm writing this last

time.
I don't hate you. But I don't know what I should say instead.
Besides goodbye.

Oliver

Jackson

All told, I don't get out for another two years after Oliver's last letter. It's dumping sheets of rain when I walk through the prison gates, blowing desolately into my eyes. I figured the parking lot would be empty, but there's a piece of shit black hatchback idling all by itself in the middle.

For a second, even though it's impossible, I think it's Oliver.

The driver's door opens and a boy of about nineteen gets out, the rain flattening his hair and running down his bare arms. He has a cigarette in his mouth that he was smoking in the car. Pinning me with his calm gray eyes, he drops it and stamps it out.

"Scout?"

One of his eyebrows quirks in a gesture I recognize, even though I haven't seen him since he was fourteen. He's still lean and wiry, watching everything so intensely it's like he's trying to set it on fire with his stare. Most of the boys in the trailer park are animals, but he's always been smart, and all the more dangerous for it.

He tilts his head toward the car, but I hesitate. "Are they going to kill me?"

Pursing his lips, he shrugs. "Not until you pay your debts."

Maybe I just got out of prison after five years, but I'm not free. I never will be. As I walk over to the car, I switch off the part of me that dreamed about tracking down Oliver and begging him to take me back.

I drop into the passenger seat, my wet clothes drenching the ripped upholstery. One of the cup holders has been turned into an overflowing ashtray. In the other, balanced in a jumble of garbage and loose coins, is a Styrofoam cup with the smell of fresh coffee steaming out of the little hole in the lid. Scout watches me pick it up and burn my tongue on the first sip while he babies the car into starting.

"Thanks."

"Welcome home." His voice twists around the irony, but a small smile tips the corner of his mouth. As he drives, we pass the cup back and forth in silence until it's empty. I know where he's taking me, the inevitable end I won't walk away from this time, so all I can do is fall asleep with my hand shoved deep inside my backpack, wrapped around a bundle of worn-out letters held together with rubber bands.

II

Ollie and Jax

Chapter 11

OLLIE

"Ew. What the fuck?" My best friend, Tristan, comes up behind me and rests his chin on top of my head while he studies the photos of large, reddish-brown snakes I'm scrolling through.

"Megan's birthday present," I explain, like it's painfully obvious.

"Might I suggest a new cell phone or a bike or anything that can't strangle you in your sleep?"

I elbow his ribs and shake him off. "Don't let her hear you talking like that. She's been asking for a red-tailed boa since she turned eight. I said maybe for her thirteenth birthday." Propping my face in my hand, I sigh. "It sounded so far away at the time."

Reaching around me, he starts cleaning up all the out-of-date sticky notes I've left scattered over the sides of my work monitor. "Don't those things get massive?"

"Six to ten feet," I mumble.

"Jesus, Ollie." The big nerd with his boisterous voice and unruly dark beard sits on the counter next to me, almost mashing my PB&J with his ass. "I hope you're okay with sleeping in the car while she fills your room with snakes."

"It was inevitable." Tapping *print* on some of the juvenile boa listings, I spin my chair around and scoot toward the copy machine. "I made peace with it a long time ago."

"Did you get a date for this weekend?" I can feel his eyes boring into the back of my head.

"No. Did you?"

"I did, in fact. A lovely veterinarian." He *tsks*. "I'm gonna kick you out of the *SSTMBDC* if you don't pull your weight."

The *Sad-Sack, Too-Much-Baggage Dating Club* has just two members: Tristan, whose wife died four years ago, and me, who let a couple of fucks with a stranger in a cave destroy his ability to form relationships for the rest of his life. As far as Tris knows, though, I'm just a late bloomer who can't keep a girlfriend because I'm a single dad with too many reptiles. It's easier that way.

"Fine." I slap my phone on the counter and launch the dating app, Tris hanging over my shoulder. "What about her?"

Tristan bats my finger away from the first profile. "Way too corporate. She looks like she has standards, which eliminates you." He grins when I finally give in and smile in spite of myself. Tris and his antics and his constant, unquestioning acceptance are the only reasons I've been able to hold down this job at the local bank and stay even remotely sane.

After a few more minutes of arguing, we settle on a teacher from the next town over. Just as I hit *send* on an invitation to chat, the front door squeaks open and we both snap to attention. Tris tries to look professional, while I shovel my phone into my pocket and grab a spray bottle to wipe down the countertops.

Everyone remotely modern in this town uses the big chain bank down the road, so we only get suntanned farmers pulling out cash to buy second-hand equipment or old ladies depositing their profits from the Saturday market. The guy standing in the doorway is definitely neither of those. I can hardly make him out with the sun behind him, but he's broad, with a buzzed head and hard, stubbled jaw.

He takes another step inside, body tensed like he's going to turn around and sprint right back out, and lets the door swing shut behind him. Instead of coming up to the counter, he beelines to one of the chairs on the far side of the lobby and sits down. He folds his hands in his lap and sits perfectly still, staring at his feet and letting his shoulders sag a little. He's wearing a worn black button-down, faded black jeans, and heavy leather boots.

Tristan raises a bewildered eyebrow at me, and I shrug. "*Should I talk to him?*" he mouths exaggeratedly.

"*Your funeral*," I mouth back. This looks like the kind of guy you wouldn't want to meet down a dark alley.

Shuffling around my chair, Tris disappears in the direction of our boss's office. A few minutes later, he pops his head around the corner. "Sir? She'll be right with you." The guy grunts, barely glancing up.

"Stace says he's here to interview for the janitor position," my friend stage-whispers, incapable of being quiet.

Craning my neck, I study the stranger over the top of my monitor. After two years in the neighborhood, I can recognize most of the locals. "I've never seen him before," I murmur.

"Me neither."

"Tristan." The bank owner, Stacey, appears down the hall. "There is money in the back that is *not* counting itself, if I had to guess."

"We keep money back there? Who knew?" Grinning, Tris pops up and heads toward the vault. The guy in the lobby ignores our stupid antics; he just sits there with his head down, like he might have fallen asleep. "Gaming tomorrow night?" Tristan whispers on his way past.

I spin around. "I thought you had a date."

"I lied."

"You *prick*," I hiss at his back.

Stacey ignores us. "I'm ready for you, sir. Come on back."

He slowly unfolds himself from the small plastic chair and crosses the room with his hands stuffed in his pockets, no resume or anything. His muscles fill out the sleeves and shoulders of his shirt, but he looks too thin, his jeans loose around his hips. Nothing about him says podunk Iowa. Everything about him says he doesn't want to be here or anywhere else.

I don't realize I'm gawking until he lifts his head, his eyes catching on mine. They're a moody brown, like bitter coffee with no sweetener. He looks…tired. Really fucking tired.

I offer him my brightest smile and a thumbs-up. "Good luck!"

Glancing away, he disappears into Stacey's office. Instead of doing real work, I loiter for the next thirty minutes, waiting to see if he got the job. I sit up when the office door opens, but he strides across the lobby and straight out the door with barely a glance in my direction. Stacey doesn't leave her desk, so I give up and head for the vault to help Tris clean up for the day.

We clock out at four, then stop on the way out the door to water the beds of tulips and crocuses out front. The sun's just starting to sink in the pastel sky, the air clean and sharp. It's that time of spring where it's cool enough in the shade to want a jacket, but warm enough in the sun to take it right off again.

While Tristan drives the battered Accord, I take his phone hostage and read dating app profiles to him, because hell if I'm suffering through a date this weekend while he goofs around. I say "uh-huh" to his feedback, then message them all anyway. A gorgeous woman with a sense of humor who labels herself a nerd messages back right away, and I drop the phone in his lap with a "you're welcome."

Gravel pops under our tires as he swings into the end of my driveway, which is so badly paved you can't get out if you pull up any further. We're right at the edge of town, in a neighborhood with decaying old Victorians and overgrown rose gardens. Our crooked white house has cracked steps and mold in the double-glazed windows, but I think it's charming. My flowerbeds burst into a riot of colors and species in the summer, because I can never decide on a theme.

Waving at Tris, I pick my way across the scrubby lawn and push open the front door. Two years ago, I said I'd have someone out to fix the way it screeches and leaves a scar in the wood flooring, but like most things, it never happened. Megan's normally a tidy kid, so the purple sneakers and camo backpack scattered across the entry mean she's in full snake parent mode, where the rest of the world ceases to exist. I nudge them aside with my foot and wander into the living room.

The squashy couch and old TV look pretty normal if you ignore the reptile tanks crowding the wall. We have a few small ones for frogs that she slipped past me when I was in a good mood—at this point, I've resigned myself to a kind of Stockholm syndrome, where everything that isn't a massive snake feels like a casual purchase. Mr. Scalypants the aging lizard lives in one corner, while the other is taken up by the fucking palace that belongs to Mars the python. In addition to sunning spots and a jungle of plastic plants, Megan redecorates his boring snake hides to look like castles and hobbit holes. Right now, he has a colored-pencil drawing of a beach taped to the back of his tank like a backdrop. She's created a whole set to match his moods, from snowy mountains to deserts to the stage at a rock concert.

He practically lives on her arm or shoulder when she's home, but today is shedding day. Megan's balanced on a chair at the dining room table, sprinkling moss into a large plastic container. She huffs impatiently, blowing back the white-blonde hair falling out of her messy braid. The girl has on what I call her uniform—pink jeans and a vintage metal band t-shirt from her wide collection.

"Mars having trouble shedding again?" I wrap my arms around her from behind and kiss the top of her head.

"Mhmm." She's too focused to greet me, squirming in my grip. "Could you get me some water, please?"

Tristan was right about me sleeping in the car once the boa comes along. This house belongs to my daughter and her snake. I just live here.

Grabbing a pitcher of warm water, I help her sprinkle some over the moss. She snaps the lid on, double-checks the hole I perilously carved out of the side with a box cutter, and skips over to deposit the shedding box in Mars' tank. "Here you go, buddy." Sliding onto her butt on the floor, she watches intently to make sure the four-foot-long black ball python slithers inside.

"How'd your history test go?" Grabbing the pressure cooker from the cupboard, I start dumping in frozen chicken breasts and curry seasoning. I used to enjoy cooking and baking, but a lack of time and money means that we mostly stick to cheap, hearty, healthy, and fast.

When she doesn't answer, I put the chicken down and stick my head around the wall to narrow my eyes at her. "Megan…"

She flops onto her back on the floor, throwing out her arms dramatically. "I tried, I promise."

"What's the damage, Skip?" She thinks the nickname Skipper came from the pirate boat at the playground we used to visit when she was little, but it's secretly because, between the two of us, she steers this damn ship.

Reluctantly, she holds up one hand in a C-shape and the other flat, like a minus sign.

"Hey!" I grab her wrists and swing her scrawny body up, dropping her on her feet. "You passed! I'm so proud of you!"

"I wanted a B." She wrinkles her nose at her bare feet. "We studied every single night."

"Alright." I crouch in front of her and look up into her stunningly blue eyes. "What's our rule?"

Her face scrunches up in frustration. "But that rule's for you when you feel scared at the grocery store or call Uncle Tris to drive us somewhere."

I shake my head, pretending the words don't sting. "It's for both of us, and I want to hear you say it."

She rolls her eyes, but she's smiling now. "If you give your all, then you succeeded, even if it doesn't look like everyone else's success. God that's so corny, Dad."

"Put your boots on and get the apples. And don't cuss." I tug her braid and go back to the pressure cooker.

"I'm old enough to own a boa, but not old enough to cuss?"

"One, you don't own a boa because it's not your birthday yet. Two, if the naggy moms at your school hear you cussing, they'll run me out of town and we won't be able to afford a boa."

"So I can cuss once the boa's here?"

A grin stretches my mouth as I slide the lid onto the pressure cooker and set the timer. This girl owns my smiles and my laughter; everything good in me belongs to her. That's how it's always been and always will be. She's standing in the entry with her boots on waiting for me, swinging a bag of over-ripe apples in one hand, banging it against her leg. The sun from the front yard, golden and sleepy, blooms around her in a halo of blond flyaways, and I can hardly look away as I slide on my own shoes and follow her outside.

She slips her slim hand into mine and bumps her shoulder against my side as we stroll down the dirt road that leads from our house into a stretch of farmland. We've walked this way almost every day for the two years we've lived here, clambering through snow, kicking fallen leaves, having mud fights in the spring. We talk about snakes and school and boys, my anxiety and her struggles making friends, what movie we should watch on Friday and whether she misses having a mom. I'm always completely honest with her, in an age-appropriate way. She even knows a little about the friend I used to have, the one who took care of me, the one I've never forgotten even though he didn't answer our letters.

A mile down the road, Megan hops onto the lowest bar of the rail fence and whistles. Four Shetland ponies come trotting across the pasture in a jumble of shaggy bodies, angling straight for the bag in her hand. She almost falls backward off the fence, giggling and squirming as their fuzzy noses all attack her at once. "No, Frodo, stop it!"

Putting the open bag on the ground, we go about feeding the ponies we've named after the hobbits from *The Lord of the Rings*. It's a game to make sure they each get two apples, because they keep rearranging their nearly identical faces and trying to snatch each other's treats. Megan watches them like a hawk, but secretly feeds her favorite, Pippin, an extra.

Scratching Frodo's mane, I squint toward the beautiful farmhouse in the distance, the trees behind it, and the sharp horizon beyond. When Gray Freeman told me about life in Iowa of all places, suggesting it might be good for us, I thought he was crazy. But Megan has everything she needs here, and I have the space to grapple with my slowly spiraling mental health.

"Anything cool happen today?" Megan cocks her head at me, wiping horse spit all over her pants even though I've told her a million times not to.

"A mysterious stranger came to the bank. He wore dark clothes and sat silently in the corner."

The gap between her front teeth flashes in a huge grin. "It's Strider!" She rubs Pippin's ears. "Hear that? He's going to come take you on an adventure. Did he do something cool?"

"He had a job interview and went home."

"Oh." She deflates. "Well, if he gets the job, find out where he's hiding his sword."

I roll my lips into my mouth and bite them to stop myself from cracking up at the innocent euphemism. "I will be sure to ask him."

Stuffing the empty apple bag in my back pocket, I throw my arm around her shoulders as we head for home.

"Can I read *The Lord of the Rings* again tonight?" She skips, her braid bouncing. "The part where Strider comes."

"It's not really reading practice if you have the book memorized, is it?"

"Then you need to write more of your story, so I have something new to read." Slipping away from me, she hopscotches across the rutted, muddy road.

I snuggle my chilly hands into my jacket pockets and slow down, savoring the smell of spring grass. I don't know why this can't be enough, simple and perfect. A moment where I'm not sick in my head, where my child doesn't "need a mom," where the ghost of someone who never wanted me isn't holding me back like an anchor around my feet.

Chapter 12

JAX

"The address on your job application is *1 Main Street, Byrock, Iowa*." The bank manager sits back in her chair and raises an eyebrow at me. Her perfect blouse and pressed skirt suggest that she takes this job a lot more seriously than the idiots working her front counter.

I decide to double down. Not like I have anything to lose. "Yes, ma'am."

The corner of her mouth turns up. She seems to think my ballsy-ness is funny. "We don't have a Main Street, and no one in this town has ever seen you before."

I watch her in silence for a minute, waiting for her to throw me out. When she doesn't, I spread my hands. "You need clean toilets, and I need money."

She chuckles, shaking her head. "The thing is, I can't hire someone who doesn't have an address—" she points at my bad handwriting on the application form "–or a real name, Mr. *John Martin*."

I stand up wordlessly to leave, but her voice stops me. "Wait." Her eyes can see right through my one nice shirt to the tattooed piece of garbage underneath. "I watched you ride into town this morning while I was getting coffee. You had a sleeping bag and a big pack on your bike." She glances down my too-lean body. "When was the last time you ate?"

Crossing my arms, I watch her silently until she sighs and her face softens. "I was homeless once, before someone gave me a chance. I can't hire you, but this whole building is falling apart. The plumbing leaks, the heating and cooling are broken, and the locks are all stiff. The interior and exterior both need painting, carpet pulled up and flooring laid, furniture refinished. If I'm satisfied, I can leave $500 a week in cash lying around."

It's all I need. As soon as I can afford enough fuel to keep riding, I'll be gone again.

"Thank you." I stare at the corkboard behind her head, dotted with pictures of her family and drawings from her kid. One of the photos in the corner shows the slight, fair-haired man from the front counter, holding an employee of the month award and beaming like it's a million-dollar check, squinting with the sun in his eyes.

"You won't thank me when you see the state of the place." She starts digging in a drawer. "Don't say anything to my actual employees. Let them think I hired you; it's simpler that way."

"Understood."

"Show up at nine each day." Pulling out a red polo, she tosses it at me. "Wear that so people won't bitch if they see you hanging around. If you so much as look at the money or the vault, I will prosecute your ass to hell. I have plenty of security."

"Yes, ma'am." Realistically, the word of a transient stranger means nothing. But it's not surprising that people would be too trusting in a no-name bank in the middle of nowhere.

"One more thing." The woman grabs her purse from under the desk and digs through it. She holds out a crisp $100 bill, but I just stare at it without moving until she shakes it at me. "Get something to eat and a place to sleep tonight. And don't make me regret helping you."

Taking the money and folding it carefully, I offer her a nod.

"See you tomorrow, *John*."

I raise my eyebrows at her, refusing to take the bait and tell her my name. "You too."

As I leave, I see out of the corner of my eye a tousle of gingery hair bouncing up from his seat and watching me curiously over the top of his computer. He has another smile prepared, a kind of cute one, but it dies when I turn my back on him and walk out.

Making sure there's no one watching, I add the hundred to the stash of money under the insole of my boot before walking back to my motorcycle and riding across town. I blend in better in this neighborhood, where it's not all planters full of pansies and little consignment clothing boutiques. Pulling up to a crummy-looking bar, I park at the end of a row of bikes out back, counting on the fact that some of them will stay there all night.

It's windier here, with fewer trees, and I have to turn up the collar of my jacket and dig my tattered hat out of my bag. I've been hit with a few late freezes as I cross the Midwest, waking up with frost on my sleeping bag, and it's going to be a bitch to sleep out tonight.

Hunching my shoulders, I stride across the empty street to a convenience store. Even on the poorer side of town a stranger draws attention, and the college-age clerk stares at me while I watch a single hotdog spin slowly in one of those heated racks. "How old is it?"

He leans over the counter and blinks at it, like he didn't know it was there. "That one might be from yesterday."

"Can I have a discount?"

His eyebrow arches. "They're only two-fifty, plus a bun for a dollar."

I hold up the last two one-dollar bills in my pocket. Every other penny goes toward getting me out of this place before someone catches up with me. "Make it the hot dog, your oldest bun with the mold cut off, and a soda for two dollars."

He snorts. "Whatever, man. You're saving me from having to take out the garbage."

Cradling my prize, I head back across the street and sit down in the smoking area outside the bar. It smells like grass and melting asphalt, gasoline and old brick. I want to make the food last a long time, but it disappears in thirty seconds and I don't feel any fuller. The hunger eases a little when an old man gives me one of his cigarettes, plus an extra for later. I doze off and on against the wall, waiting for dusk to fall as my awareness slides between the ache in my joints, the tight pain of hunger in my belly, and anxiety-fueled half-dreams where I'm always running.

The gang didn't kill me last year when Scout and I drove into the shithole we called home. They did worse—put me in the ranks, set me to work paying off a made-up debt equal to all the problems I'd caused them. I couldn't even find it in me to care when the debt kept growing instead of shrinking.

I always wondered, growing up, how I'd die first. Whether someone else's gun could get to me before mine did the job. Day after day, the answer got clearer—it was always going to be me, and my time was almost up. But some fucking stupid part of me, the one that has never for a second stopped loving a dorky single dad named Oliver, crawled out of the darkness and forced me to fight one more time.

Calling the cops on the gang as a distraction while I ran was the dumbest thing I could have done, but also the most satisfying. I think people with big vocabularies would call it poetic. Now, after riding across two states, I have no idea how much further I have to go before they stop chasing me. Part of me hopes they never will. Because I'm pretty sure running is the only reason I feel the need to keep living.

By the time darkness has mostly choked out the twilight glow around the bar, I've decided there has to be a strip club operating in the back of this place, because they have way too many customers who leave looking way too happy. The name *Dolly's Den* kind of gives it away, too.

When I can't see across the parking lot and all the lamp posts along the street have turned on, I fetch my backpack and sleeping bag and prowl along the chain-link fence I scouted earlier. It circles a small trailer park, behind which I spotted a few abandoned cars rusting in the trees, weeds tangled around their tires and pushing under their hoods.

Wading through tall grass that clings to my jeans, I lean on the fence and watch the park for a long time, looking for dogs and people. It seems quiet, so I dig my toes into the chain link and scale it, dropping into the dirt on the other side. When I don't hear any movement or see any lights come on, I keep my head down and fade away into the shadows around the cars. I pass on the one with no windows that reeks of mouse piss. The second is locked, but the third has a window open far enough for me to force my arm through and pop the lock. The door squeals as I yank it open and stick my head in. It smells like smoke and worse, but it still has seats and I can't see any shit, animal or human. That makes it a three-star hotel compared to some of the places I've slept, so I unpack my sleeping bag and lay it out in the passenger seat.

Sometime in the night, with the full moon sharply outlining every blade of grass, I scramble out of the car and vomit up the rancid hot dog in the bushes. I crouch there for so long, with my head heavy in my arms and spit hanging from my mouth, that I fall asleep that way until dawn. Shaking with cold and sore as hell, I peel off my damp shirt and pull on a long-sleeved tee under the clean bank polo.

My backpack fits perfectly under the back seat of the car, so I leave it behind and climb the fence before everyone wakes up. In the convenience store bathroom, I wash myself with paper towels, slap on some deodorant, and brush my teeth. My haggard face in the mirror looks like shit, my eyes hollow and dead. I can count way too many of my ribs. Forty is only a few years away now, and every inch of my body *hurts*, every muscle and joint and organ, protesting the kind of abuse I used to shrug off like it was nothing. If my life is a joke, then the thing staring back at me through the mirror feels like the fucking punchline.

OLLIE

"Get it together." Pulling my shoes up onto the edge of the toilet, I rub my face against my khaki slacks, trying to wipe away that one lonely, frustrated tear on the side of my nose. Tristan told me to take a long lunch after the bank got busy this morning, but I shouldn't have to. Normal people don't have to. I wish I knew what I did to deserve losing the privilege of being normal. The therapist I saw for a few months after the tunnel collapse said that agoraphobia isn't really a fear of being outside like most people think. It's a cycle of self-feeding anxiety triggered by the trauma of having panic attacks in places where you feel trapped—the line at the store, a movie theater seat, buried alive. You can't escape the cage when it encompasses the whole world.

The dizziness and tightness in my chest ease when I step out the back door of the bank with my sandwich baggie in one hand and an apple in the other. That makes me hate myself even more. As soon as I leave the situation, I feel perfectly fine again, like I was faking it the whole time. My brain is fucking petty.

Normally, the cracked, weedy parking lot behind the bank has the same few cars parked in the shade, employees of the businesses across the street. Today I stumble to a stop and gape at the gorgeous motorcycle sitting all by itself, dark blue paint and chrome gleaming in the noon sun. It sports a classic, almost vintage design, with the word *Indian* emblazoned on the fuel tank. I know fuck-all about motorcycles, but I love how pretty they look, not to mention the fantasy of how effortlessly cool I'd be if I rode one.

Setting my lunch on the curb, I circle the bike to admire every angle. It looks perfectly maintained except for the mud caking the tires and bottom of the chassis, like it's been ridden hard. That just makes it even sexier. I stand there for a long time, chewing my lip, trying to decide if I should do something really stupid just to win a bet with my child. In the end, the answer was always going to be *yes*.

Pulling out my phone, I double-check the parking lot to make sure it's deserted. After trying for ages to get the camera propped at the right angle against a concrete planter, I screw up my courage and set the self-timer. Yelping when the fifteen seconds start, I sprint to the bike and swing my leg over the smooth leather saddle, reaching for the handlebars. Now the kid will have to admit that Dad's still got it. If he ever had it in the first place.

Fuck. It's a lot bigger than it looks, and I'm balanced on the very tips of my toes as I try to strike a pose. Right when the shutter flashes, someone clears their throat behind me.

"*Shit*," I squawk, trying to turn around and get off the bike at the same time. My thigh hits the seat and the whole thing starts to fall. "No, no, no, no." I manage to throw myself under it, staggering with the weight, but I'm too weak to push it upright. Trapped, I look up to find the mysterious visitor, Strider himself, leaning against the corner of the bank with his arms crossed. Instead of pipe-weed from Middle Earth, he's just smoking a Lucky Strike. His dark eyes flick over me expressionlessly. I open my mouth, but nothing comes out except a groan as the bike slowly crushes me to death.

Pushing off the wall, he picks up my phone from the planter and studies the screen. The corner of his mouth twitches. He strolls over, in no hurry at all, and rests a big, beat-up hand next to mine on the seat. His eyes flick between mine for a moment, then he hoists the bike out of my hands and props it back on the kickstand.

He's even more intimidating up close—the hard set of his jaw, the roughness of his buzz cut, the scars scattered across his scalp and neck. But there's something else in his eyes. Something intelligent and warm, buried deep.

My face flames as I wait for him to yell at me. "I'm so sorry. That was incredibly rude. I have this bet with my kid. I told her I'd totally ridden a motorcycle before, but she said she wouldn't believe me until she saw photographic evid…dence…" I trail off as he drops my phone in my hands and turns toward the back lawn, where I spot a pile of old lockboxes and filing cabinets sparkling clean in the wet grass. The bottom half of his jeans looks soaked.

Flexing my sore arms, I trail after him. "You got the job? Congratulations. This looks more fun than what I was doing." He doesn't answer. "Were you taking lunch?" Shrugging one shoulder, he holds up the mostly finished cigarette.

"That's not lunch," I reprimand automatically, like he's Megan trying to convince me a cookie counts as a meal. Grabbing my food, I sit on the planter nearest to where he's leaning.

"I'm not hungry." It strikes me as a weird thing to say, not *I already ate* or *I'm eating later*. His eyes track my hands as I unwrap my ham and cheese sandwich, with mustard you can smell as soon as the bag comes off.

I hold half the sandwich out to him. "I'm Ollie. Welcome to town."

His jaw tightens a little, his gaze shifting from the food to my face before he stamps out his cigarette and moves toward the hose lying uncoiled across the lawn. The man stops with his back to me for a long moment, his shirt hanging soft over the ridge of his broad shoulder blades. In one quick movement, he turns back, swipes the sandwich, and walks away, swallowing it in a couple of bites. "Thanks."

"I'm sorry again about the bike," I call after him, but he doesn't even turn around.

Chapter 13

JAX

Friday night marks the end of my first four days of work. I've already gotten sloppy, vaulting the trailer park fence before it's completely dark and not checking my surroundings carefully.

My steps slow to a stop twenty feet away from the car. The man leaning against the side isn't as big as me, but his aura is huge and dangerous. I know this kind of guy, and I know he's packing a loaded gun in the back of his jeans.

He watches me carefully, not moving a muscle, waiting to see if I'll bolt. I was a fucking fool to leave my pack in the car. I could do without the clothes and shit, but I need the bundle of worn-out letters at the bottom as much as I need food and warmth and fuel.

I hold out my hands placatingly. I could reach the knife in my pocket, but not as fast as he can shoot me in the head. "Can I get my stuff and go?"

"This is my neighborhood. What are you doing here?" His dark, slicked-back hair looks greasy in the setting sun.

Taking three cautious steps closer, I lower my voice. I'm sure he has guys watching, but I don't want to draw any extra attention. "I'm just passing through and needed a place to sleep. I have to work for a couple of weeks, but I'm not here to cause trouble."

My heart hammers my ribs as he looks me over. I should be used to this by now, but I don't have it in me to be hard anymore, to play these fucking mind games. Finally, he reaches into the car and pulls out my bag, dangling it from two fingers. "Get out and find somewhere else to sleep."

"I will. I'm sorry." When I try to take the bag, he tightens his grip.

"You look like you've seen some things. I might have better work for you." My empty stomach cramps as he watches me knowingly.

"I'm not interested."

He releases the bag, letting it bang into my chest, and quirks his cracked lips into a smile. "Find me if you change your mind. If you bring trouble, or I find you back here again, I'll put you down like a stray dog. Got it?"

I don't know how long I have before trouble catches up to me, but I have to take the chance. "No trouble, I promise."

His eyebrows go up mockingly. "Big promise."

Holding his gaze, I back away until I have no choice but to turn my back to him and speed-walk out of the trailer park. Every inch of this place feels like home, from the rusting buildings to the sad-looking dogs chained to porches. I can feel eyes on me, even though I can't see anyone. Putting my head down, I force myself not to run.

Back in the bar parking lot, I slump over my bike and rest my forehead on the handlebars, catching my breath. I should fill up the tank with my first paycheck and ride out tonight, but I'll go broke again in the next state over. A few more weeks at the bank will keep me going all the way to the East Coast.

I can feel *it* sitting close by, watching me as I pull in lungfuls of secondhand smoke and sweet night air. My dark animal, I called it. A huge wolf made of shadows that engulfs me until I can't see or hear, until I can't do anything but hurt myself. It runs with me while I ride, and sits by me while I sleep. It invites me to the place where I can't fail anymore, because I can't try. On nights like tonight, it offers. When I refuse often enough, it just takes.

Luckily for me, I'm too broke to even get drunk, let alone do anything worse. I head into Dolly's Den, noting the unmarked door at the back with a steady stream of men coming in and out. Nursing a small glass of their cheapest beer, I find a shadowy booth at the back and stretch out, trying to keep my eyes open and make the drink last as long as possible.

At four in the morning, the bartender shakes me awake. "Get out of here, man. We're not a hotel."

"Sorry." Between the hunger, the beer, and the drowsiness, my head spins when I move to stand up. I blink hard, trying to clear my vision.

"There's a business fair going on this afternoon downtown," the bartender offers, his face softening a little at the state of me. "They have free food. But if you sleep in here again, I'll have to ban you."

I think the lowest point in my life was the moment the gun went off in my hand. Or maybe when the person I almost died to protect told me she hated me. But standing alone in a dark strip club parking lot, dirty and starving and hunted, with a gaping, festering hole in my heart from the moment a man let go of my hand six years ago…fuck me if this doesn't come close.

"Hey, sweetheart!" The woman in the pink *Byrock City Small Business Fair* t-shirt blanches a little when she sees who she's talking to. I washed up and covered my tattoos with my nicest shirt, but I'm never going to blend in with the families and elderly couples buzzing all over the place like a swarm of hornets. "Would you like a brochure and a sticker?"

"I came for the…" I gesture helplessly in the direction where I can see people carrying plates of burgers and corn on the cob. My stomach gurgles loud enough for everyone within ten feet to hear.

"Fantastic! Once you have seven stamps in your Byrock Passport, you can turn it in for a meal ticket." She drops a glossy booklet into my hand. I've never actually seen a passport, but I think that's what it's supposed to look like. The inside has a spot for each booth at the event to add a stamp. I stare at her for a minute, every part of me wanting to ditch this goofy shit and walk away. But I can't think straight with the smell of barbeque sauce and freshly cooked meat floating through the trees.

"Got it." Keeping my head down and avoiding eye contact with everyone, I circle the park and collect the stamps as quickly as possible. Their sales pitches dry up as soon as they look at me; it's pretty clear I'm not in the market for insurance or soy candles. I can feel eyes on my back every time I walk away, like they're watching to make sure I don't snatch a child or piss in someone's lemonade.

The obnoxious red tablecloth on the last booth looks familiar. It's covered in flyers for the bank—Ollie's bank. Our bank, I guess. There's no one manning the table, and the big glass candy bowl is getting fucking pillaged by little monsters running away with giant fistfuls. Without thinking, I pick it up and carry it behind the booth. The folding chair has a green jacket hanging from the back, but I can't see anyone around.

Like an idiot, I carry the dish of candy off across the park, searching for its owner. A hundred yards away, in a lonely corner, I spot a slim body with a familiar head of gingery curls. He's pacing back and forth along the top of a retaining wall with a phone to his ear.

When he sees me, he stops sharply, flinging out his arms to keep from twisting his ankle and falling. "You scared me." Stuffing the phone in his pocket, he balances with one foot on top of the other. He's wearing red canvas sneakers to match his bank polo. "Did you need something?" His voice sounds tense, and he won't look me in the eye. He blinks at the candy in my hand and tilts his head.

"You were being robbed blind."

A vague, tired smile pulls at his mouth. "Thanks. Not a good look for a bank, huh?"

Digging the bent passport out of my pocket, I hold it up.

"Oh, shit. I'm sorry. Here." He hops off the wall and trots over to me. I stare at the top of his head, all soft and tousled, while he pulls out a pen and scrawls a star in the last square. Handing it back, he flexes his fingers nervously. "I lost the stamp, but that should be alright."

"Okay."

Like a nervous reflex, he checks his phone screen again, his face falling when he finds it empty. Gnawing his lip, he starts to text someone, then gives up. "I should get back. I just needed some air." As if there wasn't air everywhere.

When he tries to walk around me, my body moves without asking my brain and steps into his path. He stops abruptly and stares at me with bewildered eyes. I don't know what the hell I'm doing. Maybe I feel like I owe him for the sandwich last week. Maybe he's starting to pull at my brain like madness, because if there's one thing I need more than oxygen, it's someone to take care of. "How long does this shit go on for?"

"The fair?" He hugs himself, glancing toward the noisy crowd. "We set up at noon, and it goes until eight."

"Where's the other guy? The loud one?"

"Tristan?" Checking his phone for a third time, he shrugs. "He got a call that his mom's dog ate a hairbrush or something. He said he'd be back by three. I was just trying to call him, actually." When I check my own phone, it's almost five.

"And they don't have anyone else to step in?"

This time he grins without much humor. "We're a one-branch bank with about ten customers. Of course we don't." His chin tips up. "What makes you think I can't do it?"

"Nothing. Forget it." Shrugging, I drop the candy bowl in his hands and walk away, toward the food.

They have about sixteen grills going and mountains of food, but the stingy assholes only give me one plastic plate and one turn through the line. No one notices when I stuff eight bags of chips, a handful of ketchup packets, and some extra burger buns in my jacket pockets.

Pausing at the end of the long buffet tables, I scope out the chaos of the packed park. I want to take my food somewhere quiet, but I can feel that trailer park guy watching me whenever I go—whether he actually cares enough to do it or not—waiting for an excuse to end me. The crowd feels safer, even if it gives me the mother of all headaches.

Since I'd probably get arrested if I tried to use the family picnic area, I wander back toward that red tablecloth like it's a beacon. Ollie's slouched low in his seat with his head down, staring at his phone. The candy bowl disappeared, which means most of the customers have dried up, too. When I pull out the second folding chair and drop into it, the creak has his head jerking up.

He frowns, eyes troubled. "What are you doing here?"

Shoveling in a mouthful of pulled pork, I tap my plastic fork on the table. "I work here, don't I?"

Sighing deeply, he pulls off the glasses he only wears when he's concentrating and rubs his eyes. As he slides the thick, gray frames back on his nose, he plasters on a bright, fragile smile. "It's nice of you to worry, but I'm fine. I don't need you to babysit me."

His eyes follow my hand as I grab the M&M cookie off my plate and drop it in front of him. "Eat that. For the sandwich."

After a startled pause, his face relaxes into a genuine chuckle. "If you insist." He nibbles delicately along the edge of the cookie, like he wants to make it last for hours. Unlike everyone else, this man never looks at me with fear or disgust, only curiosity and something I can't grasp. "I gave you one other thing, too."

"What's that?"

"My name."

"Oh, I see how it is." I snatch back the rest of the cookie and pop it in my mouth whole. "I'm Jax."

He lights up with a soft, million-dollar smile. "Nice to meet you."

"All this stuff," I nudge the table with my boot and nod to the chairs and the large banner attached to a PVC frame. "Do you have to pack it up by yourself?"

Cringing a little, he nods. "I hoped Tris would be back by then, but it's just me. I can handle it." He sticks out his arm and flexes. Absolutely nothing happens. He flexes harder, grunting, then cracks up so hard his narrow shoulders shake with laughter. The faint wrinkles around his eyes tell me he's close to my age, but he laughs like a little kid—loud and free, with his nose all scrunched up.

I set my empty plate on the table, desperately wishing for more. "I'll stick around and help you pack up. I'm an employee, right?"

"You don't have to." But he looks so fucking relieved. "Thanks."

For the rest of the evening, I scoot my chair back under a tree and doze while listening to Ollie try to woo customers. No one's interested in a shitty bank, but he never stops trying, even as I can hear his energy draining away. By the time fairy lights come on in the trees and people start to head home, he looks completely exhausted.

"Fold up the small shit, and I'll take the tables and chairs to the truck." When I bend over to pick up the table, three bags of chips and half a hamburger bun tumble from my pocket onto the grass. Ollie glances from them to me with a weird look on his face, but I just snatch them up and lug the table away into the twilight, where a white pickup truck waits in the parking lot.

Ollie stuffs the tablecloth, candy bowl, and flyers into the cab, then sags against the side of the car with a groan, letting his eyes drift closed. "Thank you so much." He fidgets with his fingers, winding and unwinding them, then stuffs them into his pockets. "I'll see you on Monday."

"You alright?"

It takes him a minute to respond, like his brain keeps getting stuck. Blinking, he nods unconvincingly. "Just sleepy. I'll take this stuff home for tonight."

I can't exactly keep asking the same question until I get a different answer, so I nod and take off across the parking lot, trying to figure out where the hell I'm going to sleep tonight. At the edge of the park, I stop under the shadow of a tree and look back. Ollie has the truck running, but he hasn't gone anywhere. Leaning against the lumpy bark of the oak, I cross my arms and wait. Five minutes pass with him just idling all alone in the empty lot, headlights illuminating a dumpster.

Just when I convince myself he's fine, the door of the truck flies open and he drops back onto the asphalt. "Jax?" he calls, his voice strained. "Are you still here?"

I sure as hell shouldn't be, so I back into the shadows and turn to leave. When I check one last time, he's dropped to sit on the running board with his face buried in his arms, dwarfed by the massive vehicle. Everyone else went home twenty minutes ago.

He looks up quickly at the sound of my boots, his deep blue eyes and pale eyelashes a little teary. Scrambling to his feet, he stands there shivering, hugging himself tightly. The night air isn't that cold, but he only has the thin t-shirt and no extra fat. His whole body stiffens when I shrug off my leather jacket and hang it around his shoulders. As I step back, he pulls it tighter and sinks into it like a turtle trying to hide in its shell.

"What's up?"

"This is mortifying." He shoves his glasses up and roughly wipes his eyes. "Um, I was wondering if you'd be able to drive the truck to my house. I'm kind of stuck."

"How are you stuck?"

It's very quiet now, except for the buzzing of old, cobwebbed street-lights that glow pale yellow against his skin as he stares into the distance. Finally, his gaze finds mine again; he looks defeated. "I have agoraphobia."

"Okay? I don't know what that is."

My reaction confuses a weak smile out of him. "It's a panic thing. I can't drive when I'm having a rough day. If I try, I get dizzy and confused and most of my body feels numb. It's dangerous." He kicks a rock and watches it skitter across the parking lot. "And today's not a good day. But I need to get home and put my kid to bed."

He has a kid, but no wedding ring. I'm like a sad crow, collecting useless trinkets of information about a stranger I'll never see again. "No problem. I'll drive you."

Our eyes meet and hold. "Thank you," he whispers. "I'm sorry."

I take a step closer. "Hearing you apologize ticks me off." That wasn't supposed to come out of my mouth.

"I'm sor–" When I tilt my head, his eyebrows go up incredulously, and the corner of his mouth twitches. "Understood," he says quietly, fighting a grin. "I'll never apologize to you again."

"Good. Hurry up and get in the truck."

It's been a while since I drove something with four wheels, so I study the dashboard and test the pedals while Ollie climbs into the passenger seat and buckles up. He slides his arms into the sleeves of my jacket, the shoulder seams hanging halfway down his biceps. As I pull onto the street, he turns off whatever Korean-sounding pop music his friend put on this morning and rides in silence, his hands pressed together between his knees. The orange dashboard lights play across his face as he cranes his neck, watching block after block of decorative fences and yard ornaments roll by. He doesn't speak except to tell me to take a left or right until we're in an old neighborhood, run-down but very peaceful.

At the very end of a quiet street, he points to a single-story house with a few lights on in the windows. When I pull into the driveway and cut the engine, he doesn't move. "I have a question," he bursts out finally. "But you'd better not get offended, because apparently I'm no longer allowed to apologize."

"That's not part of the deal. I can still get pissed at you. You just can't do anything about it." Some distant, confused part of me tells me that this might be flirting, what I'm doing right now. But it can't be true, because I don't know how to flirt. Because someone whose cock doesn't work has no reason to flirt anyway.

He squirms around until he's facing me, resting his tired head against the seat. "I heard you brushing your teeth in the bank restroom the other day. Do you have somewhere to live?"

"What, no employee ever brushes their teeth at work?"

Maintaining eye contact, he stuffs his hands in the pockets of my jacket and pulls out two giant fistfuls of chip bags, sprinkling them across the seat.

"The fuck? I'm not the only person who likes chips."

Out come the squashed hamburger buns. He looks down at them in his hands and sighs. "I'm not trying to give you a hard time or pry into your business. But my friend Tristan has a couch in his garage that he would let you use for free. No questions asked."

This is how everything falls apart–getting entangled, owing favors. Bonds that hurt when they break. "I'm fine."

"Please, Jax." When I start collecting my chips, he grabs my arm for a second, frowning at me. "You didn't like seeing me anxious and overwhelmed today, right? Well I don't like seeing you hungry and exhausted." He lets go, flushing a little, and stares at his dented garage door.

If I had even a single idea of where to sleep tonight, I would turn him down. "Fine."

"Yeah?" His eyes brighten. "Here, let's exchange numbers and I'll text you his address. It'll only take you ten minutes to walk. He said he's staying with his mom tonight, but he never locks the garage. I'll let him know you're there."

My empty contacts list now has one name on it. Part of me, the stupid part, likes seeing it there. The rest of me hates it. Sliding my jacket off, he hands it back to me. I can't imagine his body makes much heat, but the lining feels warm. "Thank you for your help, and for introducing yourself." He sticks out his hand. Like we're meeting at a party or in a bar. Like it matters. Like someone did six years ago—except this person can see me clearly, every disastrous, unapproachable part of me, and does it anyway.

Chapter 14

OLLIE

"No, no." I flap my hands impatiently at Tristan. "You have to come at me, like you're trying to kidnap me."

He puts down the customer file he's trying to organize and looks me up and down. "Who the fuck would want to kidnap you?"

"Come on. I'm gonna flip you on your back." I dance from one foot to the other like a *Street Fighter* character.

Tris wheezes a laugh. "*You* are going to flip *me*?"

"Megan flipped me." Her school put on a self-defense class, and we've been pulling the moves on each other all week. "My back will never be the same."

"That's because she's a fucking badass and you're an old man." He shakes his head. "What are you on today? For my sanity, please go outside and run laps or something."

I'm on *something new and exciting happened for the first time in two years*. In this case, *new and exciting* happens to have a bad attitude and sullen, dark eyes that brighten when he sees me. He's been showing up to work alert and clean ever since he moved into Tris's garage, which has me patting myself on the back.

Grabbing my satchel from the staff room, I carry my laptop to the sunny patch of lawn behind the building. Fresh grass tickles my back where my shirt rides up as I flop down and stare at the endless, empty sky. When my eyes get tired, I open my tiny computer with all the letters worn off the keys and squint at the screen, trying to remember where I left off last month.

It started to rain as Samvir reached the top of the

And that's it. Wow, past Ollie, way to leave off. I don't even remember what he's climbing. A mix of stress and writer's block looms up in the back of my mind, so I quickly tab down and skip to a new scene I've been looking forward to: Samvir entering the temple of the dead. I get so engrossed in describing the cold, ancient shadows that goosebumps come out on my arms.

At the creak of the back door, I look up to see Jax. As soon as he notices me, he turns right around and goes back inside without a word. Sighing, I blow the hair out of my eyes. Why didn't I just say I was too tired to drive last weekend? I learned a long time ago that throwing the big a-word at people makes them treat me like a bomb that's about to go off. For some reason, Jax's face just pulled the truth out of me before I could think.

Listening to the blossoms of the cherry tree above me flutter, I focus on the holy knight as he enters the most profane place in the world to rescue his love. His love started out as a beautiful maiden, of course. After the cave-in, when I was pining for Jackson, I tried changing her to a man to see how I felt about it. I even jerked off to some potential gay sex scenes, until I realized I was only climaxing because I'd replaced the characters in my head with me and Jackson. So now she's a maiden again, because I don't need my heart broken in fantasy as well as real life.

The door slams open a second time, and I squint up at Jax's towering form. He's dangling an orange Tupperware container at me. "I found this on top of my jacket."

"Cool." I shade my eyes with one hand, watching him.

"It has food in it," he accuses, like someone played a horrible prank on him.

"I accidentally packed too much. Figured you could help me get rid of the extra."

He crouches, glaring at me, and I sit up against the tree trunk to avoid feeling so weirdly vulnerable. "You accidentally packed two sandwiches, two apples, two bags of chips, and two brownies?"

"I hadn't had my coffee yet. Want to eat with me?" I grab my own matching lunch out of my satchel.

Holding my eyes, he drops the Tupperware in my lap. "Stop doing shit for me. Just because I needed a couch to sleep on doesn't mean I'm your pet charity now."

"Hey," I call after him as he starts to walk away. "Don't say stuff like that when I'm not allowed to apologize."

He stops, but doesn't turn around. "I don't want you to spend time with me." There's a deliberate heaviness to each word, like rocks dropping into a still pool.

"I'm not spending time with you," I grouse gently. "Just sit down and eat the damn sandwich I made and pretend I'm not here. I swear you're more stubborn than my kid."

To my surprise, he eases down on the grass a few feet away and accepts the Tupperware in silence. I watch from the corner of my eye as he considers the contents carefully, like he's making a life-or-death decision. The sandwich wins, and he inhales it in a few bites, licking mustard off his fingers so as not to waste a single calorie.

Once the chips are gone, he lies back on his elbows and takes thoughtful bites out of the apple. The brown of his eyes looks lighter and warmer when he watches the clouds, like a rich mahogany. It's not until they turn to meet my stare that I realize I'm gawking at the way his shoulders bunch up in his polo, how his throat moves when he swallows, everything about him. Panic sparks in my chest. I haven't felt this way in so many years, which is *completely right* because Megan needs a mom and Ollie needs to think about his family's future, not give his heart to another strange, untouchable man. But I'm not strong or good enough to turn away the chance to feel happy again, even if just for an afternoon.

"What were you working on?" Jax asks finally, as I pack away the remnants of my own lunch.

"Nothing," I mumble. No one knows about my old writing dreams except Megan and Tristan. Jax just raises an eyebrow at me and waits until I crack. "Okay, so I'm writing a book. Or I was. My kid loves fantasy, so I tried to make something new for her to read. But I don't have the time or energy to do much with it anymore."

Tossing his apple core into the bushes, he flops onto his back and closes his eyes. "What's it about?"

"Um." I fixate on the screen so I have something to do with my eyes besides take him apart. "Do you want the long version, the longer version, or the polite conversation version? The last one is *just a fantasy adventure, yeah totally like insert-popular-franchise-here.*"

Before I can react, he rolls onto his stomach and grabs the laptop from my legs, dragging it across the grass to rest between his elbows as he frowns at my document. "*The gold-plated skulls lining the walls leered at Sir Samvir, as if they knew his God couldn't follow him here. It would take the last of his courage to face hell and come out alive,"* he reads painstakingly, batting away my hands as I try to grab my computer back.

"Seriously, cut it out. Don't make fun of me." I snatch at the laptop again, and his hand shoots out to grab my wrist. We both freeze for a second, his scarred thumb brushing across my pulse point.

"I'm not making fun of you." He studies my face. "It sounds interesting."

"Yeah, right." I yank my arm away. "You're a fucking hardcore biker dude and I'm a scrawny nerd with anxiety, writing stories no one will ever read."

He shoves the computer back toward me. "Read it, then. From the start." Stretching out his legs, he rests his head in his arms. "I'm waiting," he prompts when I just stare at him.

Not sure what else to do, I scroll to the top of the document and start reading aloud. I wrote this stuff years ago, before the cave-in, and it feels like visiting one of those friends who has their shit together, where you leave their house feeling messy and inadequate and a bit jealous.

When the embarrassment becomes unbearable, I cut off and bang the laptop shut. "I should get back to work." Jax doesn't move, and I realize he's dozed off with his face mashed in the grass. I'm not sure what that says about the quality of my writing.

Hugging my computer tight to my chest, I fold up my knees and watch his shoulders slowly rise and fall, his relaxed fingers twitch occasionally. No matter how many times I try to move, I can't look away. I sit with the ghosts of everything I wanted, everything I lost, the man I can barely remember, the promise I made myself afterward that I didn't need love to be content. The fear that if I do somehow find love, I'll erase him completely.

Reaching out, I grab Jax's shoulder to shake him awake. The warmth of his skin through his shirt shocks my hand and I just stop, with my fingers spread against his back, watching him sleep in the lazy spring afternoon.

Chapter 15

JAX

The garage stays chilly all night and day, but not as cold as sleeping outside. Tristan brought me a pile of old blankets big enough to keep fifteen people warm, and a space heater that looks like it's ready to start a house fire if I so much as touch it. He tries to make conversation every time he sticks his head in, but doesn't seem bothered when I only offer *yes*, *no*, and *thanks*. After I turned down his invitation to come in for pizza and a bad sci-fi movie, I found a plate stacked with slices of pepperoni sitting on the garage steps. I ate them so fast I burned my tongue and made myself sick.

Falling asleep next to Ollie scared me, a sign of how far I've dropped my guard with him and how much I'm losing focus. Self-loathing and frustration dog me all the next day, until I cave and buy a bottle of cheap vodka on the ride back.

I don't like being drunk, the way it replaces my feelings with someone else's, but the dark animal does. And today I'm happy to sink into it, to lie back on the tattered couch and drift. If I had drugs, I'd probably take those, too. Anything to get my malfunctioning heart away from him.

As I sat in prison, watching my memories of Oliver melt away, I told myself that at least it was over. I found the light that could pry me open and shine into my darkest corners, and I let it go again. There would never be anyone else. Now I've stumbled across another man—with almost the same fucking name, because life is a bitch—who has the sun in his chest and needs to be protected the same way I need to protect.

The vodka's gone, swimming in my empty stomach, and I'm inside out and drifting. If I had a little more, I might be able to erase myself completely and save myself the pain of walking away a second time. Because I know from experience how much it's going to fucking hurt, and I don't know if I can take it. My phone, the one that only has a single number, pings. *The hell could he want now?*

O: Wat's a pee trap?
Me: Excuse me?
O: In the sink. The video says the pee trap is broken.
Flopping my head back, I cover my eyes and groan.
Me: The *p-trap* is the u-shaped pipe.
O: Oh.
After a very long silence, I give in and send another message.
Me: What did you do to it?
O: Ask my damn kid. Water won't go and it smells like shit.
Me: Buy a new one. Ask the guy at the store how to put it in.

When he doesn't answer, I assume he's gone to wander around Home Depot looking confused. Just as I throw my phone aside, it goes off again.

O: Wat's it called where u have sandpaper but u plug it in so it goes fast?
Me: A sander?
O: kk thx where do I get one?
Me: Same place as the pee trap.

This time I just watch the screen, counting down in my head. After three minutes, it lights up with another text.

O: How do I make this ratchety thing go the other way?

Letting the vodka do the thinking, I hammer the video call button in the corner of the screen. After a second, it displays a very blurry ratchet shoved up against the camera. "Seriously, how?" Ollie shakes it.

"There's only one fucking lever on the thing." I try my best not to sound as drunk as I am.

Setting the camera down, he cocks his head at the tool. He's sitting cross-legged on a concrete floor next to a bicycle, wearing denim cutoffs, a tatty sleeveless shirt, and a backward hat with wisps of curly hair sticking straight up out the front. It might be the cutest thing I've ever seen. "That's a lever? I thought it was decoration."

"Are you having a mental breakdown?"

He grins. "It's Saturday. I'm fixing everything in my house."

"Sounds like you're taking everything in your house apart with no idea how to put it back together."

"I'll have you know—" he points the ratchet at me threateningly "—that I have been a single dad for twelve years and I can fix fucking anything, given enough time. Sometimes that means years, but who's counting?"

As I roll my eyes, my heart's going nuts in my chest, fighting the booze, fighting the darkness. I want to go over and fix all his shit for him. But I also want to go over and just sit, handing him tools and watching him fuck things up and figure them out again, answering his questions.

"Hey." The world tilts and blurs a little as I struggle into a sitting position. My throat feels strangely tight. "Should I come help?"

An almost guilty look flits across his face. "I can't. I have a thing later. But we could hang out while I do this bike tire?"

"Sure."

He picks up his phone and studies me for a minute, like he's reading my mind. "You should grab some water and a blanket first." I start to protest, but he shakes his head. "Go on. I'll be right here."

When I come back, holding on to furniture to keep myself stable, he's sitting there flipping the ratchet lever back and forth, trying to figure out which way he actually wants it to go. He smiles at me when I slide down under a blanket, propping my phone against my thigh. I sip some water and clear my throat. "Counterclockwise."

"Oh, thanks."

Leaning offscreen, he switches on a classic rock radio station and gets to work, bobbing his head to the beat as he pries the tire off the wheel rim.

"You into biking?"

He chuckles, not looking up. "Anything that involves coordinating more than two of my limbs at once is a no-go. But my daughter signed up to do this 20k bike ride for the local animal shelter, and I want to ride it with her. If I get my face scraped off or my nuts ground into paste, at least it will be for the puppies."

I try to imagine his child, what kind of person you become if you have a father who loves you this much. Ollie just putters away, commenting occasionally as he wrestles the floppy tire onto the rim and reattaches the wheel. "There you go!" Hopping up, he slaps his hands on the butt of his shorts to get rid of the dust. "I told you I could do it." But he sounds genuinely surprised.

"You couldn't pay me to sit on that."

"You're an asshole." Glancing at his watch, his smile fades and he picks up the phone. "I have to go. Maybe don't drink any more tonight?"

"I wasn't," I grumble, but he just raises his eyebrow.

"Tris is on a date. He has an Xbox in the living room you can use if you're bored, and an ass-ton of freezer snacks he won't even miss."

It doesn't occur to me until he hangs up that he probably has a date, too. I picture him in a nice shirt, facial hair trimmed and the tousle on his head slicked back, helping a beautiful woman with a flowery dress into his car. I wonder if she knows about the thing—*what's it called?*—agoraphobia. I hope she's ready to take him outside if he gets overwhelmed and talk to him, help him drive home, make sure he knows it's not his fault.

If I had more alcohol, I'd drink it all. I never made any promises. But I don't, so instead I venture into the quiet, dark house in search of pizza rolls and video games.

OLLIE

"I just had a quick question." Trying to sound casual, I prop the phone between my ear and my shoulder so I can button up my shirt. Getting hung up chatting to Jax has me running late. "Would you be willing to take my birthday and Christmas present money this year and put it toward braces for Megs?

Apparently, she needs them soon." The bank definitely doesn't offer its employees dental insurance.

"Honey," Mom chides. "You don't have to do that. We can just give you the money."

Biting back a sigh, I pull on socks, hopping around the closet on one foot. "I don't want you to give me the money. It's what I want for Christmas, I promise."

"If you're having that much trouble, Ol," Dad chimes in, "why haven't you just asked us to help?"

Because you sided with her. Because the minute I take your help with no strings attached, I've lost the independence I fought so hard for. My parents distanced themselves from Kay when they saw how easily she accepted losing custody of her daughter, but they've never apologized or acknowledged what she put me through. They're only sorry because they lost the fantasy of a perfect family Kay dangled in front of them. I've tried to mend fences for Megan's sake, but it's slow, slow going. "Because I don't need help. We're fine, Dad."

In the awkward, disbelieving silence, I flop onto the bed on my back and stare at the cobwebs in the corners of the ceiling. "We've been talking." Mom puts on her peacemaking voice, the one I came to loathe during the custody hearings. "Megan's getting to the age where she needs opportunities for her future. An absolutely beautiful private school just opened up here, that feeds into the best high schools and colleges. There's a science lab with connections to the local zoo and reptile house, and a huge library. They have story writing contests every year, guitar classes...she'd be in heaven." *You're still not enough for her, Ollie. You'll never be enough.*

I squeeze the bridge of my nose until my head aches. "I'm not moving back to New York. Our whole life is here."

Dad clears his throat. "We'd be more than happy to take her during the school year, and she can go back to Iowa on breaks and for the summer."

"No fuc—" I jerk upright, struggling to swallow the words. They're probably fucking right. But I'll search to the ends of the earth for any other answer. "No, Dad. That's never going to happen. I provide for us just fine. All I was *trying* to do was ask about braces."

"We're sorry, hon." Mom hurries to smooth it over. "We just know it's hard to do this alone." They don't even know about the agoraphobia, that I'm digging us into a hole because I can't drive or hold a normal job. They'd probably fly all the way out here to stage an intervention, bombarding me with offers to pay for a doctor or move us back home where they can keep an eye on me.

"I'm actually seeing someone," I deflect, picking at a loose thread on my chinos. "We're going on our second date tonight." Closing my eyes, I wait through the onslaught of *that's wonderful* and *we can't wait to meet her at Megan's birthday*. I'm never sure if they want me to marry again so Megan and I will have a complete family or so they'll have a second chance to turn me into what they want.

"I'm late, gotta go. Think about the braces."

Jamming my phone in my pocket, I roll off the old quilt and head to the living room to give Megan strict instructions on how much ice cream had better still be in the freezer when I get back.

"Are you sure you're alright?" Alice slips her hand into mine as we cross the parking lot to the movie theater. "You're really quiet."

"Just a little argument with my folks. You know how it is." Fuck, I've been living in Iowa long enough to start calling my parents *my folks*.

She laughs, tossing back her long, chestnut hair. "Sometimes I think dealing with my son's grandparents might be harder than living with my ex."

Tris and I hashed through every detail of my first date with Alice over pho and beer one night, and we concluded it couldn't have been more objectively perfect. We clicked right away, "blabbing nonstop about your kids like there are no other interesting topics in the world," as Tris kindly put it. When the waiter spilled wine on her dress at dinner, she just laughed it off and left him an extra big tip. If I had to marry again, I'd want it to be someone like her, someone comfortable and kind and funny. My parents would be over the moon. I caught myself imagining, as we said goodnight, what our blended family might look like. I almost asked how her seven-year-old boy feels about snakes.

Tonight, I manage to score an end seat in the row at the theater. The only way I can handle sitting in a crowd for more than a few minutes is if I have unblocked access to the exit. I haven't mentioned agoraphobia to Alice yet, and it sits awkwardly in my chest to know that I spilled everything to Jax an hour after learning his name but can't bring myself to tell her.

As we wait for the movie to start, she leans in and hugs my arm. "Ollie? I was wondering...Kyler has his last soccer game this weekend, and I was planning to take him out for mini golf and ice cream." She offers me a hesitant smile. "I know it's soon, but I wanted to invite you and Megan to come with us."

"Oh." I blink at her, trying to process the idea. Until now, I haven't let dating touch anything else in my life. Once I do, Megan and I and our safe, cozy little world will never be the same. There's something crawling under my skin, something frantic, but I'm so used to anxiety that I brush it off. "Thanks, Ali. That's a great idea. I'll think it over and talk to Megan."

"Absolutely. I understand it's a big step."

During the movie, she rests her cheek on my shoulder, her soft hair smelling of strawberries where it brushes my neck. I lace my fingers between hers, warm and intimate, and try not to think about how it would feel to be the one leaning against someone bigger and stronger than myself. To have an arm pulling me closer, a firm jaw resting on top of my head so that I know I'm safe. These weird, passing fantasies taunted me even before Jackson, but he sure as hell didn't make them better.

This is it, I psych myself up as we leave. *You're going to lose your child if you keep stalling. And if it has to be someone, it should be her.* I try to let myself lean into the faint attraction, stoke it into a flame. Because she's not just second-date material, but third and fourth and fifth, the kind that you introduce to your parents, spend picture-perfect holidays with, propose to in the summer at sunset. Together we could make a beautiful family.

I managed to get us here in the car I almost never use, pretending I wasn't nauseous and dissociated the whole way, so I focus the last of my energy on driving her back to her cottage after the movie. She turns the radio to a quiet folk station and rests her hand on my thigh, offering smiles that tell me I'm doing all the right things. I beg myself, my brain and my heart and my dick, to get with the program. It's starting to work; by the time I walk her to the front step, a faint, electric heat has started spreading from my chest all the way out to the tips of my fingers.

She turns around and presses close to me, searching my eyes. "I had a great time tonight."

"Me too." I try not to startle when she puts her hands on my face.

"Come inside," she breathes, smiling invitingly. "Kyler's with his babysitter, and I won't keep you from Megan for too long."

I haven't kissed anyone in years, but I brush her hair back and lean in anyway, because this has to be it. The part where I convince myself the butterflies in my chest are for this stunning woman, and not a belligerent loner who walks away from me every time I say something he doesn't like, but always comes back again.

At the last minute, my phone vibrates against my leg and every nerve and synapse in my body lights up with a single thought, as giddy as a teenage girl: *maybe it's Jax.*

"Fuck, I'm sorry." I pull back, scrubbing my hand through my hair. "I'm so sorry."

Her face falls. "What's wrong?"

I squeeze her hand, trying to communicate that I respected her enough to try. "You're incredible and brilliant. I...I have a pile of issues the size of Mt. Everest. It wouldn't be fair for me to take this any further."

Hurt flashes in her eyes, but she puts on a smile. "Thanks for being honest. Can we stay friends?"

"Absolutely." I gesture toward the door as I back down her walk. "I'll make sure you get in safely."

She shakes her head, laughing. "Because there are so many big, bad, dangerous men in old-town Byrock."

I picture Jax leaning against the wall by his bike, dressed all in black with his buzzed head and intense eyes, the scars and muscles. And I'm walking away from the most beautiful, nurturing woman I've ever met because I want to tap that. I really do have problems.

Before I can even get to the car, I check my phone. The text was a coupon code for two dollars off a delivery pizza. And just because I'm in a mood now, I order one and put pineapple on it, so that Megan can't eat it all.

Chapter 16

JAX

Dropping my roller in the tray of white paint, I head over to the window, shove it open, and suck in a deep breath of fresh air. Since there's no screen, I stick my head out and prop my elbows on the sill, letting my paint-splattered hands dry in the breeze. It's hot in here, my clothes are covered in tiny white specks, and I'm dizzy from fumes. I thought the manager was a soft touch, but as I end every day with a backache and a bunch of new cuts and bruises, I'm realizing she got the better end of the deal.

Something scuffles, and I look down to find Ollie sitting directly below the window, staring up at me with his head tilted all the way back. We keep stumbling into each other all the damn time, like some power out there thinks it's funny to watch our conversations swing from awkwardness to badly disguised flirting to God knows what in the space of a single sentence. This building is too small. This whole town is too small. I should have left a week ago.

"I was looking for you!" He scrambles up and starts digging through his worn-out satchel. "I have something to give you." Instinct tells me to slam the window and run, but this clumsy, gentle, sweet thing has me too well and truly fucked to ever hurt his feelings. I'm saving that for when I leave without saying goodbye.

Standing up, he thrusts a gift wrapped in a grocery bag toward me. His fingers tighten around the crinkly plastic, and his fair face with its dusting of almost invisible freckles turns pink. "Please don't think I'm weird."

"Too late." Goddamn it. I'm teasing him again before I know it, just to get any glimpse of that smile. He's made me an addict.

He rewards me with a shy grin. "Fine. I just...I make a lot of crafts, and I'd rather give them away than have them sit around at home. Don't think of it as a big thing."

When he tries to pass me the bag, I pull my hands back. "They're covered in wet paint. Just show me."

He screws up his nose, turning redder. "I wasn't planning on being here when you saw it."

"You're killing me."

Yanking open the wrapping, he pulls out a beanie made from chunky, gray yarn, with a rust-colored stripe running around it. It doesn't look dorky, like most knitted stuff—just soft and comforting. Since I can't touch it, he flips it over so I can see the other side. "Is it okay? I didn't know your favorite color, but something about you said orange."

I peer up into his worried face. "I thought you said you didn't make this specifically for me."

Stepping forward, he plants the hat on my head and pulls it down over my eyes. It's warm and thick, perfect for sleeping outside. "Stop being mean and just say thank you."

"Thank you," I tell the dark interior of the hat. For a moment I think he bolted, but then he tugs it up so I can see again. Avoiding my stare, he fusses with the sides until they sit right on my ears.

"It looks good," he says very quietly. His hands when he pulls them back are tensed into tight fists, and he takes a quick, ragged breath. "Would you like to go on a date with me?" he blurts, so fast it comes out as one word I have to piece together after the fact. As we stare at each other, I want it to be a ridiculous question, to be able to say *what the hell are you on* or *what gave you that idea?* But it's not. I can only ask myself *how could you let someone do this to you again?*

And my only answer is the man in front of me, waiting with his chin up like he's about to be decked. The mix of emotions on his face looks just as complicated as my own.

"Where do you want me to take you?" I listen to the words come out of my mouth like they don't belong to me. I'm *leaving*. But not today.

His mouth opens and shuts a few times before anything comes out. "You want to be the one doing the taking?"

"I should probably buy you a drink first."

The man looks puzzled for a second, then laughs so loudly that he claps his hand over his mouth. He can't stop smiling. "We have no idea what we're doing, do we?"

I just shake my head, unable to take my eyes off him.

"There's a bar about twenty minutes from here that's having a band I like on Friday," he offers tentatively.

"Okay then."

"Well, alright." He presses his hands to his flushed cheeks and huffs out a slow breath. "I guess that's that." Neither of us seem quite sure what just happened. It's almost impossible to believe the moments that change your life can slip by so simply, in the breathless second between a question and an answer.

He picks up his bag. "I need to get back inside. See you later."

"Uh-huh." Before I can straighten up, he steps closer and pulls the hat off, setting it gently on the windowsill. His eyes flick between mine, the quiet look that holds more wisdom than he knows. Then he grabs one of my hands, paint and all, leans in, and pecks me on the cheek. Face burning, he steps back and makes a break for the door. Something tells me I won't be seeing him again before Friday.

Studying the intricate knit of the hat, I try to imagine his hands working on it, turning a piece of string into a beautiful thing that's mine now.

Everyone deserves something that's soft and something that smells good–those are basic human rights.

I put my nose in the yarn and inhale. It smells like sunlight and his woody deodorant, with a faint hint of coffee. Something in me aches, that fucking organ in the middle of my chest that insists on delivering blood even when I want it to stop.

I've met someone, Oliver. He reminds me of you, so much it hurts. He takes care of me even when I try to drive him away. I think you'd like him.

Rubbing my sleeve roughly across my cheek, I go back to work.

Chapter 17

OLLIE

I'm regretting a lot of things. Not my arms tight around Jax's waist, my face buried in his shoulders as we speed down the country roads on his bike. But everything else. I've put myself in a high-stakes situation with someone I don't know well, in a town I'm not familiar with, in a fucking bar on a Friday night. A twenty-minute cab ride stands between me and home if everything goes south. When Jax pulled up to the house, I hopped on the bike without a word instead of asking if we could go somewhere quieter. I can't shake that eternal stubbornness, the insanity of putting myself in the same situations over and over, hoping for a different result if I can somehow try harder. I deserve the panic attack at the end of this, and I deserve to have my ass dumped.

I'm a windblown mess by the time we pull into the parking lot of the bar, tugging my helmet off and trying to fix my hair before Jax shuts down the bike. My heart plummets; the place looks packed. I don't realize I'm clinging to the bike like a life raft until Jax climbs off and holds out his hand. As he helps me down carefully, his strong fingers squeezing mine, it hits me that he's taking this seriously. Maybe he didn't only say *yes* to get me to stop harassing him.

"I like the..." He reaches out and tugs on the edge of my navy blue cardigan, which I pulled on over a white tee. "Did you make it?"

"Yeah. You want one of these, too?"

His lips quirk as he snorts a laugh at the mental image. "No thanks." He's wearing the neat button-down he had at the job interview, but part of me misses his casual, faded long-sleeve tees and battered jeans.

My feet start to drag as we approach the doors, and I stop dead when I see backs and shoulders crowding the glass. I can delude myself all I want, but being forced to stand up in a tight crowd is a hard limit I can't cross. "Jax..."

He glances over his shoulder at me. Before I can start babbling apologies, he inclines his head toward the side of the building. "This way."

Bewildered, I trail after him to a secluded strip of landscaping between this building and the next. There's a table that clearly came from inside sitting in the gravel, with two chairs next to it. Napkins, salt and pepper, menus, the whole nine yards. "What is this?"

He shrugs, with a *duh* face. "You don't like crowds."

Someone cracked open the tall windows nearest the table, so we can hear the music, and my whole chest hurts. "You've really never dated someone before?" I keep my voice light, like I'm not exploding from the inside out.

"No?" He shoots me a weird look.

"Fuck, man." I shake my head. He doesn't even think it's a big deal. "You have game."

His scruffy eyebrows go up. "I don't even know what that means. I just asked if they'd–"

Impulsively, I grab his arm and pull him into a hug. "This means a lot. Thank you."

"Sure, I guess." The stiffness in his muscles eases gradually, until his hand comes to rest against my back. It's the first time I've really smelled him, and something about the scent of his skin sets off a tidal wave of endorphins–words like *safe* and *mine*, feelings that stretch from one horizon to the other–and I have no idea where it all came from or why. When I let go, we both look awkwardly at anything but each other.

"I'll go get drinks and food." He stuffs his big hands in his pockets. "What do you want?"

I dig out my wallet. "I can pay."

After considering it for a moment, he shakes his head. "I've got it." And maybe the table was no big deal to him, but I can tell that this means something.

Smiling my thanks, I search for the cheapest food on the menu. "A rum and coke, and we could split the wing platter?"

He just nods and disappears around the corner. The chairs wobble when I sit down, the napkins keep trying to blow away, and the air smells faintly of cigarettes, but it's all so fucking beautiful I want to cry. For the first time, I don't have to spend the whole date managing myself and my surroundings. Jax gets it. He built us a safe place. And for some unknown reason, he wrapped his fingers deep in the messy core of me and said *I want you the way you are*. Though he might take it back if he returns to find me sobbing and hugging the table.

I press my hands together in my lap and stare at my sneakers, enjoying the gentle acoustic guitar through the windows and fighting a new kind of nerves I've never had the space to feel before, the kind that tingles and fizzes with uncertain anticipation. A breeze tickles my arms, the sky turning purple and hazy as the sun sets.

"Hey." I look up to see Jax balancing two glasses and a serving plate, with two bottles of water tucked under his arm. Scrambling to my feet, I help lay everything out on the table. My body's going haywire, sparking every time our skin touches, making it impossible to settle down.

"What do you think of the band?" I sip my drink, wondering what kind of music he listens to. He tilts his head and concentrates for a minute.

"The guitarist is solid. He's playing two melodies at the same time."

Dropping a couple of barbeque wings onto a napkin, I nudge the rest of the plate subtly in his direction. "Wait, do you play?"

He shrugs one shoulder, concentrating on his food. "I guess." The man doesn't look as starved as he did when he first came to town, but he starts mowing through wings like there's no tomorrow. If we kept dating, if we somehow in some universe got together for real, I'd make sure he was never hungry again.

"You guess you play the guitar?"

Hearing the teasing in my voice, he glances up. "Okay, sure. I play the guitar. Played."

"Were you good?"

"I don't know." Something about his matter-of-fact tone makes me sad.

"My daughter wants to learn. I got her a second-hand guitar, and she looks up the choruses to her favorite songs on YouTube and tries to pick them out. But I haven't been able to pay for lessons."

He swallows the last bite of chicken and studies my face. "Yeah?"

I shrug, not sure how we managed to dig this deep on a first date, like we've known each other for years instead of weeks. "Her mom...left...in a big blowup. I lost the financial security from my family, and with my agoraphobia I've had a hard time holding down work that pays enough. I know that's pathetic."

"What about your book?" Wiping off his hands, he slides down in his chair until his knee gently bumps mine and stays pressed against it. He's watching me with that intensity he always has, and tonight it feels like a flame held to my skin.

"What about it?"

"Couldn't you have a job writing books?"

I laugh before I can stop myself, even though I know he's serious. "Very few people are lucky enough for that, and they're a hell of a lot better than me."

"I thought it was pretty good."

"How many books do you even read?" I realize immediately how rude that sounded, but he grins.

"Zero. But I didn't fall asleep for five whole pages. That's a record for me."

"We'll add that testimonial on a sticky note when I send the manuscript to publishers. That'll do the trick."

He shakes his head impatiently. "You can't bitch about not getting published when you've never finished the book, can you?" It's almost completely dark now except for the windows and a few lights high up on the side of the building. His hand finds my knee under the table, squeezing gently. Part of me wondered if he even got what a date meant, where it could lead. But he seems to get it perfectly fine, and I'm the one breaking out in a nervous sweat. I've only had sex with a guy once, and it was not exactly an informative scenario.

"I'll bitch about whatever I want." I flick my napkin at him, and he catches it lazily with his free hand, his eyes still on mine. Everyone flowing in and out of the bar has to be wondering how a dork in a cardigan managed to land the most effortlessly cool guy on the property.

For a while we just relax and enjoy the music, his hand a soft, unmoving weight against me. His eyes drift half closed, and I notice his fingers shaping guitar chords in his lap. The band's set steadily picks up energy, from background music into rich, acoustic ballads. "Good evening, everyone," the lead guitarist rumbles into the mic. "We've cleared out the tables up front, and I want to see some of you beautiful couples out here dancing, alright?"

My gaze slides to Jax, who's still lost in thought. I nudge his hand with my knee. "Wanna dance?"

He widens his eyes at me, like I just asked if he wanted to get castrated. "No." When he realizes I'm serious, he looks pained. "You want to dance?"

"I always thought it looked fun to come to something like this and have someone to slow dance with. But it's fine," I add. "Really it is. I was mostly joking."

Relieved, he buries his face in his mostly empty pint of beer. I get up curiously and cross to the nearest window to prop my forehead against the glass. Now that it's dark, the yellow light pouring out makes it easy to see. Between tightly packed shoulders, I can make out four or five couples with their arms entangled, swaying to the music with swoony looks on their faces. The lead guitarist is singing now, something about how every person you fall for changes you, and it's beautiful enough to make me wish I was normal, that I could be in the thick of the crowd dancing with someone I loved.

I hear movement behind me. Before I can turn around, Jax's hips lightly bump my ass. His arms slip around my chest and pull me back against him, his chin resting on top of my head as he looks over me into the room. "I don't know how to dance," he murmurs. He has to be able to feel my heart stuttering like

I just staggered across the finish line of a marathon. His beats steady and strong against my shoulder, and for a moment the rhythm of it, the song that our two heartbeats make together, feels familiar.

"Neither do I." My voice has gone all wobbly. "I think you just glue your bodies together and sway."

"There's this move too, something like this?" And the motherfucking man lifts one of my hands over my head and *twirls* me slowly once, twice, until I'm facing him.

"I think you know perfectly well how to dance," I breathe.

Instead of answering, he takes my chin in his fingers and presses his lips to mine, tentative and searching. Pulling back a little, his dark eyes search my face. He grunts when I wrap my arms around his neck, go up on my toes, and kiss him back harder. His mouth tastes sweet and spicy, like the top-shelf bourbon my dad broke open at his retirement party. Wrapping his hands around my waist, Jax holds me steady as I lower myself back down.

"So we just sway?" He gives a small, crooked smile.

I nod, unable to speak, and rest my forehead against his chest as he holds me close and rocks us back and forth to the music. I don't know why I look down just then, at his arm. His right sleeve has ridden up his forearm from reaching out to twirl me, exposing a complex pattern of ink. That must be why he never wears short sleeves. I'm not surprised a guy like him would be tatted, but I am curious. Squinting in the dark, I try to make out the shapes.

Every part of me, head, heart, and body, shuts down at once.

"What about here?" Pulling his unhurt arm away from my chest, I touch the inside of his wrist, the pulse and tendons.

"I have a chain and barbed-wire bracelet around my wrist. What?" he demands when I snicker.

"That's really emo."

"Shut the fuck up."

Jax stops moving when I do, tilting his head in confusion. I let go of his shoulder and run my shaky thumb along the letters wrapped around his forearm. S-C-O-U-T. Trying to remember how to breathe, I step back and press the heel of my hand against my mouth, just staring at him.

"What?" He sounds scared, like he knows we're on the edge but he hasn't fallen off yet.

"Jackson?" It comes out strangled, barely recognizable as a word. "Jackson Moreno?"

I see everything falling into place behind his gaze, the answer to a puzzle that's been in front of us the whole time but so unthinkably impossible that we never even tried to put it together. "Oliver?" When it clicks, a feral panic fills his eyes and he starts backing away.

Knowing exactly what's about to happen but unable to do anything about it, I reach out my hand. "Please don't."

Jackson bolts. I can hear his shoes hitting the asphalt, then the roar of his bike engine. For a moment I let myself believe he wouldn't abandon me here, but I stand helplessly in the chilly night and listen to the sound grow fainter and fainter until it's gone. The music's still going strong inside; they're playing my favorite song, the one that got me interested in the band. I wanted Jax to hear it.

Dropping into my chair, I bury my head in my hands and struggle to follow the box breathing I learned from some meditation app. Four seconds in, hold for four, four seconds out, hold for four. Over and over. But it's just making me panic harder, my chest constricting until I'm gulping in air with no success. Because wherever Jackson's going, I'll never see him again. If he didn't want me six years ago, he sure as hell doesn't now. This is so ridiculously, existentially unfair that I can't even wrap my head around it.

Hands shaking so hard I almost drop the phone, I fumble to call Tristan.

"You alright?"

"Please come get me."

As soon as he hears my voice, he unleashes a string of curses targeted at Jax. My friend couldn't care less that I decided to go on a date with a man, but he did grumble something about why that man had to be a scary biker who communicates mostly in grunts and glares. Now I'll never hear the end of it.

"Hang in there, buddy. You're alright. I'm coming." He calls me twice on the way, just to make sure I'm still functioning. After twenty minutes, headlights spill over me where I'm sitting curled up in a ball on the curb. For a second, I hope it might be Jackson. But it's just the crappy blue Accord with my friend fuming behind the wheel.

"I'm kicking him out of the garage," he declares before I can even buckle my seat belt. "The bastard."

Shame burns in my chest. I hate that he's witnessing one of the happiest moments of my life go to shit, and I can't even tell him why. I just want to get home and knock on Megan's door and ask if she minds sharing a bed tonight.

"He's probably never coming back," I croak, turning up the heat to try and stop my shivering. "But if he does, you should let him stay. He has nothing and nowhere to go."

"What happened, Ollie?" He frees one hand from the wheel to touch my arm. "Did he hurt you?"

He fed my heart through a fucking wood-chipper over the course of less than thirty seconds, and I'm not sure I'm strong enough to put it back together a second time. "Of course not. We just had a misunderstanding, and the date ended."

"He shouldn't have left you alone at a bar at night."

"I know it doesn't seem like it sometimes, but I am a thirty-six-year-old man. I wasn't in danger."

When he starts to protest again, I turn up the radio and we pass the rest of the drive with Tris in sulky silence and me staring at the ghost of my reflection in the window. My brain tries over and over to process the last hour and keeps failing, like I'm a computer stuck on a corrupted file. Even as I wrapped my arms around Jax on the back of the motorcycle earlier tonight, some tiny part of me wondered what it meant that I could fall for another person besides Jackson. Maybe I could finally move on. Now it's all come true, the thing I feared most for the last six years: my heart's defective. There's only one person in this world who can make it whole, and no matter where we are, no matter *who* we are, I can't have him.

Chapter 18

JAX

I spent what was left of the night locked in the bathroom of the convenience store across from Dolly's Den. The latch on the door didn't seem strong, so I dozed with my back pushed up against it. No one ever came, because who the fuck would want to be here?

When I do sleep, I dream of darkness and Oliver hurt somewhere in the cave, sobbing. No matter how far I search, I can't find him. Then Ollie starts crying too, their voices mixing together and filling the whole world as I dig at the rocks until my hands are bleeding.

Running on minutes of rest instead of hours, I get up before dawn and ride to the other side of town. As I park my bike at a gas station a few blocks from Tristan's, I resist the urge to stake out Oliver's house until I prove to myself he got home safely. Instead, I walk to Tris's and sneak into the garage to grab my backpack and jacket. Maybe they aren't the kind of people who will steal my stuff and destroy it to get back at me, but I can't break the instinct.

I still don't know, even as I'm walking back to my bike, if I'm leaving today or not. I'm trapped, pacing between all my shitty options like they're the prison walls I memorized for five years.

That fucking guy from the trailer park is standing next to my bike in a white t-shirt and ragged jeans, smoking. He must have heard my engine loitering around the trailer park and followed me across town. When I stop at the edge of the gas station lot, looking around for an ambush, he just holds out his box of cigarettes. "I want to talk."

"I didn't do anything. I haven't come near your place."

He waits impassively until I give in and cross the lot. I've been trained since I was a little kid to obey men like him, because the alternative is the kind of violence I'll never purge from my memory. He taps a cigarette into my palm and lights it for me, but I just hold on to it instead of smoking and stare at a neon sign that flashes the *Bud* in *Bud Lite* over and over, blue light reflecting off puddles on the asphalt.

Shifting his weight, he studies every inch of me. "I thought you were just passing through."

"I am."

After a long moment, he smirks and shakes his head. "It seems to me you're awfully content to camp out in my territory for a while, get cozy."

"I—"

He talks over me without raising his voice. "I've heard rumors there are guys riding around the state looking for someone. That wouldn't have anything to do with you, would it?"

I shake my head, but I know he can smell the fear rolling off of me. "You want me to go? I'll get on this bike right now and head out." The words tear me up inside, like someone's wrapping barbed wire around my heart.

He watches me flounder like he thinks it's funny. "I'm not stupid, and you're not a random vagrant. You're from this life."

"I'm not." I fumble the lie out lamely.

Shrugging, he taps his cigarette on the fender of my bike. "Either you get the hell out, or you earn your place here." His smile turns nasty. "I guess this isn't relevant, since you definitely, absolutely aren't the person those guys are looking for, but I do protect my people. Whoever they're looking for would be safe with me. Especially if he's the kind of man who's worth chasing across the country."

Everything I did, everything I lost, was to get away from this life. "No."

"Fine." He brushes past me and heads for a car idling on the far side of the lot. "You have twenty-four hours to change your mind or get out and never come back."

I should be saving fuel, but I'm desperate for wind in my face. As the sun starts to rise in a splendor of gold over the farmland, I ride out of town until I spot a wide river with the silhouette of a railroad bridge spanning the banks. Hiding my bike behind a tree, I wade through the uncut, wild grasses until I almost trip over the tracks. The rails look shiny and recently used, but I walk down them anyway.

The old, knotty ties creak faintly as I stop from one to the next. I can just see between them, a hundred-foot drop into sluggish water. I sit down on the edge, letting my feet dangle into empty air, then prop my arms on the railing and bury my face in them. Sometimes I look down past my elbow at the drop and watch streaks of sunlight unfurl across the river. A few fish splash, and once a raccoon comes to the edge of the water and washes its hands.

I really try for a while to find the words to say goodbye. Because he deserves it this time. But there aren't any words, and eventually I just switch my head off and drift without feeling, barely breathing.

I won't jump. But if I heard a train coming right now, I'd stay here and enjoy the view for one last second. I'm not as brave as Oliver.

At some point, between one blink and the next, the river goes from dark to reflecting a bright blue sky. My back screams in pain as I sit up, stretching and rubbing sleep from my eyes. It's been hours, and there are dark thunderheads all across the horizon.

Ollie

"Hanging in there?" Tristan bumps his wheely chair against mine, his eyes full of worry. I look like shit, with messy hair and dark circles under my eyes from lying awake while Megan snored in my face and kicked me all night. Despite his concern, I know Tris is buzzing to hear more juicy details about what went down, especially now that I've spent the whole day jumping up to see if every little sound might be Jax–Jackson. Part of me thinks he never stopped driving; he could be in the next state by now.

"I'm fine," I grumble, folding a sticky note over and over in my lap. "It was a bad date. Everyone has them. Did Jax sleep in the garage last night?"

He shrugs. "He wasn't there when I got home. I thought I heard something super early in the morning, but when I checked later the place was empty. I haven't seen his bike anywhere."

I stare at my PC monitor, the reflection of my face laced across with the rainbow streamer screen saver. This whole thing already feels like a dream, the kind of story so unlikely you'd make fun of someone for trying to pass it off as true. The front door shuts, and I snap to attention. It's just Lionel from down the street, coming in for his weekly wire transfer to his son in London. I rest my chin in my hand and doze as Tristan walks him through the familiar steps.

"You and Megan should come over tonight," he announces when the bank's empty again. "We can have a fuck-bad-dates party."

"Megan hasn't had any bad dates. And I don't want a party. I want to cry and eat ice cream by myself." I throw my mangled sticky note toward the trash, but Tris catches and unfolds it.

"What do you have against the sticky notes?"

Flopping back in my chair and staring at the ceiling, I rotate slowly. "Did you know it's impossible to fold a piece of paper in half ten times? No matter how big it is. I was just checking if even one fact in my life is still true."

He stares at me with his mouth open. "Nuh-uh. That's bullshit." Grabbing an extra-large sheet from the printer, he starts folding with his tongue sticking out of the corner of his mouth. I rest my head on the desk and watch his confidence fade as he gets to five, then six folds. "This can't be happening." By his fourth attempt, he's graduated to crawling around on the floor with a four-foot by four-foot sheet of poster paper from the back room. It's a relief to find that I can still laugh.

The sky gets darker and darker over the afternoon, our first real thunderheads of the year boiling deep purple over the outskirts of town. Halfway home, the squall breaks, pounding rain and hail on Tris's car. The beater can't get uglier, so he just keeps going, creeping past all the nice vehicles hiding under awnings and thick trees. By the time we get to my house, the streets are overflowing like miniature rivers. The lawn tries to swallow my shoes as I wave to Tris and sprint inside with my jacket over my head.

Toeing off my filthy sneakers, I strip off my drenched polo and duck into the living room. Megan turned on the ancient gas fireplace for warmth, and the whole place reeks of burning dust. She cradles a mug of coco in one hand and Mars in the other as she labors away at her homework. Girl and snake both stare at me as I grab the fuzzy *Seattle, Washington* hoodie I save for rainy days and drag it on over my head.

"Good job on the homework, Skip." I offer her a high five which she returns with her non-snaked-up hand. "I'm proud of you."

"You're always saying that, but you can't be proud of me all the time," she points out cynically, crossing her legs and coaxing Mars to climb her arm.

"You have no idea." I kiss the top of her bubblegum-smelling hair. "When are Gray and Eli picking you up?"

"Fifteen minutes."

My old lawyer, Gray, and his partner, Jonah, live in a town about forty minutes away with their kids. Eli's only a little older than Megan, and they're inseparable. His younger sister, Kenzie, chases after them like a shrill and very opinionated shadow. The men have a river property where the kids roam for hours, pretending to be knights and probably doing all kinds of dangerous things I don't want to know about. Part of me wants to ask Megs to reschedule tonight and watch a movie with me, so I don't end up alone in a silent house, but she's been looking forward to this all week.

"I'm going to shower." No matter how miserable I am, I can't deny the bliss of hot water cascading down my chilly skin as

I listen to rain hammering on the roof and dripping from the eaves. Toweling off, I slip back into my hoodie, along with some sweatpants I cut into shorts a long time ago. When I get back to the living room, Megan's kneeling on the window seat, staring out at the storm, her slippers dangling from her toes.

When she hears my feet, she turns around. "Dad?"

"Mmm?" Wandering into the kitchen, I switch on the coffee maker to brew a fresh pot. I haven't decided between caffeine and alcohol for my night in, but I want to keep my options open.

"There's a creepy person just standing in the yard."

"It's Mr. Walters," I mumble through a mouthful of chocolate chips I snag from the baking cupboard. The neighbor on our right has some form of dementia, and occasionally he wanders the neighborhood and stares at peoples' houses. Though if he's out in this weather, I should probably go check on him.

"I'm serious." She sounds freaked out, which never happens. "It's not Mr. Walters."

Coming up behind her, I put an arm around her shoulders and prop my head against hers to peer out the rain-streaked glass. My mouth goes dry when I see the broad-shouldered figure leaning against the fence between our property and the next, not moving. He's got his arms wrapped around himself, his t-shirt clinging to his body.

"Stay here." I sprint around through the mudroom and fling the front door open, stumbling to a stop at the edge of the steps, under the shelter of the overhang.

Jackson's eyes shift from the house to me. He looks wrecked in a way that has nothing to do with the water pouring down the sides of his nose and dripping off his chin. He shivers hard, every inch of his body soaked.

"Come inside," I call, raising my voice over the roar of rain.

He shakes his head, jaw set.

"You can't just stand there." My heart clenches when he takes a step back, but he doesn't run.

"I just needed to say goodbye." He takes another step toward the motorcycle parked at the bottom of the driveway. "And I'm sorry."

"You need to dry off. I have coffee."

Paralyzed, he looks from the bike to me. Bracing myself, I step out of the shelter of the porch and hop on bare feet through the sludgy mud, my dry clothes darkening with raindrops. He watches me approach with troubled eyes, until I stop in front of him and cross my arms. "And you once told me *I* was extra."

After a long moment, he reaches up and brushes water off of my eyebrow with his thumb. His hand lingers there for a moment, against the side of my face.

"If you ever cared about me at all, Jackson, come inside and say goodbye properly. And do it before the mud reaches my knees."

His jaw tics, but at last he raises his chin in agreement. As he follows me back to the porch, I check behind me every few seconds to make sure he's still there. He waits in the entry while I hand him a spare towel and use the other to scrub my hair and wipe mud off my feet. "You can put your shoes on the rack."

"I'm not staying." He stops right in the doorway to the living room, stubbornly refusing to come any further.

I'm so focused on getting us hot coffee that I forget about Megan. When I turn around, she's perched on the back of the couch with Mars cradled against her chest, staring at Jackson. In the years between meeting Jackson and realizing he wasn't coming back, all I thought about was the day I'd get to introduce him to my daughter. Now it's happening by accident, with no fanfare, in the middle of the saddest goodbye of my life.

Megan's eyebrows pull together in a suspicious frown as she watches Jackson intently. He shifts his weight, his eyes flicking from her to me, and I know he feels the weight of this moment as much as I do. Rubbing water out of his eyes, he clears his throat. "Nice snake," he offers.

Like a useless guard dog when you toss it a juicy steak, my daughter brightens up and bounces off the couch to give him a closer look. "I'm Megan, and this is Mars. He's a super black pastel ball python." She always says that part in a rush, like it's all one word, and I can tell Jackson isn't following in the slightest. "Do you want to hold him?"

"Megs," I chide, finding my voice. "I told you to stop throwing the snake at people. Wait until they ask."

"Is he friendly?" Jax pulls his hands out of his wet pockets, examining the sinuous, black creature. "I like his color."

"Of course he is." Sounding offended, she grabs his hand and dexterously transfers Mars from her arm to his own. "It can take him a minute to get used to a new person, but he's really social because I have him out so much."

Jax watches uncertainly as Mars coils himself into a more comfortable position, wrapping around his hand. "Is he saying hi or trying to kill my arm?"

The doorbell chimes, and before I can say anything Megan sprints out of the room, leaving Jackson dripping on the floor, gamely clutching a snake he's never met before. "Here." Grabbing a mug of black coffee, I take it over and trade it for Mars, who's getting annoyed at all the passing around. I deposit him back in his tank, then step around Jax toward the sound of Gray's voice at the door.

I still find my old friend intimidating as hell, even though we've known each other for years and share a love of books. He's towering and broody and perfectly put together, with piercing eyes and flawless suits. Even though he's only a few years older than me, I always feel like a messy child around him. Megan once suggested I should share my writing with Gray, since he likes to read. I told her that if she ever showed Gray my manuscripts, I'd murder her and bury her body in the back yard. The brat thought that was hilarious, and asked if I was going to stab her with my knitting needles or boil her to death in my favorite crockpot of cider.

Megan grabs her purple duffel bag and barely swipes a kiss across my cheek as she gallops past me into the mud after Eli and Kenzie, arguing about who gets shotgun. "How are things?" Gray asks, ignoring the kids and leaning on the doorframe.

Not exactly in the headspace to hold a normal conversation, I land on the easiest topic. "I'm about halfway done with your project. It's looking great."

His face lights up. When he heard that I knitted, he took me aside and asked if he could commission a pair of gloves as a birthday present for his husband. The catch—Jonah's left arm is amputated just below the elbow. I've had a great time designing a sort of stump-cozy for one side, with a matching glove for the other. "I won't ask to see it tonight." The horn goes off in the truck behind him. "They're about to drive away without me." He flinches, but his wry grin hints at just how much this buttoned-up lawyer loves not only being a father to his own kids, but a second father to mine, too.

His gaze shifts over my shoulder and his brows furrow. When I look back, Jackson's still standing in the entryway, staring at his feet. Gray studies me, lowering his voice. "Is everything alright?"

No, absolutely not. But that's not what he means, so I just smile and nod. He takes one more look at the bulky, scruffy man covered in tattoos, then meets my eyes carefully. "Do you want me to stay a while longer?"

This time I shake my head, finding my voice. "I promise it's fine. He's a friend. Coworker. Friend. Go ahead."

Backing down the steps, he tries to find a way across the lawn that will save his shoes. "Call me if you need anything and I'll come right back. Seriously."

"I will." Waving, I shut the screen door, then the inside door, cutting off the chilly, rain-drenched air. For a moment, as the energy in the room shifts, I regret not taking Gray up on his offer. Aside from the name of his brother and the knowledge that he probably killed someone, Jackson's a mystery to me. But I can't find it in me to be afraid of him. I never have.

"Sit down for a minute." I step around him, my bare toes next to his heavy boots, and sit on the edge of one of the bar stools by the kitchen island.

He shakes his head. "My shoes are dirty."

I take a sip of my coffee, but it's already cold. My mug scrapes loudly against the countertop as I push it away. "Why are you here?"

"I told you. To say goodbye." He sets his drink on the side table where I keep my keys and backs toward the door. "I'm sorry this happened. You're a great guy, and I don't want you to worry about me."

I snort unexpectedly, bitterly. "Because you cared about that so much for the last six years."

"Jesus." His gaze darkens as he crosses his arms, all his muscles bunching under his wet tee. "What was I supposed to do? I was in fucking prison, Oliver."

I'm on my feet before I know it, slapping the countertop hard enough to make my hand sting. I've never been this angry, fire itching and crawling through all my veins. "And I was beating down the fucking door, begging to hear your side of the story. Don't you dare tell me you didn't have a choice. Did you read a single one of my letters, or did you just use them as toilet paper?"

He watches me in silence, lips pressed together.

"Do you want to know what I asked myself every single day?" Running my hands through my damp, tangled hair, I pace frantically back and forth between the kitchen and the living room, spewing words I've held in for so long. "How did I misunderstand what happened down there so badly? How do I have all these memories of giving myself to this person who upended my entire world, when apparently for him it never. Fucking. Happened."

He takes three quick steps forward, scattering mud across the floor. "Look at me." I shake my head, turning away, but he takes another step and says it again, louder. Shifting to face him, I grit my teeth and force myself to stand still with my arms wrapped tightly around myself, breathing fast and shallow.

"You think I had a choice, but I didn't. Everything you've heard about me was true." My eyes follow his unsteady hand as he holds out two fingers and his thumb up, like kids play at holding guns, and levels them in my face. "I shot a guy in the head, just like this. As close as you're standing now. And then I did it ten more times." I can feel my nostrils flaring, trying to get more oxygen, but I don't flinch. Finally, he lowers his hand. I don't think he's ever said this many words at one time in his life. "My life is a fucking nightmare. There's no place for you. There's no place for cute little girls with pet snakes. I made such a mistake, agreeing to go out with you. I was being selfish, playing with something I can't have. You think I didn't want you, Oliver? I fell in love with you *twice*. You're the only good thing I've ever known. But it doesn't matter what you want, or what I want. It's already decided. Do you get it now?"

Something in my head explodes in a shower of pain and absolute, raw frustration. I never yell, but I'm yelling at him, loud enough for my voice to break. "Then *why are we fucking here*, Jackson? What did we do to deserve this?"

The room goes quiet for such a long time, with just the dull thunder of rain on the roof, neither of us moving at all.

"I don't know," he says quietly. "I really don't."

One pathetic sob escapes from my mouth before I press my hand over it. My breathing's fucked up, just hitching and catching over and over. Because this is it. There's nothing else we can say or do or want or change. None of it matters. "You should go now," I manage thickly, trying to hold it together long enough for him to walk out the door.

Halfway there, he stops and turns around. "Close your eyes." I just stare at him, but he waits until I finally obey.

It's dark.

I can feel air stirring against my skin. I can hear the floor creak. When Jackson's hands take my face, I shiver and almost open my eyes again. "What are you–"

"Keep them closed. Smell me." A battered thumb traces along my cheekbone. "Feel me. Pretend we're back there, nothing in the world but us." His forehead rests against mine as his voice drops even more, until I can barely make out the words. "I was waiting there for you this whole time."

"Jackson." My voice comes out a whimper. I bury my face in his shoulder, rubbing my cheek against him, drowning in his scent.

"Shh," he breathes, pressing his nose against my jaw. He wraps his arms around me and *inhales* me, kisses my neck, my collarbone, runs the flat of his tongue up under my chin. He pulls back, and I feel his breath stir on my lips, our noses touching. "I missed you so fucking much," he whispers. Then we're kissing so hard it's not about lips anymore, just tongues and moans and the fracturing of our breath as Ollie and Jax do this for the first time and Oliver and Jackson do it for the last.

Chapter 19

JAX

He can't tell, but my eyes are closed too. He still smells like tea and houseplants and sweat and arousal, and his skin is still sweet, fierce sunlight. Maybe we're the universe's sick joke, but if the world is really this unfair, I'm going to force it to pry him out of my hands.

Grabbing under his thighs, I pick him up and sit him on the edge of the counter. His legs wrap around my hips and his arms circle my neck as I sink into his mouth again. He still loves to play with my tongue piercing, tugging and nipping at it. When we stop, I feel eyes on my face. I open mine to see him studying me with so much intensity and tenderness it takes my breath away. Looking back, I can't understand how I didn't recognize Oliver from the moment he jumped out of his seat behind the bank counter and beamed at a broken, empty stranger, like he'd waited his whole life for me.

His fingers slowly rub the back of my neck, teasing my hairline. "What are we doing?"

"We're in the cave," I repeat with more confidence than I feel. "And we're not getting rescued until tomorrow."

I can hear the faint buzzing of heat lamps from the living room, the ticking of the coffee pot, the never-ending rain. Neither of us moves or says anything for a long time, like we're deciding how deep we can go without breaking. Finally, his face relaxes into a weak smile. "Are we gonna have to conserve body heat again?"

"Definitely. Otherwise we won't make it."

His grin fades slightly. "There's..." He sighs. "There's something else I should show you first, in case it's a deal breaker. I was going to tell you—Jax—about it after our date, if things got physical."

"I'm sorry I left you last night." I grab his hand as he slides off the counter and pulls me down a short hall to his bedroom. Through a door on my right, I spot a room with a purple, leopard-print bedspread, life-sized sword replicas, and Metallica posters that could only belong to one person. Ollie's room feels unfinished and plain—the most basic Ikea bed, bins of yarn against the wall, and a big, messy watercolor landscape on the wall that looks like it was painted by either him or Megan. He's poured all his energy and resources into the parts of the house that have to do with his daughter, and let himself disappear.

"Unlike Tristan, I don't hold it against you." Oliver shuts the door, even though there's no one else in the house, and my body starts to grow warm and electric as it resurfaces more and more memories of his skin, his sounds, the things he did to me that I haven't felt before or since. "People do wild things when they're panicking. I should know."

He leaves the overhead light off and switches on a dim bedside lamp, spilling a circle of yellow light like we finally figured out how to make a fire in our cave. Feeling a little uneasy, I follow his gesture to sit on the edge of the bed. Oliver stands a few feet away like he's going to give me a speech, pulling his sleeves down around his hands as he shifts from one foot to the other. "Do you remember in the tunnel, when I asked you not to touch my dick?"

Of course I do. Like him, I've worked over every detail of that week a million times, picking at scraps of memory like meat on a bone, trying to find something left to sustain me. I never could figure out what to make of his request. I just nod, unsure what to say.

"I'm going to show you, but if you hate it, just please don't say anything mean."

I'm freaking out a little, wracking my brain to figure out what the hell he could have in his pants that could possibly make me want him any less. When he drops his sweats, it takes me a minute to figure out. First, I notice the navy briefs decorated with white stripes, because of course Ollie wouldn't settle for plain underwear, then the bulge of his soft dick—and there it is.

He's fucking massive. Even tucked away in his underwear, I can tell it's the length of my erect cock. I can't imagine how big it is hard, or how he manages to keep it discreet.

I realize he's watching my face, his jaw tight and his eyes full of a shame I don't completely understand. "Maybe this wasn't a good idea," he says unsteadily, trying without much success to cover everything up with his hands.

He studies me warily as I stand up and cross to him. "May I?"

After a long hesitation, he nods once and ducks his head. Crouching down, I hook my fingers in the waistband of his briefs and slide them down his thighs with their pale ginger hair. His cock unfurls to hang heavily between his legs. It's thick and uncut, with big balls tucked away underneath, and even though it's completely out of proportion with his body, it's just as beautiful as the rest of him in a different way.

Working his sweats and underwear around his ankles, I tug gently. "Step out." He slips his feet out and curls his toes against the carpet. His hands keep moving to cover himself, then dropping away again, flexing uneasily as he waits for something bad to happen. Wrapping my hand around the back of his thigh, just under the crease of his ass, I tilt my head up at him. "I don't get it. What's wrong?"

He sounds defeated. "*Ten-inch uncut cock* is a bad porn video or a thread in a fetish forum, not a person. I don't know how to use it, and women say they're into it until they actually see the fucking thing or I try and end up hurting them. Kay and her friends joked about it behind my back all the time. I've never told anyone, but I hate topping. I hate fucking people. After...us, I thought maybe being gay would mean I didn't have to do that anymore. But when I watched porn, I only found one bottom with a big dick and the whole video was about making him top because it would be a waste otherwise." Ducking his head, he burrows his face down under the collar of his hoodie, until I can only see the vulnerable expression in his eyes. "I'm sorry it doesn't match the rest of me," he mumbles.

Grabbing his fingers and pulling his hand out of his sleeve, I rest it against my cheek. "Is that true? I think I need to check." I tug the hem of the hoodie, uncovering his face. "Can we get rid of this?"

A tiny smile starts playing at the corners of his mouth. "You're so cheesy."

"I'm serious."

Rolling his eyes, he yanks his sweatshirt over his head, almost getting tangled up in it. "There. Are you–" He trails off as I run my eyes over every inch of the body I've tasted but never seen. Just like with his cock, his hands move reflexively to cover himself up, then fall to his sides again. His shape is slender but curvy, flowing into the dip between his hip bones and the round swell of his ass. At thirty-six, his body has some wear and tear, but his skin's still soft and smooth, with only a faint scattering of hair around his navel. His narrow chest rises and falls quickly, his pink nipples hard.

I can feel lust, the hardening of my cock that answers only to him, but more than anything I'm overwhelmed by awe and a rush of thankfulness. He's my only and everything, so fragile and strong at the same time, and this body has kept him safe and given him back to me for one last night together. In my world, something this precious would already be broken and ruined. Just now, I'm a little afraid of breaking him myself.

Pausing with my hand on his thigh, I check in with him. "Can I touch it?"

He hesitates, pinning his lip in his teeth, but his gaze has gotten hazy with want. "If you'd like to."

He squeezes my shoulder as I run my fingers from the base to the tip. I've never seen an uncut cock up close, and I don't really know how it works. When I brush the end, where the skin gathers together, he stirs and whimpers, grip tightening on me.

Fascinated, I grasp the shaft and pull the foreskin back, watching it stretch to reveal a dark, wet head and the sensitive, untouched skin beneath. "Fuck," I breathe. It's so raw and viscerally sexual compared to mine. When I let the skin glide down again, then draw it back up, he makes a louder sound, rocking into my hand, and his cock starts to harden. There's so *much* of it, so many ways for me to make him feel good.

I try to put into words the first thing that crossed my mind when I pulled his pants down, the picture he makes in my head when I look at him, so that he can see it too. "I don't get why any guy wouldn't want to see you kneeling there with your knees open and this massive, needy hard-on, begging them to make you come."

His eyes widen and his mouth drops open. "*Oh.* I...that's...wow. Jesus, Jackson." He flushes again, all the way down his chest this time, but it's not from shame. "Can I take your shirt off too? This is getting awkward."

Pulling off my jeans and stepping out of them, I perch on the edge of the bed while he stands between my knees and drags my shirt up my body. He gasps as he takes in the tattoos covering my torso—a mess of thoughts and feelings, old and new, hurt and anger and the need to feel. I've invested so much thought and pain into them, but I don't even like to look at them anymore. I hate him looking, too, seeing my past carved into every inch of me, twisted stories that I'd never want him to hear.

His hand comes to rest in the center of my chest, his thumb tenderly stroking the edge of my pec. Our skin remembers every piece of each other, even the things our hearts forgot. I tense up as he climbs on his knees across the bed until he can see the huge expanse of black ink that spans my shoulders and goes all the way down to the middle of my back. It feels like a brand; no matter what I leave behind, it will literally follow me for the rest of my life. I shiver when his fingers trail along my spine, then his mouth. "Did it hurt?" he murmurs.

I nod. "I should have gotten them lasered, but I could never afford that. Some hack said he'd do this coverup for free. It was kind of a nightmare."

Humming quietly, he rests his forehead between my shoulder blades. In the solemn silence that follows, he blurts out, "How many pull ups can you do?"

"Huh?" I turn around and frown at him. "I don't know."

He huffs irritably. "Figures. I hate people who are so fit they don't even bother to know how fit they are. I'd be bragging about it nonstop."

"How many can you do, then?"

Grinning, he bounces up on his knees, forgetting to be nervous. "Two. If I just ate a pizza, then one. Or three, if Megan holds up my feet." His smile turns rueful. "Zero when she tries to hang on my legs and sends us both to the floor and I have to take her to the ER to get stitches where her head hit the bathroom counter."

He's such a fucking dork. Even when I'm falling apart inside, even now, he always manages to make me laugh somehow, blowing fresh air and sunlight through all the parts of me I locked up and abandoned long ago. I throw my arms around him and toss him on his back on the bed, climbing on top of him. "I met her for all of thirty seconds and I totally believe that story."

"Check it out." He's staring down at our bodies. "We look hot together." Arching his back, he rubs into me, his nipples brushing my chest, and he's right. There's something crazy about his innocent, soft body pressed against my roughed-up one. "Fuck," he murmurs, and suddenly everything makes sense to me. I'm still learning what my body wants for itself, but I know beyond a shadow of a doubt what I want from him. It's my one chance, less than twelve hours before I have to go, and I want him so turned on he can't think, helpless to it, coming harder than he has in his life, all because of me. I want to make it happen, and I want to watch.

Our mouths find each other again, more frantic this time. He's almost completely hard now as he shoves down the front of my boxers and thrusts his hips, rubbing his insanely thick cock against mine. When I wrap a firm hand as far around our shafts as I can reach, he cries out and fucks erratically into my fist, his excess skin dragging back and forth along my dick until the sensation is almost too much.

The man looks stunning–the flush on his skin, his mouth abused by our kissing, gasping for breath with that giant cock resting along his belly and the dark tip jutting obscenely out of the foreskin, slick and leaking. I can't wrap my head around the fact that he's *here*, under me, hot and alive. Not a cold shadow in the back of some rapidly fading dream. He's coming apart at a hundred miles an hour, because he's never been allowed to let go before, never been worshiped, and he needs it almost as much as I need to give it. This feels like the best thing I've ever brought into this fucking shithole world.

"Open your mouth."

He moans and sticks out his tongue, still trying to hump against my thigh. When he tastes my messy fingers, his moan deepens and he sucks hard, shivering and pushing his tongue up between them.

"Should I turn you over now?" I pull my slick fingers out and show him.

"Please," he begs. "Fuck, please Jackson."

I help him flip onto his belly and kneel like he did in the cave, with his ass up. My eyes explore the faint constellations of freckles scattered across his back. When I gently pull his right cheek to the side so I can see his hole, he gasps and bucks. I've never seen a guy's ass before, and I wasn't sure how I'd feel about it. But it's just another piece of Oliver he's offering to me, and I could never want anything more than that.

Guessing what might turn him on, I nudge his knees apart wider, until the head of his cock is rubbing into the bed. He groans wretchedly, and I can see how tight his balls have already pulled up. I want to stroke them, but I think he'd go off if I did, no matter how hard he's trying not to. When I touch his hole, he jumps and smears precum across the sheets. This time

I know how to go easy, so I just work one spit-slicked finger past the rim, then another. His insides feel exactly the same as when they hugged my cock six years ago. I spread my fingers wide so he feels nice and full.

"*Shit*," he whines. "Jax, fuck. I haven't played with it a single time. Can you feel? It's tight because I saved it for you."

I come. It hits me like a wrecking ball, without touching myself, harder than I ever have before. When my cum lands on his ass he gasps, jerking against my fingers as it drips into his crack and down his thigh. "You feel that?" Still flying high on my climax but completely focused on his body, I fuck my fingers deeper into him. "You did that, Oliver."

He groans my name into the bed like he's about to cry. When he reaches toward his cock, I push him away and stroke him with my free hand, playing with how his foreskin moves, fast and slow, to see what he likes. "I'm gonna make you come so hard, Ollie. I'm gonna empty you all over my hand so you can see how much cum your giant cock makes."

His body convulses. Part of me wants to toss him on his back and put my mouth around his dick, but I'm not brave enough to take a load like that on the first try. Instead, I push him onto his side and lap at his slit as he comes, the salty, pure mess of it, his hands gripping my head.

When he finally runs out, he goes limp and lies there with his eyes shut, struggling to catch his breath. I climb over him and pull his back to my chest, where he belongs. After a few minutes, he wriggles free to lie on his back and opens his eyes, blinking in the muted orange light. As soon as they find my face, he relaxes into a brilliant smile, like a reflex he's not even aware of. It breaks every piece of my heart. I throw an arm and a leg over him and slide down to bury my face in his neck, where I don't have to look at him.

Shifting, he kisses the top of my head and strokes the shell of my ear.

"Okay?" I mumble.

He chuckles hoarsely. "I think you know the answer. That was madness."

I can't help but smile against his shoulder.

Oliver doesn't have a clock ticking on the wall, but I can hear each second pass just the same as we doze off, counting down until we're rescued again, dragged into the sunlight. Until his hand lets go of mine for the second last time.

But for now, we fall asleep naked with every part of our bodies intertwined into a knot that no one would be able to untangle. Our breathing synchronizes, our heartbeats too, sharing secrets with each other in the dark.

You and Me

Chapter 20

JACKSON

I jerk awake in an unfamiliar room, sprawled naked across most of a queen-sized mattress. My heart bolts out of the gate in a panic, but when I realize my pillow smells like Oliver's hair, everything calms. I rub my face all over it before forcing myself to sit up and untangle my legs from his quilt.

A shaft of sunlight pours between simple, gray curtains that wave gently in a breeze from outside. When I finally manage to find my jeans on the floor and dig out my phone, the screen shows noon. I restart the entire phone in disbelief, just to make sure, but the time doesn't change. After months of old cars and restaurant booths and couches, that damn bed must have swallowed me whole. For the first time I can remember, my mind feels nimble and my joints aren't aching.

I've slept straight through my twenty-four-hour time limit. If I'm lucky, I can ride down the dirt road next door and disappear before that guy catches on. Part of me wants to walk right out the front door without a word and disappear. Ollie deserves better, but I'm not a fucking saint. Ever since the first day my dad and his drunk friends hit me, I've spent my life trying to avoid pain. The only force strong enough to overwrite that instinct is my need to look into his ocean eyes one last time.

As I pull on my clothes, the sound of laughter floats through the open window, mixed with music that sounds like The Beach Boys. Warm light spills over my body as I pull the curtains aside and look out. I can smell the yellow roses climbing all around the window, but I can't see anything from this side of the house. It's so quiet in here, a dusty, peaceful kind of hush that invites me to sink into it and never leave.

When I move toward the rest of the house, my sock feet stop halfway across the room. Peeking out from the bathrobe and jackets Ollie hung on the back of his door, I see a familiar strip of flannel. The brown and white plaid feels so worn in my fingers that I'm pretty sure it's going to crumble in my hands. Tidy mending stitches mark all the spots along the seams that he's tried to repair, but it's more hole than shirt at this point. When I put it to my face, it smells like years upon years of Oliver, and all the places he's taken it—campfire smoke, sea salt, fresh-cut grass. I want to wrap it around him and wrap myself around it, until he's laughing and swallowed up in me.

Putting it down, I open the door and explore the hall, feeling like an intruder. I pee in the tiny bathroom with its chipped countertop and water-stained tub, then stop in the entrance to the living room. Everything's old and worn, the floors and walls, the furniture and fixtures, but it might be the homiest place I've ever been. My eyes move from the two dents in the comfy couch cushions—one big, one small—to the jungle of houseplants in the dining room and the wall covered in dozens of photos of Megan and Oliver over the years. Everywhere I look, I only see love and memories and mementos that are never going to get broken or sold for drugs.

Crossing to the sliding glass door in the dining room, I take off my socks and step out onto a cracked patio slab. It looks like a garden store exploded back here—ripped-open bags of potting soil, trowels, gloves, shovels. Those flimsy plastic trays that plants come in are blowing empty across the grass and getting caught on the fence.

"I'm done. It's water time," Megan hollers, jumping up from a bed of haphazardly placed, crooked flowers. She's wearing leggings caked in dirt and an old t-shirt of her dad's that hangs down to her knees. Her chaotic high ponytail bounces as she marches toward the hose coiled against the side of the house, not noticing me.

"I told you, Skip: it's not water time until all the plants are in the ground, not just the ones you think are interesting." Oliver's kneeling with his back to her, carefully filling in dirt around the root ball of a tree sapling.

I lean back against the door and watch as Megan uncoils the hose, tucks it under her arm, and turns it on.

"Megan," Ollie chides at the sound, still focused on his work. "It's *not* water ti–" He screams, high-pitched, when she nails him straight in the back of the head with a stream of water, knocking him onto his hands and knees. As he spins around and dives for her, I realize they're wearing matching sunglasses, the red plastic ones that the bank gave away for free at that business fair.

They wrestle for the hose in a geyser of water that glitters in the sun before Oliver claims it and chases his daughter until she's shrieking and thrashing around on the grass like a drowning cat.

When he notices me, he stumbles to a stop and stands there, panting and dripping as Megan grabs the hose away. He pulls off his sunglasses, revealing his bright eyes, and watches me with an apprehensive expression halfway between scared and hopeful.

Megan follows his gaze and spots me. She throws down the hose, letting it soak wastefully into the grass, and waves. "Hi again! Did you come to garden? Dad says I'm a bad helper."

"I can see that." I study the way Ollie's wet t-shirt clings transparently to every angle of his body.

She steps closer, wringing out the hem of her top. "I was gonna feed Mars his mouse. Do you want to watch?"

"Kiddo." Oliver turns down the music on his phone, still watching me carefully. "Go put on dry clothes and feed Mars, okay?"

Frowning at him for a minute, like she's trying to read his mind, she shoots me a curious look and scampers inside.

"You were nice to Mars last night, so you're her best friend now." He tries to peel his shirt off, but it's so drenched he gets stuck halfway through with his arms up. I push off the wall and rescue him. Water droplets cling to his skin and hair, flawless in the light. Wrinkling his nose, he tosses the shirt in the grass. "You alright? I wanted to let you sleep."

It's past time for me to go. I can't make my feet move.

He tilts his head when I don't say anything, his eyes worried. "Do you want to hang out with us for a while? We're trying to landscape and plant some vegetables in the corner. Later we're going to grill burgers, then set up a tent and watch movies out here." He smiles sheepishly, running his fingers through his wet curls. "We do this every spring."

I feel like I'm disintegrating. Goodbye is just two syllables, but my mouth can't manage it.

"You can help Dad set up the tent because I'm too short and he curses the whole time he's trying to do it," Megan pipes up behind me. She backs out the door, dragging a giant tent bag. Oliver winces every time it makes clanking and tearing sounds.

"We don't make guests do work, Megs." He eyes me a little defensively. "Believe it or not, we do teach manners in this house. You just haven't seen any yet."

"She seems cool to me."

Megan flashes me an approving thumbs-up, and I feel myself smile. This is something I've never seen before, not survival or sex or drugs or money. It's family. I get why people die to protect this.

Stepping over the lake in the grass, I turn off the hose. Oliver looks startled when I pull off my new flannel and drape it over his bare shoulders, but he slides his arms into the sleeves and hugs it tightly around himself.

I'm on borrowed time now, so I might as well live it.

And I do. I set up Oliver's tent while he's still trying to read the directions and Megan lounges on a patio chair, pointing out all the ways it's crooked. When I finish, she races inside and carries out armloads of pillows and blankets. Distracted from gardening, she curls up in her new palace with a tablet and starts watching some show full of teenage girls who talk insanely fast.

I wander over to the raised bed in the corner, where Ollie wanted to put vegetables. He's sitting on the edge with seed packets spread across his lap, sunglasses back over his eyes. The tops of his nose and cheeks are starting to turn pink with the sun. He smiles up at me when I stop in front of him. "Want to plant some lettuce? Skip's lack of delayed gratification draws the line at seeds, so I usually do this myself."

Crouching between his knees, I pull off his sunglasses. I need to see him this afternoon, all of him. My fingers linger behind, tracing the edge of his ear. Then I slide his glasses on top of my own head. "Show me how."

He swallows, eyes searching mine, his drying hair getting all mussed and fluffy in the breeze. Turning around, he draws lines in the dirt with his finger. "I want this row to be lettuce, this one carrots, and this one pumpkins." I watch his thumb press deep into the freshly turned soil. "I just make a little hole every few inches and drop a couple of seeds in, then cover them up." Brushing off his hands, he fumbles for his phone. "I got a good-sized pumpkin last year—at least I thought it was good. I have pictures somewhere; I tried to carve a dragon in it for Halloween, but it looked like a hippo."

Wrapping my hand around his phone, I cup the side of his face and press my lips gently to his. He makes a soft, longing sound of surprise, then kisses me back. If this ends up being the last time, I'm content with that—the smell of fresh earth and growing things, the sun on our skin, and a perfect, tousled man wrapped in my shirt, telling me about his vegetable garden. When I pull back, his eyes are full of questions I don't have answers for.

"Let's do this." I offer my palm, and he pours in a ticklish pile of seeds. Imitating his instructions, I work my way down the row, trying not to waste a single one. I've never done this before. I've destroyed a lot of things, but I've never made something new. No one ever showed me how.

Every once in a while, I can hear Megan laughing hysterically at her movie, and I notice that Oliver smiles at the sound every time, without realizing he's doing it.

Oliver

When we're finished planting, I water the delicate parts and let Megan go ham with the hose on her flowers. I'm pretty sure half of them float away, but she has to learn somehow. While she has her back to us, pretending the hose is a flamethrower and she's roasting an army of zombie vegetables, Jax puts his arms around me from behind and rests his chin on my hair. I don't understand what's going on in his head, whether I'm keeping him or losing him. He's made of walls, like a hedge maze with no map.

The three of us here, like this, brings back the fantasies I've tried hardest to forget—where Jackson and I somehow made Megan together and Kay never existed. I have to pull away from his arms before I go insane. "Will you help me get the burgers ready for the grill?"

He checks the sun, checks the time on his phone, and hesitates. Then, like a wild thing being lured to my hand, he follows me inside. I kick off my wet sandals next to his socks, then start digging through the fridge. "Tris taught me how to make burger patties with salsa verde and chia seeds mixed in. They sound weird, but wait until you try one."

Clutching the ingredients to my chest, I turn around and find Jackson leaning on the counter, frowning at a piece of paper he picked up from next to the fruit bowl. My chest constricts. I dropped it there last night and never got around to hiding it.

"I didn't mean to leave that out." When I swipe for it, he pulls it out of my reach and keeps reading. "If you're leaving, then you don't get to pry into my shit," I argue, holding out my hand.

He drops it in my palm, but it's too late. I look down at the thick, black letters: *DEBT COLLECTION - PAST DUE*. Hot shame curdles in the back of my throat like I'm about to be sick. I don't know any of his secrets, but now he knows one of mine, something I haven't even told Tristan.

"Is everything alright?" he rumbles quietly.

"Absolutely perfect."

He narrows his eyes.

"It's none of your business. You're not my–" I stop, because there are both too many and not enough words to finish that sentence. "Everyone gets behind on bills sometimes."

"That's a lot of behind."

"Have you ever even paid a bill?" I explode petulantly. "Or do you just ride your bike around brooding and seducing lonely single dads before moving on to the next town and doing it all over again?" When he doesn't answer, I run my hands down my face and groan. "You just touched a very raw nerve. I'm sor–"

"Remember," he warns. "No apologies."

"Is that really still a thing?"

Coming around the counter, he picks me up and sets my ass on the counter, sliding his fingers up under the edges of my shorts and squeezing my thighs. "You promised. You said never."

I cross my arms and stare miserably out the window. Megan folds the hose in half to cut the water off, but her hand slips and she sprays herself in the face. "Fine. I'm not sorry." Taking a deep breath, I pull his warm flannel closer around me. "This agoraphobia thing...I can't afford therapy, so it's just getting worse. I can't work normal jobs unless they're willing to accommodate me, like Stacey does. I've been piecing together all the work I can find and couponing like one of those homeschool moms with twelve kids, but it's not enough."

"It's not your fault," he murmurs in my ear. "The tunnel would fuck anyone up."

"It didn't fuck you up."

He leans back, raising his eyebrows at me, his brown eyes intent. "I was already fucked."

"When I got custody of Megs, I promised the court, and her, and everyone else that I was the perfect parent who would always take care of her. Now she's missing out on things she deserves, like guitar lessons and summer camp. Don't even fucking get me started on college. My parents, her grandparents, keep offering to take her and put her in these dream schools, give her everything she could ever want." I throw up my hands. "She's been my everything since the first time I took her out of the crib at the hospital, Jax. I'd die if I lost her."

"I know." He squeezes the back of my neck. "You're her dad, and she needs you. Could your parents help with the therapy instead, if they want to do something?"

I shake my head quickly. "They just want me to be their perfect son with his perfect wife and child, even if I'm miserable. I decided not to cut them off, but I refuse to accept charity from them. And if they find out what a mess I am, that I need shrinks and psych meds or whatever the hell, they'll never respect me again. I'll never respect myself again."

"Oh." A shadow crosses his face. The silence stretches out, because in the end neither of us have any answers.

"Thank you for staying," I murmur, taking his tired face in my hands. "Will you at least think about changing your mind? Not saying goodbye?"

He looks uneasily at the rooster clock over the sink, like every movement of the second hand is hurting him. "I can't."

Wrapping his arms around my shoulders, he pulls me against his chest and clings to me, face buried in my hair. The man I've dreamed about for six years is standing in my kitchen, real and everything and about to walk away. I start babbling, desperate. "Do you remember the Tower of Shadows? Megan and Tris and I get together with our friends every week to play that game, the one we did in the tunnel. I put the tower in, just for fun, and they're about to climb it. I guarantee you my friend Jonah is going to set off the mimic—and he's an amputee, right—so when it bites his arm off he's going to die laughing. If you came next week, you could—"

"Ollie." Cutting me off gently, he pries us apart. I can see the *no* on the tip of his tongue. And the *goodbye* and the *I'm sorry* after that. I grip his shoulders until my knuckles turn white, like I can physically force the future to change. Jaw tight, he stares down at the floor. He stays that way for a long time, then takes a deep, unsteady breath and leans in to kiss my forehead. "Maybe."

"Wait, what?" I gape at him, my heart stumbling to a stop in my chest. "Does that mean you're staying?"

I can see something wrong in his eyes, but I can't put a name to it. Instead of answering, he tips my chin up and kisses me, hungrily this time, like he's taking instead of giving, parting my lips and pushing his tongue inside to taste mine in slow strokes. Then he steps back, grabs his shoes, and runs out the front door without another word.

Chapter 21

JACKSON

Scout found me first, in the aftermath. He was only fourteen, but he didn't bat an eye at my face swollen beyond recognition, the dried blood, my broken hand. Or the bullet-riddled body at my feet. He poured water on my face until I was mostly conscious, then checked to see if I still had all my teeth. Propped against the wall, I stared blankly at nothing while he cleaned and bandaged my wounds using a first aid kit he stole from an ambulance once while the EMTs were busy resuscitating an overdose.

He told me the other men had already called the police on me, one of the cops on the gang's payroll. While I was bleeding in the dirt, they were planning how to ruin me for what I'd done.

"You're completely fucked," he tells me matter-of-factly, in his cracking adolescent voice, as he sanitizes one of my gashes. "It would have been better to let them kill you."

Over and over I thought back to those words, how right they were. Because no one can keep living this way. I told myself every day after that if I somehow found the courage to run from this life for good, nothing in heaven or hell or this godforsaken planet could ever bring me back.

Riding straight into the middle of the trailer park is a good way to get killed, but I'm over it. I just sit there with the motor idling and my arms crossed, waiting until whatever-the-fuck-his-name-is comes out of a trailer and strolls over with his hands casually stuffed in his pockets. It's a pointed insult I've seen many times, a flex that says *I consider you so little of a threat I don't even care how long it takes me to reach for my gun.*

He waits, making me talk first.

"I'll do it."

"Do what?"

"Whatever you wanted me to do." What a massively stupid thing to say, but there's nothing left in me except recklessness. "As long as I can stay here, protected, like you promised."

"Of course." I hold eye contact as we shake hands, keeping my shoulders square, but my stomach's twisting and aching. "Come back tomorrow night, before dark. We'll get you started easy, see how things go. I'm Garrett, by the way."

I could try and hide my name, but I'm pretty sure he already knows it. "Jax."

"Glad to have you, Jax."

As I watch him walk away, the familiar smells of this place creep into my nostrils—filth and decay and cruelty. Pulling a fast turn, I accelerate onto the road and let the wind wash away the stink.

I've taken my first step against the universe. I've offered a trade—the thing that matters most to me in exchange for the one thing I need more. It can't be enough. I, of all people, should know that fate takes everything and demands more. But if I can't fight it, I'll gladly take a chance to fuck with it before I go down.

I skip work the next day, even though I'm halfway through fixing the bathroom sink and no one will be able to wash their hands. Since Tristan's at the bank, I drag the hose from the side of his house and wash my bike in the driveway. After digging through his garage, I find a screwdriver shaped like that trash can robot from *Star Wars* and a wrench set that's never been taken out of the plastic wrap. Listening to my favorite blues guitarist on my phone, I work on tuning everything up and checking the tires and oil. Now I have a like-new motorcycle and nowhere to run with it.

After I wash my hands, I find a text Ollie sent a few hours ago.

O: Are you still here? Is everything alright?

My body itches to go find him, but I need to make sure this shit with Garrett is real before I see him again. Because when he's in my arms, I start making promises whether I can keep them or not.

Me: I'm here.

O: God, I'm so glad. Thank you.

When I pull up to Dolly's Den, I sit and read that text about ten times, running my thumb over the words, before I make my way into the trailer park. There aren't many lights except the small ones outside each door, covered in spiderwebs and moths. I can hear TVs playing in some trailers, yelling in others, and loud fucking from one. Since I don't know where to go, I head for the trailer Garrett came out of yesterday.

Someone opens the door as soon as I knock, like they were watching me come up. I'm hit in the face by a wave of alcohol breath, body odor, and traces of meth. The men sitting on couches and leaning on the counters all stare as I step across the threshold. My heart stops fighting when Garrett appears and takes my shoulder, pushing me to sit between two men on a mattress with no sheets. "This is Jax. He'll be working as backup. Arm him, but keep an eye on him. I don't give a shit what happens to him if he takes a wrong step."

I just sit still and keep my eyes on the floor until someone drops a Glock into my hands. A rushing sound fills my ears—*the most scared I've ever been in my life, the blood-slick handle of the gun, eleven deafening shots.* I automatically check to see if it's loaded, make sure the safety's on, and slide it into my jeans.

"Put this number in your phone, and answer it every time." Garrett watches to make sure I do it. Now I have two contacts, *G* and *Ollie*. After Garrett moves on, I add a bunch of blank contacts named *H* and *K* and *M* so that their names aren't touching anymore.

I don't remember the rest of the night very clearly. We get into tightly packed, run-down cars and go places where I and the guy assigned to show me the ropes stand around in parking lots until deals are done, then move on to the next one. I think we hit four or five towns around Byrock, but I don't try to keep track. They'll probably become familiar, in time.

A few more hours. Then you can go home. Not home where I was born, not home in Tristan's garage. Home is Ollie's bed, with his soft body pressed to mine and his sleeping breath in my ear. The only world where I get to be everything he sees when he looks at me.

"He's pretty good," the guy tells Garret when we're finished. It's so much easier to come back to this world than it was to leave, like switching to my native tongue after struggling to speak a foreign language. I've already made the wrong choice. I can feel it. I'm setting fire to my last hope of leaving this life behind, just so I can stay warm while everything burns down around me. But I don't know what else I'm supposed to do. I don't want to be cold anymore.

Oliver

At first, the tapping on my bedroom window sounds like a tree branch in the wind. When I remember there aren't any trees on that side of the house, I slide down and pull the covers over my head so the ghost or axe murderer will pass me by and go straight for Megan.

The taps turn into proper knocking, quiet but persistent. "The fuck?" I slur, staggering out of bed with my eyes still mostly shut. Half scared, half pissed off, I wrap my mostly naked self in Jax's flannel, which hangs almost to my knees. When I yank open the curtain, I have to slap my hand over my mouth to smother a shriek at the human face less than a foot from mine.

Recognizing the ghostly figure, I struggle to yank open the old, stiff window that's been painted shut a dozen times. "You motherfucker, what is the matter with you? Did my front door stop working?" When I squint at the numbers on my phone screen, the indignation leaves my voice. "Jax, it's three-thirty. Are you okay? Didn't Tristan let you move back in?"

He grunts affirmatively, but I don't know which question he's answering. Folding his arms on the windowsill, he props his chin on them and stares at me like he's dying of thirst and I'm an oasis. He looks wide awake and fully dressed, like he never went to bed. "I didn't want to wake up Megan," he rumbles.

I shiver as the breeze from outside plays on my bare skin. "I appreciate the effort to channel some Romeo and Juliet, but can we continue whatever this is inside?"

"Never heard of them." Reaching through the window, he tugs on the hem of the flannel, then brushes his fingers along my thigh.

"Did you come to take it back?" Possessively, I hug it closer around myself.

His mouth quirks a little. "Add it to your collection."

My face heats up as I glance over my shoulder at the plaid on the back of my door. "You weren't supposed to notice that." When he doesn't answer, I touch his fingers where they're resting on the peeling, splintery wood. "Why did you come?"

"Can I sleep here?" His eyes have changed. Yesterday, they were all turmoil. Today they feel heavy, almost broken. I have no idea what he's been doing for the last thirty-six hours.

"Of course." I turn around to go open the front door, but he just lifts himself up in one smooth motion and swings his leg over the sill. "Well then." I grimace, rubbing my forehead. "Thanks for demonstrating how easy it is to invade my house."

I mostly wanted to make him smile, but he just strips off his shoes and jeans without saying anything. Stepping so close I have to look up to see his face, he pushes his flannel off my shoulders so it drops around my elbows. His fingers trace up my bare arms as he presses his face into my neck. Night air pours off his skin, like he's been outside a long time, and he smells like something new—an acrid tang of smoke and unfamiliar sweat.

"What's wrong?" I murmur, hugging him closer.

"Nothing," he says against my skin. "I wanted to make sure you were safe."

"Why wouldn't I be?"

He runs a hand through my hair, then steps back, not looking at me. "No one's ever safe."

I make an aggravated gesture at him behind his back as he climbs into my bed and flops down, stretching his arms over his head. He's fucking impossible sometimes. When I kneel next to him, he pulls me down to curl against his side, and I slide my hand under his t-shirt to rest against his warm chest.

I watch him take in the glow-in-the-dark stars Megan stuck on my ceiling with Blu-Tack when we moved in. She tried to make Ursa Major, but half of them have fallen down, so it's just a scattering of spooky green shapes.

"Are we a thing?" Jackson asks abruptly, his voice hoarse with exhaustion.

Confused, I prop myself up on my elbow. "Jackson, you know we are."

"Is it real, though?"

I rest my forehead against his shoulder. I have no idea what it is. In some ways we barely know each other; in other ways we're the only ones who have ever really known each other. Of course it's real. "Do you want us to give it a name?"

He nods slowly, eyes still fixed on the dusty, fake sky with its plastic stars.

"Does that mean you're staying?"

Another nod, and my heart unclenches. "I'm so happy."

The smile he tries to give me isn't all the way there. "I need a name for when I think about you."

Leaning up, I kiss the corner of his mouth. "I can be your boyfriend. I'm not ashamed of that."

To my surprise, he frowns. "It sounds cheap. It's not enough."

Not enough for six years and a thousand miles and the rush of absolute peace whenever I meet him for the first time. "What, then?"

"You're..." He rests his fist on his chest, over his heart, like it's clutched in his palm. "You're this. You're the reason it's still beating. But I don't have a word for it."

I want him to explain why, if that's true, he won't tell me everything about himself. But I know it's not the time. "You're the reason I made it out of the cave and left Kay. The reason Megan and I are here."

Tipping his head back, he closes his eyes. "I've never had a reason for anything before."

"So you're my reason, and I'm yours. Is that good enough?"

His eyes blink open and fasten on mine. This time our kiss is quiet, sensual, sealing our words like some kind of promise. Then he rolls me over and holds me pinned to his chest, one hand gently wrapped around my throat as he kisses every inch of the back of my neck, slower and slower until we're both asleep.

Chapter 22

OLIVER

I should recommend my mattress to more people with insomnia, because the hypervigilant Jackson absolutely knocks out every time he sleeps here. He doesn't even stir when I pry myself from his arms after I've waited so long my bladder's about to explode.

Once I've relieved myself and taken a rapid shower, I pull on some gym shorts and duck into the kitchen to get coffee going and toast one of the biscuits I stress-baked yesterday evening. Peace and quiet fill the sunny room—which means my other favorite person hasn't gotten out of bed either, even though it's a school morning.

"Skip?" I knock on her door-frame, but she stays in a ball underneath her covers. "What's up, sleepyhead?"

When I perch on the edge of her bed, making the mattress bounce, she groans and stirs. "Go 'way." She sounds like she's talking with her fingers up her nose. When I brush her hair back from her face, her forehead feels warm.

"*Another* cold? Are you rubbing your face on the bathroom door handles at school?" The Megan-shaped pile of blankets giggles a little, then relaxes as I stroke her hair some more. "I'll call your teacher. If I leave some soup for you to microwave, can you sleep and watch TV until I get home? Or should I call off work?" We can't afford for me to take extra sick days, but maybe I can beg Stacey for some overtime hours.

"I'm fine," she croaks. "You can go."

I start to leave, then drop back down on her neon purple comforter. "Megs, can you look at me for a minute?"

She thrashes around until her flushed, sleepy face is turned toward mine, blinking like a mole that just got ripped out of its hole. "Huh?"

"You remember my friend Jax, right?" Maybe this makes me a bad parent, but my gut trusts Jackson with her as much as I'd trust Tristan or Gray. "He and I were...hanging out last night and he accidentally fell asleep."

She raises an eyebrow at me, but I pretend not to notice. It's not about the sex talk—we've had that. It's the *your dad's sharing his bed with a strange man you barely know* talk I'm not ready to have.

"He'll wake up soon and leave. I just didn't want him to scare you. Is that okay? I can make him go now if you want."

Patting my arm with one floppy hand, she offers a thumbs-up with the other. "Now go 'way, please."

Since I can't afford to get sick either, I kiss my fingers and tap her forehead, then wash my hands. When I return to the bedroom to put on my polo and slacks, Jax is spread-eagled on his face, his boxers twisted and pushed up to show the bottom half of his ass cheeks. He's got one of those butts that looks nonexistent in pants, but toned and pert once you get it out. I never thought I'd be calling another guy's ass pert. After Jackson, I gave the whole *maybe I'm gay* thing a try. It went about as well as the *maybe I can find Megan a mom* thing. None of it has ever felt right, except standing here and ogling Jax's pert butt.

Grabbing a notepad, I scrawl *Gone to work, Megs home sick, don't worry about her. Grab a biscuit and jam before you go. And text me later.*

Love you almost spills out the end of my pen, without even giving me a chance to think about it. That's not something I'm ready to tackle at 8:00 AM on a Monday in Tristan's car, where there's been a K-pop cassette jammed in the player for four years and the passenger seat rolls forward and back if you don't brace your feet. Signing my name feels too formal. In the end I scrawl a heart, like Megan and I do at the end of all our notes, and bolt out of the room before I can regret how cheesy it looks.

Jackson

I can still smell Garrett's trailer on my skin, and my body convinces me I'm back on a dirty mattress, trying to force myself to sleep longer before I get up and face the things I did last night and the things I'll have to do today. If Scout wakes me up, I'll get a kick to the ribs. If someone else gets here first, it'll be a boot in my face.

But when I open my eyes, I see plastic stars spangled across the ceiling, and a crocheted blanket draped over my legs. My phone says eleven. Rolling over, I read the note on Ollie's pillow. He just left me here with his kid, as casually as if it was my house, too. He even nagged me to eat his food. I look at the heart at the bottom for a while, then fold it up and tuck it in my wallet.

Tiptoeing so I don't wake Megan, I scrub last night off my body with the hottest water I can get. Once I'm dressed, I sneak toward the front door. I don't realize the kid's sitting in the living room until she clears her throat behind me.

"Shit. I mean—sorry."

She grins weakly at my language. Her eyes look puffy, her hair a giant tangle, and her nose is already turning red from the pile of dirty tissues scattered around her. Cross-legged on the couch in plaid pajama bottoms and a wrinkled t-shirt, she's clutching a guitar on her knees. "I won't tell Dad you cussed at me."

I realize I have no idea how Ollie explained me strolling out of his bedroom. I figure I'll keep my mouth shut. "See you later. Hope you feel better."

"Dad told me I'm fired if I let you leave without taking a biscuit." She sneezes violently.

"I don't need one."

The girl flashes fake puppy eyes at me. They're perfect copies of Ollie's eyes, a vivid blue that makes me feel like I'm on a vacation by the sea—if I knew what that felt like. "You're seriously going to get me fired? I thought you said I was cool."

"Fine." As I go poking around the kitchen to find the biscuits—and stumble across a bunch of Oliver's junk food hiding spots instead—I hear the opening bars of "Highway to Hell" playing from Megan's phone. After a little while, she pauses the song and launches into a painful, halting, and mostly wrong attempt on her out-of-tune guitar, interspersed with sniffles and coughs.

"Damn it," she grumbles, and starts again. By the time I heat up a biscuit and spread it with jam, she's made five goes at it, each one worse than the last. The more wrong she gets, the louder she plays—another thing that reminds me of Ollie.

When I can't stand it anymore, I come into the living room and sit down on the edge of the coffee table, catching pieces of biscuit in my hand as they crumble off. "Your dad said you were into guitar."

She pulls a sarcastic duck lips face. "Yeah. I love being the worst guitar player in the history of the entire world." But whatever words come out of her mouth, I can see how she's cradling that thing with almost as much care as her snake. "I want to take real lessons someday, when Dad's feeling better." There's not an ounce of bitterness in her voice, just a love almost as vast as Ollie's for her.

"Tuning it first would sure help."

So I'm not a natural teacher. But she doesn't seem to mind. "I had a tuning box thingy, but it broke."

"Can I?" Swallowing the last of the biscuit, I wipe my hands on my jeans and hold them out. Her eyes widen.

"You can play?"

"Maybe." I carefully lift the instrument from her hands and settle it on my lap. I haven't held one in probably eight years.

"You're going to catch my cold if you touch that," she points out.

I shrug. "Colds are scared of me, not the other way around."

She snickers, then sneezes again.

"Should I go buy you some medicine?" I've never done that before, but I can work it out or call Ollie if I get confused.

"Dad's got an entire drug store in the bathroom. I'm good." Her eyes stay fixated on the guitar in my lap.

"Alright, so I'll tune your E string, then you can do the rest." Part of me worries I forgot everything, but those six notes are burned into my body. I dial in the top string, then hand it back to her. "You're gonna use the fifth fret–" I guide her finger into place on the neck "–and make each string match the one above it."

It takes us a while, because she's got no ear yet, but we make it in the end. Her face is all screwed up with concentration. When her nose keeps dripping, she stuffs wads of tissue up her nostrils so it won't interrupt the lesson, and I have to struggle not to laugh at her.

"Play the song!" she bursts out as soon as we finish. "You can do it, right? I don't have the music, though."

"Run it for me?" I point to the phone, and listen to the opening as she gives me the guitar back. "Let's see." My hands try to run ahead of me eagerly from chord to chord, because it feels so fucking good. I sink into the music like I always used to, where I don't need to feel or hear anything else. I'd take my guitar to the riverbank or out in some abandoned field and play and smoke until two in the morning. Eventually, someone stole it, just like everything else.

When I look up, stopping the song in the same spot she paused the video, she's watching with her mouth hanging open–partly in awe and partly because she can't breathe any other way. "That was soooooo cool. You just figured out the notes from hearing them one time?"

"They're chords, not notes. Want to learn them?"

She practically snatches the guitar back. First, she shows me what she's taught herself; she sucks, just like I did at her age, but I can tell that she's been training her hands to contort into the more difficult fingerings. She's a hell of a lot more patient than I ever was. I figure she'll get bored or tired eventually, but she's obsessed with getting everything perfect. After an hour, she starts "Highway to Hell" again. It's shaky and slow, with a lot of mistakes, but now it's almost recognizable.

As the last chord of the intro rings out, she bounces up on her knees and squeals with absolute joy. "Did you hear that? I did it, I did it, I did it!"

"Good job."

"Can we call Dad? He needs to see this right now." Before I can say anything, she fumbles with her phone and rings Ollie on video chat. I can't see the screen, but after a couple rings I hear a clatter and Ollie's muffled voice.

"Is everything okay, kiddo?" I notice that Megan and I both start smiling at the sound of his voice.

"Daddy, Daddy, look, watch me." She throws her phone into my hand, and I find myself staring at Ollie's face outside the back of the bank.

"Hi." He furrows his brows. "You're still there? It's past lunchtime. You're going to catch her cold."

"He said he's too scary for colds," Megan yells as she messes with her strings, and Ollie's lips twitch.

"Oh, I see. My mistake."

"Film me Jax, please. Make sure he can see my fingers and everything."

Shrugging at him, I rotate the phone and check the angle. The second try at the song goes even better than the first. Her nose plugs fell out while she was bouncing around, and snot glistens on her upper lip, but she's oblivious. Jamming the last few chords dramatically, she looks up with her eyes shining. "Did you hear me?"

"*Skip*, that's *amazing*." He sounds like she just got accepted to Harvard. "I'm so proud of you."

She grabs the phone back and plops herself on the table next to me, turning the lens to show both of us at once. When I try to lean away, she just scoots closer. "Jax taught me. He's, like, a pro."

"Make sure to thank him, then." Ollie's looking at me instead of her.

"Thanks, Jax!"

I hold up my fist, and she bumps it. Instead of a normal fist bump, she makes a firework sound and explodes her hand backward, waggling her fingers.

"Now *please* go wipe your nose," her dad frets. Before either of us can say anything else, she hangs up the call and gallops away toward the bathroom.

Walking out on a sick kid doesn't sit right with me, so I wait around for her to come back. After fifteen minutes, I stick my head in the open bathroom door to find her sitting on the counter. She wore herself out so hard that she fell asleep leaning against the mirror, with a box of tissues clutched in her lap.

I stand there a while, trying to decide what to do. Touching Ollie after what I did last night feels wrong, let alone her. There's a gun in my jacket by the door, for fuck's sake. But I can't just leave her there.

Trying to get it over with fast, before I mess up somehow, I scoop her into my arms and carry her to bed. I wouldn't want to sleep in socks with a fever, so I pull them off, then tug her blankets up. There's a worn-out knit unicorn plush sitting by her pillow, its little gold horn drooping to one side. The man carried that thing through hell and still managed to finish it. Feeling stupid, I grab the toy and tuck it under the blanket with her.

After making sure I didn't leave a single mark on the place, not even a crumb on the counter, I go out Ollie's bedroom window again and shut it behind me, so I don't leave a kid asleep in a house with the front door unlocked.

Chapter 23

JACKSON

It's finally time. I couldn't put it off any longer. Fucking fantasy roleplay night or whatever the hell it's called. I still think it sounds like a sex thing.

I've spent the week remodeling the bank during the day, and working for Garrett at night. Maybe I don't need the bank job anymore, but I feel like I should have some cash put aside for when this whole thing blows up in my face. When I'm not working, I sit around deciding if it's been long enough since I saw Oliver to have an excuse to bother him again. I knock on his door like a stray and he lets me in and feeds me.

We're still pretending to be friends in front of Megan, so I doze in their recliner and watch Ollie knit while she does homework or plays video games, with Mars always on her arm. Sometimes she takes another stab at "Highway to Hell," and I lie there with my eyes closed, telling her which of her notes are flat or sharp. Most nights I force myself back to the garage so I can't sink into this life so deep I forget it's not mine. But I live for the other ones, when he takes me to his room and we fuse our bodies together, making out and talking in whispers and sleeping peacefully.

Just when I think the hell of everything else is going to break me, those parts make it all worth it.

This Friday evening, Tristan sticks his head in the garage. "Ready to slay some dragons?"

"No."

He shakes his head at the one button-down I keep dragging out for every occasion. "Unacceptable. Come here."

Awkwardly, I follow him deeper into his house, until we're in the man's bedroom. It's surprisingly spotless. I want to judge him for the nerdy shit displayed everywhere—swords and video game posters and pictures of those big-eyed cartoon magical girls—but he has old photos next to his bed of him smiling with a sweet-looking woman, and I end up feeling bad.

He buries his head in his tiny closet and comes back with three t-shirts on hangers. One has some retro-style art of knights and wizards, one has a baby dragon sitting on a pile of dice, and the last one says *I'm the DM's girlfriend*. I grab it and throw it on the bed, giving him a dirty look. "Really, man?"

"You guys can't stop making googly eyes at each other for two seconds. Believe me, no one in the room is gonna need a t-shirt to explain it to them." Crossing his arms, he nods to the other shirts. "Pick one."

"This game has a fucking dress code?"

"No, but if Ollie sees you in that little dragon shirt I guarantee you'll get laid."

"Whatever." I pull off my dress shirt and drag the tee over my head. It shows my tattoos, which is probably a terrible idea for meeting new people, but I don't have the energy left to care.

Tristan gives my look a seductive eyebrow waggle, and I can't help but chuckle. Ollie has weird fucking friends, but I don't hate them. "Thanks. I guess."

Tris hands me a two-liter of coke and a bottle of rum, then picks up a case of cider. "If we want any decent drinks at all, we have to bring them. Gray and Jonah's house only serves artisan wine or Pabst Blue Ribbon, nothing in between."

Even though we're silent on the way to Ollie's house, listening to more of Tristan's shit music, it's not a bad silence. Oliver told me he had to talk Tris down from lighting my ass on fire after I ditched him at the bar, and honestly that makes me like him more. He's been protecting my guy for years, no questions asked.

When we pull up to the sagging, white house, Tris honks and Megan comes sailing down the stairs in one leap, a backpack banging on her shoulder. Oliver appears a few minutes later, trying to pull on a shoe with one hand and lock the door with the other. Every time I see him, my whole body gets warm and the aching knot in my chest relaxes. I'd do anything for one more hit of that feeling. When he catches me watching him through the car window, he grins shyly.

For the whole forty-five-minute drive, Megan tries to catch me up on their game. I couldn't understand it the first time, in the tunnel, and she keeps using words I've never heard before like *lich* and *paladin* and *nat 20*. I'm dead on my feet, so I just zone out and say "uh-huh" whenever she pauses for breath. At some point, Oliver sneaks his hand around the headrest from his seat behind me and strokes the skin under my ear until I almost fall asleep.

Gray and Jonah live in a beautiful farmhouse at the end of a mile-long gravel driveway, backed by a giant workshop full of what looks like tractors. As I follow everyone to the front door, I spot a muddy pickup truck and a smoking hot Aston Martin parked side by side in the garage. That must be the Pabst and the artisan wine. These guys make quite the couple.

"I like your shirt," Ollie murmurs as we wait for someone to answer the door, happily hooking his pinkie around mine for a second. And I don't care about getting laid, but that moment alone is worth thanking Tristan for.

A curly-haired little girl of maybe eight throws the front door open. "Eli got the new Pokémon game and he picked the grass starter without you even though you told him to pick fire," she announces instead of saying hello. I swear these people speak in fucking code.

"He did *not*." Megan charges through the door, and they scamper away into the depths of the house, leaving the adults to let themselves into a paneled hall with restored antique furniture and paintings of local landscapes. Houses like this make me nervous; I feel like I'm getting them dirty even after I take my shoes off. I would have covered my tattoos if I'd known. *Ollie wants me here.* I tell myself that over and over.

Tristan angles away into a cozy living room. Someone pushed the furniture out of the way and set up a long table down the middle. Ollie helps me carry the alcohol back into a kitchen overflowing with so many different smells it makes me dizzy.

The guy who pops his head out of the stove looks younger than the rest of us, maybe thirty. He's holding a tray of hot cookies in one hand and the other—doesn't exist, ending in a stump below his elbow. "Hey!" he beams, babbling just as excitedly as the kids. "I've been working on my character, and he can attack five times per turn now."

Oliver clears his throat with a stern expression. "That is one hundred percent not legal, Jonah. You'll have to show me your math."

Jonah winks at me when Ollie's not looking. "So what you're saying is that the math will look a lot better after some snacks, right?"

As he sets the tray down, my eyes take in the plates scattered everywhere—cookies, cinnamon rolls, sandwiches, veggies. I've never seen so much food in one place that I'm allowed to eat. I stuff my hands in my pockets to keep them under control.

"I promise there are only five of us." I realize he's talking to me, his chocolate-colored eyes warm. "I just like to cook. And Gray eats everything we don't finish later, when he thinks I'm not paying attention."

"I'm Jax." I don't know what to say or where to look, so I stare at the back of Oliver's head.

"Jonah." As we shake hands, it hits me that he's the first person I've met besides Oliver who doesn't assess me, studying each scar and tattoo so he can speculate on what kind of criminal I am. He's more interested in the rum in my hand. "That looks super fancy."

"It was just on Tristan's refrigerator." It drops flecks of dust every time I move it.

"But look." He grabs the bottle and turns it over. "The glass is all faceted. And it has a dog on the label. I mean..." He shows me the dog, like I might not have noticed it.

Oliver peers over my shoulder. "Aww, he's so cute!"

I look between them as they coo over the tiny hound on the label, something so stupid, and for the first time this week I don't feel like I'm coming apart. Forgetting that we're still supposedly a secret until Ollie decides how to explain our relationship to Megan, I grab the back of his neck and put my nose in his hair for a second. I pull away quickly when I remember, but Jonah either misses it or pretends not to notice.

"Come see the table." Oliver goes to grab my hand, then catches himself.

In the living room, Tris is playing with a stack of weird-shaped dice with more than six sides. I'm pretty sure none of them can be used to gamble, which explains why I've never seen them before. Megan and a boy with dark, curly hair sprawl on the carpet, bickering over a video game.

"I could tell them to make you a character sheet," Ollie murmurs as he unloads all kinds of shit from his bag—books, dice, a vinyl mat with squares on it, and plastic figurines. There's so much setup I feel like they're about to start summoning demons. He flashes me a grin.

"You're not tricking me into playing this fucking game again." I growl close to his ear, and he shivers, even though I wasn't meaning to be sexy. He really is a horny little thing, underneath all the inhibitions, and it surprises me how much I like it. I get off on spending an unhealthy amount of time thinking of new ways to make him feel good, and he gets off on finding all the things I like to do with him that aren't sex. Like we were made for each other.

When Jonah comes in, he's toting a fussy baby on his shoulder. "Someone's having trouble falling asleep."

"Hi Davey!" Megan waves at the baby, who just snivels some more. Jonah drops onto the couch at the far side of the table and lets the kid splay out on his chest, patting its back. The boy on the floor climbs up next to him and leans a head on his shoulder, while Megan snuggles in next to him. Jonah catches me gawking at them, but he just smiles and turns his attention back to the game.

I still don't get how this thing works, but I start to understand why Ollie loves it so much. When lots of people play at once, instead of just me, it's loud and chaotic and creative. Everyone listens, enthralled, as Oliver perches on the edge of his seat and weaves a word picture of the Tower of

Shadows. He's souped the place up, with more guards and traps, plus a maze of thorny vines around it.

I can't stop staring at him, my Ollie, because he's lit up and radiant, describing every enemy they meet and springing surprise plot twists on them. This is the man I glimpsed in that story he started to read to me, the stuff he wrote before that bitch and a train accident and the agoraphobia broke him down. It's still in there, like guitar is still in me, but I don't know what I can do for him to bring it back.

When the adventurers find the top of the tower, Oliver keeps glancing at me as they get closer to the monster chest. Curious what chump is gonna fall for it like I did, I sit up and start paying attention. My arm ended up around Ollie at some point—which I guess is something people who aren't fucking might do on a crowded loveseat. Except that he keeps leaning into me until we're pretty much snuggling. I'm too relaxed to do anything about it now besides drift in the sensation of his breathing against my side.

I jump at the sound of the front door, tensing up. So many bad things happened when our front door opened as a kid that I still feel the urge to cower sometimes. Ollie puts a hand on my knee under the table.

A tall man appears in the entry, pulling off his jacket and dropping his keys in a bowl. He's the guy who glared at me while he was picking up Megan the other week—not that I blame him. There's something cool and assessing in his eyes that makes me feel stripped down, like he can see everything about me that the others don't notice. I'm certain he's on to Ollie and me, even though he's been in the room for less than five seconds. I don't like him, but he has to be a good man if his family is so happy.

"Hey, everyone." His eyes catch on me longer than the others, dropping to take in my tattoos before moving on. "How many dragons have you dungeoned tonight?"

"I will cut up all your suits if you ask that question again." Jonah cranes his neck for a kiss, then gingerly passes Gray the sleeping baby. "It stopped being funny before you said it the first ten times."

"Jax." Oliver squeezes my knee again. "This is Gray. He was my lawyer."

Maybe if I wasn't so fucking exhausted, if I wasn't already on edge from the door opening, it wouldn't have hit me wrong. Gray leans across the table to offer his hand, but I'm already on my feet, hemmed in by the furniture and the room full of people and this fucking lawyer sticking his hand in my face and smiling. I need to get out.

OLIVER

I feel Jackson go rigid. When I look up, his face is completely blank. Shaking off my hand, he stands up abruptly. When he realizes he's blocked in, he scrambles over the back of his chair and walks out of the room without a word. The front door bangs shut behind him, and I'm left with five people and a baby staring at me as if I have the answers. Megan sits up, her sad, confused eyes telling me that if I don't go after him, she will.

Gray's brows furrow as he straightens up, soothing Davey's restless whimpers. "I don't understand what just happened, but I'm sorry."

I open my mouth to apologize for Jackson, then stop. He had a reason for leaving, and I shouldn't invalidate his choice before I understand it. Tristan and I have a moment of silent eyebrow communication, and he takes over. "Food break, guys." We've been eating all night, but that won't slow anyone down.

Gray follows me to the entry and watches me pull on my shoes. He's gone all intimidating again, towering between me and the door with a look intense enough to melt steel. Only the baby drooling on his shirt breaks the image. He drops his voice so the others can't hear. "I'm here to take care of my family, and that includes you and Megan. I know you've gotten...close, but that man makes me uneasy. Are you sure he's safe?"

I straighten up and meet his stare. The man can't help but look stern, except when he smiles and it all melts away. "Gray, I didn't get a chance to tell you earlier, but Jax is *the* Jackson. Jackson Moreno, from the tunnel."

His hazel eyes widen. "You can't be serious." But instead of easing up, his expression clouds even more. "The Jackson who committed manslaughter?"

"Listen." I put my hand on his arm. "Has Megan told you my rule, about how your success matters, even if it doesn't look like other people's?"

He huffs a quiet laugh in spite of himself. "Indeed she has."

"This is just a simple game night, but Jackson has fought so, so much harder than the rest of us to make it here. He doesn't look like me or Tristan, he's rough around the edges, and yes, something horrific happened in his past. But he's been through so much to get here. I need you to trust me, if you can't trust him. And yeah, we're together, which is why I need to go take care of him."

He studies me for a moment, then nods slowly. "I'm sorry for grilling you. It's a bad habit for a lawyer. We'll keep Megan as long as you need, and if Tristan has to go, we can give you a ride home."

"Thank you." I stick my head back around the corner to give Megs an encouraging smile, then hurry out the door. The weather has started to stay warm after dark now, balmy enough that I don't miss my jacket. The air out here always smells like rich fertilizer and mowed grass. Stars span the sky in every direction, and the crickets and frogs from the river sing a soothing chorus.

Letting my eyes adjust to the dusk, I search the yard. He can't have gone far. The momentary flare of a cigarette lighting catches my attention, followed by a shadow of movement. Gravel crunches under my sneakers as I jog over, stopping a few feet away so he doesn't feel crowded. His eyes, so warm and peaceful back in the living room, have gotten distant again. They rove over me, then meet my stare as he releases a trail of smoke.

"So, what happened?"

His powerful jaw tenses. "I don't do lawyers." When he goes to take another pull, I realize his hand's shaking.

Frustration surges in my chest, not at him but at all the secrets he feels forced to keep in some form of self-torture I don't understand. "Alright. Here's how this is going to work." I take a step closer as he watches me warily. "We're going to talk, and you're going to tell me some things about yourself."

His face hardens. "Don't do this to me. Don't give me an ultimatum between you and telling you the truth."

"No, no." I give in and close the gap between us, resting my hands on his hips. For once, he doesn't touch me back. "You're stuck with me. Sorry. But you know all about me, my problems, and you get to take care of me and keep me safe. I can't keep you safe when I don't know what we're fighting, and that's not fair."

He huffs bitterly. "You can't keep me safe."

"Yeah, well fucking try me. You have no idea what I've gone through to raise my daughter, the things I'd do for her."

His eyes search mine, distressed. "I don't want you to learn about me, Ollie. You're not gonna—" He takes a quick, shaky breath, looking away. "I'll lose you and Megan, and then I won't have anything."

"Wait here." Stepping back, I point at him. "Don't move." I sprint back up to the house.

When I return fifteen minutes later, he's crouched against the side of the building, staring at the half-finished cigarette in his hand. He lifts his head like a startled deer, like he expects me to have brought a crowd of people to gawk at him. When he sees I'm alone, he relaxes. Kneeling in front of him, I pull the cigarette away just before it burns his fingers and put it out. There's darkness in his face, and fragility, and the constant pull between them.

I wrap my fingers around his. "I'm going to take you to one of my favorite places. Jonah showed it to me, and I used to go up there when I needed to cry about my mental health falling apart."

"I don't need to cry," he pouts, picking at the rubber sole of his boot.

"It's a good place to have a very manly sulk, too."

"That's *not*—" When he looks up and sees my smile, he mashes the tip of my nose with his finger. "Keep fucking around with me and find out, little smartass."

"Come on." When I stand up and offer my hand, he envelops it with his rough one, and almost pulls me over as he gets to his feet. "We're going in Jonah's truck." Jingling the keys, I lead the way to his tall, black pickup.

Jackson's hand finds mine in the dark as we walk, his thumb stroking restlessly along my wrist. "I thought you couldn't drive."

I sigh. "It's complicated. There are a lot of rules in my head. If I can go really slow and stop whenever I want, it's usually alright."

When I open my mouth to apologize for how pathetically high-maintenance that makes me sound, he squeezes my hand. "See? You do brave things."

That hits me too hard, and I start scrambling to make excuses. "It's not brave to fail the bare minimum a normal person should be able to do." There I go, breaking my own rule. Sometimes it's all just too much.

Jax stops abruptly. When I turn toward him, he grips the back of my neck with one hand and slides two fingers right into my mouth, so deep that I can't do anything but make a startled choking sound. They curl slightly against my tongue as I blink at him, eyes wide.

"You remember what I said six years ago? You got all hot when I bossed you around, and I said that if I don't like what I hear, you don't get to talk anymore."

I whine protestingly through my nose, fighting the urge to start sucking, forcing my tongue to stay still. He leans in and kisses my forehead. "Pretty sure you wanted to have a conversation tonight, so do you want your mouth back or not?"

I bite his fingers, not too hard, and he pulls them out. "Okay. I'm super brave. Go me." He makes like he's going to shove them back in, but I dodge away and run for the truck.

Chapter 24

OLIVER

Using the headlights, we find the dirt road stretching back through Gray and Jonah's property. It's rough, but the truck rolls through potholes like they aren't even there. We crawl along the river for a few minutes before I spot the almost invisible turnoff, just a few ruts in the grass. I feel like a badass as I take us off-roading up to the top of the hill, half-sheltered by the boughs of an old oak tree. There aren't many hills around here, so even this small one gives a wide view of the moonlight spilling across a patchwork of roads and fields, dotted with the bright specks of other farms in the distance.

I hop out of the cab and circle around to put down the tailgate. I can't work out the latches, fumbling in the dark and pinching my fingers until Jax reaches around me and flips them open. He goes still when he sees the blankets and pillows

I spread across the truck bed. Jonah has them all set aside on a special shelf for anyone who wants to use the truck for stargazing or camping out. I try not to think about the number of times he and Gray have probably fucked back here.

I'm not strong enough to hoist myself with my arms, so I scramble ungracefully into the bed and sit cross-legged in the middle. "This was my safe space. I even fell asleep a couple of times and stayed out all night. It's fun, like a pillow fort."

He looks apprehensive in an almost visceral way, like a dog that doesn't want to go inside his new doghouse and panics if you push him. For a second, I think he might walk away. Then he rests his elbows on the edge and studies the view. "When I was young, we lived near a drive-in theater. None of my friends could afford tickets, but we'd just park our truck in the hills a mile or so away. We'd bring vodka and weed and big bags of Cheetos and sit on blankets like this, watching the screen with no sound."

"That sounds fun."

His eyes burn into mine. "One of us got a bullet to the head from a drive by, another went to jail for rape and got beaten to death, and another OD'd. I'm the only one still alive."

"Jax..." I stretch out both my hands to him. "Please come here and let me hold you."

He vaults up easily and sits facing me, his knees touching mine. His body twitches when I rest my hand on his cheek, then he presses his face into my palm and closes his eyes. When I can't take it anymore, I straddle his lap and wrap my arms around his head, letting him bury his face in my chest while his arms crush my waist. I rub the back of his neck and make sure he can feel me breathe.

"You know about my brother, Scout," he says after a long pause, his low voice vibrating against my skin. "But we have a sister, too, named Jenny. A year younger than me. When she was twenty-two, she got knocked up by one of the heads of the local gang, a really evil motherfucker. We knew that he abused her, but that was just how things worked. We couldn't stop him. I did what I could—hid her when he was drunk, stole baby formula for her."

He rubs his nose along my collarbone. His voice keeps getting flatter and more monotone, empty of emotion. My mind can only comprehend his words as the plot of some miserable movie, not a person's actual life they had to wake up to every single day. "That went on for three years. There was a big feud with a neighboring gang, and her boyfriend went insane. One night I woke up to her banging on the trailer, freaking out. She was in bad shape, and she knew he was going to kill her this time."

I pull back and open my mouth, but he shakes his head at me to stop. "I let her in. When he came looking for her, I got between them. He won the fight, but I broke his nose and his arm."

"Did he kill her?" Everything I ate this evening is twisting my stomach to pieces.

"She, uh," his voice wavers almost imperceptibly. His eyes look clouded and unfocused in the moonlight. "She told him I forced her to come there and locked her in. So he forgave her. I don't blame her." Taking a deep breath, he rolls his head back and closes his eyes, talking faster. "The next day a bunch of his guys came after me. I ran for my life, but they caught me and beat the shit out of me. They stuck a gun in my mouth, fucked with me for a while to hear me cry. I don't know how, but I managed to get the gun away. I couldn't see anything; I didn't know where I was. I just started pulling the trigger. Got the guy who was holding the gun eleven times while the rest ran away."

"That's not murder or manslaughter," I protest. "That's self-defense."

He rests his forehead on my shoulder. His hand slides under my shirt and strokes my hip like he's trying to soothe himself. "As soon as they left, the guys made a plan to fuck me over and protect themselves. My brother and I put together all our savings for a lawyer, but they'd already bought the guy. He pretended to work for us while he helped them frame me. They wanted murder, but they could only stick manslaughter. After a few years, I got out on parole for good behavior."

"Why did you break parole?"

"I hadn't seen my sister since it happened, but she called me one day when she was high. I found out she was still with that piece of shit. I went nuts and left Colorado without permission to go to New York and save her. When I showed up, she had changed. She screamed that she hated me, acted like I hadn't almost died for her. She called the cops on me. And that was the worst day of my life. I panicked and ran. The day of the cave-in, I got on the train to hide from a security guard at the station who caught me trying to sleep on a bench."

"Then you went back to jail."

He nods. "Five more years. I made it worse by running."

"Have you seen Jenny again?"

"I don't..." He swallows painfully, shaking his head. "I don't think I ever will."

"Fuck. How did you end up here in Byrock?"

When he hesitates, I know I've reached the end of what he's willing or able to give me tonight. I squeeze him tighter, stroking his jaw. "Thank you. I'm so sorry for what happened to you."

"No," he murmurs, pulling away a little. "Please don't be sorry for me, Ollie."

"I'm not sorry for you, but I'm sorry you're hurting. It's the same way you felt when I needed you to drive me home, yeah?"

He nods stiffly, but hangs his head, still stroking my bare flank. He seems wrung out, paralyzed.

"Stargaze with me." Climbing off him, I flop on my back in the thick pile of pillows. The tree blocks part of our view, but the rest of the sky is jeweled with bright stars. Jackson lies down, but even after five minutes, ten, he stays on his side, watching me. "You're not looking at the stars."

He shrugs his free shoulder. His voice doesn't reach above a whisper, like he used it up. "So what?"

I study the shape of his features in the near-dark, his eyes like pools I could sink into and never find the bottom. "They're beautiful. They always make me feel better, like there's another world outside of my fucked-up head."

He still doesn't look. Scooting closer, he lays his arm across my chest and puts his mouth against my ear. "There is no other world, Ollie," he breathes. "They don't mean anything. They just watch us hurt."

We lie there for a long time, me counting meaningless stars and Jackson breathing warm against my neck. "I love you," I murmur into the dark.

He comes up on his elbow. "Don't say that."

"Why not?" We're whispering, like something might overhear us.

His thumb traces my lower lip, tugging gently at it. "If we say it, I'll lose you."

"No." I put my hand over his. "What if I promise you right now that no matter what happens, I'll find you?"

There's a bitter ache in his smile. "You'd be stupid. No one can promise that."

"Then pretend. What if I could?"

The words are right there, in his eyes, on his tongue, and I want them. I want them wholly and jealously, now and forever. His breath shudders. "Then I'd—" Breaking off, he buries his face in my neck. "*Fuck,* Ollie. I can't say it out loud. I need you."

"I know." I rub my cheek against the rough bristle of his buzz cut. "You're okay."

His fingers curl in my hair and tip my head far back, neck vulnerable and exposed. I whine and struggle a little when he kisses up the line of my throat, feather-soft, but then he murmurs "Quiet" and his lips part mine, his tongue pinning me down with the steel bar so all I can do is moan softly. The kiss gets more frantic until he's half on top of me. When he pulls back, he replaces his tongue with his fingers.

"Can I be selfish this time?" he murmurs, his eyes wandering all over my body with a raw desire more potent than I've ever seen from him before. "Can I have everything I want?" When I nod, he empties my mouth.

"Tell me what to do."

"I want you to play with yourself."

I can't help an incredulous huff. "That's not selfish, Jax."

His fingers push back in my mouth, deeper this time. When he reaches down and rubs my hardening cock through my jeans, my body spasms as I whimper and start drooling. His voice stays quiet and matter-of-fact, almost conversational. "Maybe I decided that I want to watch you make yourself come over and over until you literally can't anymore. That sounds selfish to me."

I've heard dirty talk before, in porn, and it felt cheesy, the way they growl out these awkward lines in a contrived sexy voice. Jax isn't performing shit. He's figured out what his body wants; his kink is me, Oliver Shaw, and taking me to pieces every way he can think of. And he likes to tell me exactly what's coming in a calm, intent voice, with a laser focus that isn't clouded in any way by his own cock demanding satisfaction. It's the scariest, hottest thing I've ever fucking heard.

Jackson spreads his fingers wide in my mouth and kisses me between them, adding his tongue so there's no room left for me. His hand dips into my briefs, and I groan and gag. Grinning, he pulls his fingers out, satisfied that I get the picture.

"What do you want me to do?" I pant, twitching my hips in protest when he lets go of my dick. I reach up to wipe the spit from my chin, but he stops me.

"You should take off all your clothes except your briefs." Sitting up against the cab, he watches carefully as I strip off my t-shirt. When he unbuttons his jeans and slides a hand inside, it makes me hard enough that I have to yank my pants down before I grow too much and get stuck. I am all things beauty and grace as I stand up on one foot like a drunk flamingo to peel them off, and Jax smiles as I wobble and get tangled up and almost tip over.

Throwing my jeans to the side, I drop back onto my knees and wrinkle my nose at my yellow briefs with cartoon bananas on them. I clearly wasn't planning on getting laid this evening. "Just so you know, I do not feel sexy right now."

Pulling his hand out of his pants, he stretches his legs out and pats them. When I straddle him, he runs his fingers lightly around the leg seams. "Can you put your hands behind your back for me?" My cock instantly gets harder as I obey, and he looks pleased with himself. "I like that you have a big dick but you always wear little briefs."

"I need the support." My voice hitches when his middle finger dips under the seam and brushes the edge of my balls.

"They're all colorful, but no one sees them."

I shrug. "It's just for me. I got in a bad headspace when I was stuck with Kay, so I started doing things to make myself feel, I dunno, special or something. But I wish..." I look down at my skinny, pale body and dorky underwear. "I wish I looked hot."

He rests his hands on my hips and studies me for a minute, the texture of denim against my bare legs making me feel even more naked. Reaching around, he pulls the fabric tight up into my ass crack so my cheeks are completely exposed. I yelp a protest when he tugs again so that the front of the waistband slides down a few inches. Taking my cock in his fingers, he stands it straight up against my belly so that it sticks out of my briefs and pulls at the waistband. My head's peeking through the foreskin already, and I'm leaking slowly but steadily, trailing down until it starts soaking into the fabric. He flicks my nipples just to be mean, then sits back and pushes his hand into his boxers again. "How about now?"

I can't look at him, because I don't think I can take what I'll see in his eyes. But when I glance down at myself, I'm greeted with my lewd dick and twisted-up briefs. A slight breeze caresses my ass cheeks, which makes me leak even more. Horribly self-conscious, I cup my balls through the cotton and pull my foreskin down further. When I picture him touching the exposed shaft, or licking it, I shudder and groan quietly. Everything's wet and throbbing and excruciatingly sensitive, and I'm just *sitting* here, in front of a guy with all his clothes on, letting him watch.

"I look like a slut," I murmur in wonder, staring at my hard nipples and the light flush on my skin, the way my soaked briefs keep sliding down and showing more of my cock.

"Is that what you want to be?" he asks quietly, his own hand working himself where I can't see.

To my surprise, I nod. I don't think an out of shape, thirty-six-year-old dad with a desk job–and theoretically some dignity–should want something like that. But I do. I like Jax's large, battered hands making me do things. I like being the delicate one, maybe almost pretty, turning him on. He even makes my monster of a cock feel cute, somehow.

His free hand strokes my ass cheek, kneading and squeezing it until my breath catches. "You're the only person that's ever made my dick hard. So I guess that does make you my slut, huh?"

Now that I'm his slut, now that I'm safe in those words, I rock my hips into his hand and let out all the soft, needy sounds men aren't supposed to voice, that Kay told me were pathetic instead of hot. Without overthinking it for once, I smear my fingers through my precum and reach back to pull the cotton fabric out of the way and touch my own hole for the first time. "Shit, Jax." I lean forward and rest my forehead against his. "It's so sensitive." This feels somehow more vulnerable than his own fingers working me open.

His hand speeds up as my cock drips onto his jeans. "Uh-huh," he murmurs unsteadily. "Put a finger in it."

He must sense my fear as I struggle to sink my middle finger past the tight ring, because he tilts his head and kisses me urgently. When I whimper into his mouth, he gives up and shoves down the waistband of his jeans and boxers so he can jerk off faster. He's rock hard, his hand messy as he works it with none of the finesse or skill of someone with practice. I remember how it felt to have that cock stretching me, even though it hurt. How complete I felt. My body eases and grips onto my finger, pulling it deeper as I stroke my own erection, pushing my underwear down under my balls.

Jackson releases my mouth, our faces still only centimeters apart as our hands work in sync. "Tell me how it feels."

"It feels huge, but it's not enough. Please."

"I want to hear you say it, Ollie."

I groan in frustration, my face burning. "I'm not good at this."

He pries my right hand off my dick, his firm grip trapping my wrist. Then he reaches around and pushes my finger deeper into my ass. "You said I could have whatever I wanted." The fire in his eyes is tempered with something peaceful and pure I've only seen a few times—on our first date, or when we planted vegetables.

I groan and throw my head back. I'm so close to the edge, and I know that if we can get there it will be spectacular. I want to reach it with my body joined to his. I want us to break together and make each other whole again. "Please, Jax. Please fuck me. I saved my ass this whole time and I need your cock to feel how tight it is. I need you to fill it."

His nostrils flare and he shudders a little, consuming me with his gaze. Then he picks me up and drops me on my back among the pillows, kneeling over me as he strips. His body looks massive in the faint moonlight, with the darkness of the tattoos crawling across him. Studying my face, he spits on his hand and gives his slick cock a few more slow pulls. He likes to admire my body, but the closer we get to coming, the more he fixates on the connection between our eyes.

I spread my legs for him and he moans, then catches my wrists and easily pins my arms over my head with one hand. He must see the jolt that goes through me, because he grins. "You like that? 'Cause I think you look really good just like this." He rubs his cock against my taint and kisses me, pulling away before I get my fill.

"Come on," I beg, struggling, my ass protesting the loss of my fingers.

He nuzzles my cheek, his steady, comforting breath in my ear. "Open up for me. Tell me if it hurts; it's only my second time."

The blunt head of his cock presses at my hole. I bear down this time, and there's a stretch but no sudden disasters.

Halfway in, he stops and rests his forehead on my shoulder, panting. "Fuck, Ollie. You're crushing me. I'm gonna come."

"Don't you dare, not yet," I hiss, and he laughs. In one long, careful thrust, he bottoms out, his balls hitting my ass. I give up whatever dignity I had left and thrash shamelessly so I can feel every inch, the exact, familiar shape of him, and reassure myself that I finally have him back after so many years.

He rocks into me, leaning over to kiss my nose, my cheeks, my eyelids. My cock keeps sliding and rubbing between our bodies, and I whimper his name. "You're mine, Oliver," he breathes against my jaw. "You were made for me. I'll never let anyone else touch you. Do you hear me?" I make some kind of disgusting animal sound, and his hips speed up. "Are you gonna come all over yourself for me?"

I try to say *yes, more, everything*, but he's found a place inside of me, in my body and in my soul, where everything just goes to white fire and I have no idea what comes out of my mouth as he takes my cock and milks it all over my chest.

As I finish, he looks down at the sight I must make, stretched out and wrecked, naked, cum-drenched. His slut. His Oliver. He pulls out suddenly and comes on top of my cum, until I'm covered in it. I swipe my fingers through the mess and put them in my mouth. And then I cough and gag a little, because it's really fucking overpowering.

Still breathing hard, Jax reaches out and wipes some from my facial hair. Then he collapses next to me, sweaty and spent. I've never been more of a mess in my life, every part of me throbbing and all my nerve endings lit up. Jax still doesn't look at the stars. He traces his finger along my profile—between my eyebrows, down my nose, over my lips. I turn my head toward him, and he cups the side of my face. "Jax—"

"I've never not loved you." His thumb traces my cheekbone. "You're the only perfect thing in this fucking world."

"I'm not perfect."

He shakes his head. "Well shit. I wouldn't have noticed if you hadn't said anything."

I stare at him blankly, then roll onto my face in the blankets and crack up. As I giggle helplessly, walking the sharp edge between laughing and crying, he kisses all the freckles on my back.

We fall asleep there, naked and sticky and bound together under a vast sky that may or may not give a shit about us. Maybe we'll never know.

Chapter 25

OLIVER

When I look up from taping shut a box of old filing folders, Tristan has his shoulder propped against the wall of the vault, smirking at me. "What?"

"I take it you and Jax had a really deep, uh, *conversation* after D&D on Saturday?"

I splutter and narrow my eyes at him. "What are you insinuating?"

"Jax was in a huge hurry to wash the shirt I lent him, even though he doesn't seem like the laundry type. And you've been singing female icon power ballads to yourself all day."

"Lies." Straightening up, I shove the box toward him with my foot. "I can't sing."

"Believe me, I've noticed." My best friend scoops up the box and lugs it into the storage room. "I told Jax that cartoon dragon shirt would get him laid," he yells over his shoulder, making me cringe and glance in the direction of Stace's office. It wouldn't be the worst thing she's overheard. For some reason, she keeps us around. Maybe it's boring in that office of hers.

"I'm glad you worked out the...kinks in your relationship," he offers as he reappears, brushing dust off his hands.

"Oh my God." I stop halfway through storming out and pop my head around the door. "Wait, what makes you think we'd be kinky?"

Tristan squints and holds out two fingers, like he's measuring my small stature. "The little, unassuming, repressed ones always are. And nothing about Jax screams missionary position."

"Speaking of missionary position," I snipe back, "shouldn't you be worried about your own love life?"

His grin fades, and he frowns at the floor, kicking a strip of loose baseboard that Jax needs to nail down. "Sure. I have to work twice as hard, now that the *SSTMBDC* only has one member."

"Oh, Tris. I'm sorry." I always told myself I wouldn't become one of those people—the ones who get infatuated with a new relationship and stop giving a shit about their friends. "I can still be in the club."

He raises an eyebrow. "That's definitionally impossible, my guy."

"What about that nerdy woman I found? Are you not having a second date?" Grabbing all our sharpies, tape dispensers, and other office supplies, we head back to the front to put everything away.

"Nothing's clicking, Ollie." Tris lowers his voice for once, which gets my attention. "Girls that want to date a goofy nerd aren't the same girls who are open to *oh, by the way, I want to settle down and have a family, like, yesterday*. I'm jealous of you right now."

I frown, confused. "You want your own grumpy, clingy man covered in tattoos?"

"I'd fucking take it at this point." He shoves the stapler into its cubby with more force than necessary. "At least you have a family and he wants to be a part of it. If Bee were still alive, we'd have toddlers by now." Brushing a hand across his eyes, he stomps back to his chair and sits down hard enough to nearly break it. When he looks up and sees the expression on my face, he holds up a warning finger. "Don't you dare come and try to hug me."

In a genuine lightbulb moment, I dig for my phone and fire off a quick text. "Triiis?" I sidle toward him.

"Yeees, Ollie?" I finally manage to make his face relax back into a smile.

"I just sent your number to Alice."

His eyes bug out. "The Alice you dated? No fucking way. Take it back right now."

"Why?" I throw up my hands. "What's wrong with her?"

"Only that she's a goddess in human form and I'm a mismatched sock covered in lint that you find under your bed."

"Well, you know what?" I pat his arm on my way out of the room. "Everyone's always really happy to find that sock."

"You say that like it's an inspiring comeback," he calls after me, "but it literally doesn't mean anything."

I just wave over my shoulder.

"And *stop singing*," he yells louder. "Beyoncé would like a word, and it wouldn't be a nice one."

"Amen," Stace's voice drifts out of her office.

Laughing, I stick my head in all the back rooms, looking for Jax.

"He went out for the afternoon to buy more flooring," Stace comments from the doorway of her office. "He's the only person on my payroll right now who's earning his keep."

My phone rings loudly in my pocket. I act like I'm going to ignore it and go back to my computer, but Stace waves her hand wearily. "It's already a lost cause. Go enjoy taking personal calls on the clock. See if I care."

"Hey, Mom." I put on a neutral, friendly voice, checking the caller ID as I duck into the bathroom. "What's up? Did you get your hotel for Megan's birthday yet?"

"We did." She pauses. Her voice sounds upset, like she's been crying a little, and my mouth goes dry.

"Mom? What's wrong? Is Dad okay?"

I hear my father's voice in the background asking for the phone. They argue in not-so-quiet whispers for a minute before his gruff voice comes on the line. I don't know if I should feel relieved or not–he's less emotional than Mom, but painfully blunt. "Oliver."

"What the hell is going on?"

"We got contacted last night by an aggressive cold caller demanding your address and contact information."

"What?" I prop my butt on the counter and play anxiously with the handles of the tap. "I get spam calls all the time. You shouldn't talk to them."

"When I pushed him," he continues, "I found out he was from a debt collection agency that's seeking a large sum of money from you."

The only stupid thing that manages to come out of my mouth is, "Telling you that is illegal."

"Yeah, well, so is not paying your debts."

"*Dad.*"

I can hear Mom fussing in the background as he fires off questions. "How bad is it, Oliver? Why have you been refusing our help and telling us everything's fine?"

"I don't have to talk to you about this. I'm an adult, and it's my business." I snatch a paper towel out of the dispenser and start tearing it into small pieces, balling them up and throwing them on the floor. Like an adult.

"You're an adult," Dad snaps, "but Megan isn't, and she's paying the price for your stubbornness, while she has grandparents who could give her everything."

"*Never* say that to me again. You have no right to say you know what's best for anyone."

Mom must hear me yelling and pry the phone away from Dad, because her soothing voice fills my ear. "We're not trying to take Megan away. We just want to understand what's going on so we can make up for the past by helping you now. I know you've been through a lot of jobs—are you having health problems?"

"Megan's excited to see you, and I love you, so I'm going to stop this conversation before I end up taking back your invitation to her birthday." Instead of throwing my phone across the room, I stuff it in my pocket and throw the paper towel. It hovers sadly in the air, then drifts downward onto the mess I've made all over the peeling linoleum. I grab the broom and dustpan from behind the door and start to sweep it up.

My cracks are starting to show. If I don't sort out the debt, my parents will pry everything else open and force me to get help. My only option is to sell the house. But the debt will eat up so much of the profit that we won't be able to afford anywhere to live except a shitty apartment that doesn't allow reptiles. And none of that gets me any closer to being able to pay for the things Megan needs as she gets older.

"Fuck." I wish Jax was in the building. I sit against the wall and rest my head on my knees, trying to calm down before I start spiraling.

I want to get better.

I want my daughter to have everything.

I want the debt gone.

And yeah, part of me wants my parents to step in and give me the breathing space to get back on track.

But if I admit I'm broken enough to need help, I'll prove that my parents and Kay were right all along—I never deserved to have control of my own life. All the years I've spent trying to be normal were just lies and bullshit that hurt people and harmed my kid's future until I could finally recognize what everyone else already sees—I'm defective. And I'm weak. Because I'm strong enough to keep fighting until I lose everything, but I've never been strong enough to know when to give up.

Jackson

"Be proud of me," Oliver announces, throwing open his front door. "I already bought celebratory cookies, and you may have one."

He's told me over and over that I don't need to knock anymore, but I like doing it. I like listening to him run across the floor, the welcoming click of the lock, the look on his face when we see each other through the screen door. He always backs up against the mudroom wall to let me through, curling his bare toes so I don't step on them with my boots and staring up at me through his long, pale eyelashes. On some days, like today, he makes good-tasting noises when I stop and bend over to kiss him.

"Why should I be proud of you?"

"What a rude question to ask your partner." When I just stare at him, unimpressed, he caves. "I applied to a bunch of remote work jobs this afternoon. Not just copy editing but administration, marketing, and social media. If I could get one of those, in addition to the bank, I could really start making progress."

"Uh-huh." I unlace my right boot and pull it off. There's something wrong. I can't pin it down. He's buzzing with energy, but he's not happy. "Why today?"

He doesn't answer. When I look up, he shifts uneasily and skitters away, disappearing into the kitchen.

"Where's Megan?" The place feels unnaturally quiet.

"Her school is having a lock-in sleepover for the kids who read fifty books this year," his voice calls back over the hiss of filling the coffee maker with water. "Dozens of hyped-up little Megans running around in a gym all night—can you imagine?"

I move on to my second boot as his phone rings. "It's Gray. Should I answer it?"

"Tell him to go away."

As Oliver chats to the lawyer, I wander over to Mars' tank and carefully reach inside. He watches me with disgust, so I decide not to bother him. I flip through Megan's pile of background drawings and pick one that looks like the dashboard of a sports car, replacing the beach. "What do you think of that, huh?"

"Jackson?" Oliver's holding his phone away from his ear and stage-whispering. He looks like he's trying not to laugh. "What's your stance on double dates?"

I raise an eyebrow at him. "Like where middle-aged couples all go to brunch together because they can't get it up anymore?"

A grin quirks the corner of his mouth. "Yeah, pretty much."

"If that's what you guys want to do with your spare time, then I'm not gonna stop you."

"He says he'd love to," Oliver says into the phone before ending the call. He yelps when I pick him up from behind, kicking his legs as I lug him easily into the living room and toss him into his favorite recliner, which is permanently stuck in the extended position. Pulling off my jacket, I collapse on top of him. He coughs in pain and struggles, but there's not much point when I'm mostly on top of him. "Jesus, Jax. What's gotten into you?"

"That's my question." I grab his chin and turn his face until he has to meet my eyes. I was right; there's hurt in their blue depths. He tries to go in for a kiss, but I tighten my grip and hold him still. "Oliver."

I feel his body melt a little, and his eyes drop to stare at a hole in the arm of the chair. "My parents found out about my debts."

"Oh."

"They accused me of hiding things from them." A deep crease appears between his eyebrows.

I tilt his chin up and gently bite the tip of his nose. "Isn't that exactly what you're doing?"

"It's not fair." He yanks free of my hand and drags the collar of his sweatshirt up over his head. I can hear a sharp bite in his voice. "I'm a selfish person if I don't share my private medical information with the whole world. And I should apologize while I'm at it, for inconveniencing everyone by daring to try and do something without help. I hate it."

"I know."

"I'm sad." The ball of sweatshirt curls into my side, and I stroke its hair.

"I know. I am proud of you, by the way."

He just grunts. "There's no point. Why do I even bother to get out of bed in the morning?"

Pulling the sweatshirt down far enough to expose his ear, I put my mouth to it. "I'm gonna get up for a minute. If you try to run off, I will make you regret it."

He snorts loudly into his cocoon of fabric.

"I'm serious." I smack his ass hard, then climb off him and poke around his bedroom until I find his laptop. I swing by the kitchen to grab the plastic container of chocolate-chip cookies on the counter. He stirs and frees his head when I drop all the shit on top of him.

"What's this about?"

"You're gonna work on your book."

Genuine annoyance flashes over his face, and he thrusts out his jaw stubbornly. "I don't want to."

"I don't think that's true."

Flopping his head back, he groans. "Can we just fuck instead?"

"No."

"Can I—"

I grab the cookies back before he can stuff them under his hoodie. "Only if you write something first."

He glares at me from moody, stormy eyes in the dim light of the living room. "I regret inviting you over. Did I ask for tough love? No, I did not."

He's really not okay. I can feel it in every word, in the reckless way he flips from one mood to another. We stare at each other for a minute. "Go ahead," he says hoarsely. "Tell me they're right. I can see it in your face."

"Move over."

This time he makes room for me to stretch out next to him, though we're probably going to break the chair. His eyes follow the laptop as I open it and set it on his legs. "Jax..."

"You left the guy stuck in some fucking demon temple."

"I did?" He blinks, squinting at the screen until I grab his glasses off the side table and stick them on his face. "Oh, I did. Sorry, Samvir." His eyes slide back over to me. "What do I have to do to get a cookie?"

I open the box, smell the cheap, artificial whiff, and take a bite of one, gagging in disgust. "Get him out of the temple."

"But he has an entire fight with the Lord of the Dead first," Ollie whines.

"Hurry up before I eat them all. And you have to tell me everything that's happening."

With a dramatic sigh, he starts typing. "So first, he has to make it through this maze that rearranges itself every thirty seconds. To do that, he uses a map that a ghostly maiden gave him in chapter ten."

At some point I think he takes the cookies away from me and eats them all. I keep drifting into sleep and back out, our warm bodies pressed together. Neither of us turned on the lights before we sat down, so it gets completely dark except for the glow of the reptile tanks. When I groan and wriggle closer against him, he kisses my head and goes back to typing. He's not narrating the story anymore, and the cookies are gone, but no matter how many times I wake up, he's still writing, on and on into the night.

Chapter 26

OLIVER

Part of me considers calling off the double date when I see Jackson waiting by his bike. He looks more exhausted every time we hang out, and there's an uneasy edge to him, like he's being scraped raw and blood is starting to seep through. But he never lets me see any deeper than that. I pull him to a stop as he swings his leg over the seat. "Jax?"

"I'm just a little nervous." He smiles, but his eyes aren't in it. "I don't think Gray is what someone needs to spice up their date night."

"He's *nice*," I chide, but I can't help snickering. "You know what they say about the quiet ones, though."

"What do they say?" He reaches back and runs a hand down my leg to make sure I'm seated safely.

"He's probably a monster in bed."

Jax snorts, shaking his head. "No *probably* about it. I'd be scared to have sex with him. Jonah's a brave guy. And now, when he's trying to talk to me about stock markets or some shit, this is all I'll be able to think about."

I snake my arms around his waist and hold on, my stomach churning like it always does on a ride. I've given up my dreams of being an effortlessly cool motorcycle gangster; I'll leave that to my daughter. "I don't think anyone's going to try to talk to you about stock markets."

We arrive at the outdoor mall forty minutes before we're supposed to meet the guys. I insisted we visit a men's store before I lose my mind and set Jackson's single black button-down on fire. He gets quiet and sulky as soon as he sees the clothing racks stretching in every direction, and follows me around an inch from my elbow. "This is the kind of bullshit place the kids at my school who made fun of my clothes shopped."

"Look." I gently push him away. "Can you go find me one thing that you like?"

I should have been more specific, because he comes back with a black button down so similar to the original that I could have sworn he went home and got it just to fuck with me. "Jax," I groan, resting my forehead against his shoulder.

"You don't like it?" He sounds genuinely confused.

I prop my chin on him and peer up into his eyes. "I have a dream, Jackson, and that is before I die, I will see you in a color that isn't black or Byrock City Bank red."

He throws me in a headlock. "God, you're dramatic. Can we go?"

"As soon as you look at these three nearly-identical orange Henleys, pick one, and put it on."

He grabs one at random. I was right all along—a nice, earth-tone rust is definitely this man's color. Jackson can't help but grin when he sees my face. "You like it?"

"You look fucking sexy." No one's body has ever lit me up the way his does, some heady mix of his perfect muscles and the beautiful soul inside them. This top hangs and clings in all the right places to highlight his best features, and I enjoy the jealous looks from random women who pause to ogle my man as we head for the restaurant.

"Gray must have picked this," I muse as we stop outside the upscale, modern establishment.

Jax's eyebrows go up when he sees the portion sizes on the plates going by. "I'm gonna be hungry all fucking night."

"You can eat me later if you need more." I cringe instantly and bury my face in my hand. "Fuck, sorry. That was monumentally stupid. It just came out."

He tips my chin up with his fingers, smirks, and drops a quick kiss on my lips. "You're dessert."

As we head inside, he slips his arm around my shoulders and I reach up to lace my fingers through his. Tristan was right. We're blatantly, disgustingly infatuated with each other, but I think we've fucking earned it. Dates have scared me since the night twelve years ago where dinner and a movie ended with unprotected sex and my life was never the same again. Today, instead of watching myself from a distance, I'm fully inside my own body, grounded and safe with the person next to me. After all those lonely years trying to stop myself from breaking down by playing *one good thing*, maybe I get to learn how to be happy again.

Gray and Jonah wave us over to their table. The lawyer seems pleased with his dining choice—until he realizes all three of us are looking to him to explain the menu and tell us what to order. "I'm used to this from Jonah, but I expected better from you, Oliver." He doesn't say what he expected from Jax. Gray acts put out, but he launches into a lecture on food and wine pairings so exhaustive that Jonah finally has to kiss him to shut him up. The kiss goes on for much, much longer than is appropriate for a fine dining establishment, because we're not the only disgusting couple here, until Jax is sliding down in his seat and chewing on his lip to keep from laughing as I pull innuendo-laden faces at him.

Jax consumes his steak in three bites and sits back, casting starved glances at everyone else's food. He doesn't say much, just quietly observes the conversation with his foot wrapped around mine under the table, but he seems content.

As we venture out into the warm afternoon, Jonah walks backward, expertly managing not to trip on anyone. "How about a movie?"

I have a script for when this shit happens, as natural now as breathing—*Can I do this today? What if it's too crowded? What if there aren't any aisle seats? Do I need to awkwardly remind these people that I have issues, or do they remember?* Jax cuts in smoothly. "Only if they have a seat on the end."

Jonah smiles and gently punches my shoulder. "I've got you, man." He's such a fearless ball of energy that I sometimes forget he needs accommodations, too. "This place has massive recliners and wide aisles, so every spot feels like an end seat."

I study the theater with awe as we file in. If more places were made like this, just a simple thing, my life would be so much easier. Jax collapses in his seat, resting his head back and watching me with a vague smile as Jonah and I goof around with all the buttons and levers. Gray sits perfectly upright, watching the pre-roll ads like he's going to be tested afterward. Jonah manages to break his reclining mechanism, but just before he has to go get a staff member, Jax leans over me and fixes it. When he sits back, he leaves his hand high up on my thigh, that intimate spot where only couples can touch each other, and it feels so fucking good I never want to move again.

Thirty minutes into the movie, Jax nudges me and nods toward Jonah and Gray. They've somehow ended up in the same recliner, completely horizontal and both sound asleep.

"Waste of damn expensive tickets," Jackson mumbles. Exactly ten minutes later, he's draped over the armrest, passed out with his face in my neck. I'm the only person who actually watches the movie.

"It was a masterpiece," I gush as we leave. "The part where Dwayne 'The Rock' Johnson threw their space shuttle into the sun made me tear up."

Gray starts pulling up the cast list on his phone, looking concerned. "I didn't see him on any of the posters. Was he—"

"Calm down, babe. He wasn't." Jonah rolls his eyes at me and tries to hit me with his empty popcorn bucket, which Jax snags out of the air before it can make contact. The whole plaza is thick with the smell of flowers in the breezy evening, sun glowing pink just above the horizon.

"Oh!" I tug Jax's fingers. "They put in a huge rose garden; I read about it on a gardening blog. Can we see it before we go?" I cut myself off, embarrassed, but they're all smiling at me.

"We'll come with you," Gray offers. "First I want to step into the fudge store. We need ammunition to bribe the kids into cleaning the garage this weekend."

Hand in hand, Gray and Jonah duck into the candy store. They're such an unexpected couple, so different in every possible way from their bodies to their personalities, but I've never met two people more in sync.

"You hungry?" Jax puts his nose in my hair and caresses my back. "I saw a pretzel stand around the corner." His stomach growls on cue.

Chuckling, I squeeze his arm. "I'm fine. Go ahead before you faint from starvation."

I wander over to one of the outdoor fireplaces they'll probably shut down for the summer after this weekend and watch the flames dance. It's too warm, which means I have this peaceful corner of the plaza all to myself.

At the pressure of a hand on my back, I look up. "Did they not have the—" I'm looking into the face of a stranger, a broad-shouldered, younger man with bad skin and hazy eyes. I take a quick step back. "Sorry, you got the wrong person..." My voice fades when he follows me, and my heartbeat kicks up fast and loud in my chest. "Excuse me."

When I try to step around him, he blocks me. "I was just watching you and your buddies on your little fag date." He tilts his head, grinning. "Do you let them all fuck your bitch ass at once, or just one at a time?"

In my head I say *back off and leave me alone*, but I'm so dizzy with a mixture of normal fear and panic responses that the only thing to come out of my mouth is "Please, I'm sorry," in a shaky whisper.

When I take another step to the side, he matches it and wraps his fingers roughly around my bicep, yanking me to a stop. I shove his shoulder as hard as I can, but he just tightens his grip and smiles. "Let me hear what you say when you beg to suck their cocks, huh?"

Before I can speak, everything explodes and I slam into the ground, the bricks tearing up my palms as I catch myself. When I turn over, I see Jax with his face pressed up against the stranger's, snarling a never-ending string of threats I can't make out. Every time the guy moves or tries to pull away, Jax crowds in and shoves him harder. He looks terrified now, struggling to get any distance at all, tripping and almost falling.

"Jax!" He doesn't hear me. "Jackson!" I stumble to my feet as Jax throws the guy so hard against the wall that he wails and grabs his shoulder.

"Leave me alone," he sobs, shielding his face. "I'm sorry." People are starting to look over at the commotion. If someone calls the police, things aren't going to go well for Jackson, no matter who started it.

Jackson sucker-punches the man in the ribs and he doubles over, gagging and gasping for air.

"*Jackson.*" I grab stupidly for his arm. He doesn't hit me, but he shoves me back roughly and takes the guy by the throat. Now that I'm closer, I can make out some of what he's actually saying, and I realize how deep he's gone into the world he came from, nothing like the Jax I know.

"The *fuck* did you say to him, you little fucking bitch? If you touched him, I'll fucking kill you."

Looking over my shoulder desperately, I see Gray and Jonah leaving the candy store. As soon as he notices us, Gray breaks into a jog, then a run. I doubt he's fought anyone in his life, but he's the only one of us bigger than Jax. He shoves his six-foot-six frame fearlessly between the two men and grabs Jackson's shoulder and the back of his neck, speaking firm and quiet in his ear. Jax struggles for a moment, like he's going to lash out, but then he throws his hands up and jerks away, pacing back and forth a few times before walking toward the rail fence lining the edge of the plaza. He leans his hands on it and hangs his head, breathing hard.

Jonah runs up and puts his stump around me, turning my hand over to see my scraped palms. "Are you okay?"

"I'm fine." I struggle to blink away the fear and adrenaline. "He's just a bigot. All he did was talk."

A loud clatter has us all looking up to see Jackson kick the fence hard enough to dislodge the top rail and knock it to the ground.

Gray points at the guy who harassed me. "Get out. And don't think about running to the police, or I'll be sure to press charges with security footage of you assaulting my friend." As soon as the asshole sprints away, he scans the area to make sure no one's still paying attention, then puts his hand on my shoulder. His hazel eyes are dark with worry. "Oliver..."

"I need to talk to Jackson."

"I'm not sure that's a good idea. He needs to cool off."

"No." I look across at the broken silhouette against the fence. "He needs me."

Jackson

I can't see much, but there's a bench. So I sit on the bench. Everything else is still red. My sister Jenny must be somewhere nearby; I keep looking for her. I hurt people who hurt her. She's going to say *what the fuck is wrong with you* and slam the door in my face. *I wish you'd never protected me. You ruined my life.* She's going to call the cops. I wish she'd hurry up. This time, I won't run.

I'm so tired. Evenings with Oliver and nights with Garrett are running together into a dark, rain-soaked twilight that's making it harder and harder to keep any part of myself separate from any other.

I can't see much, but there's a pair of red Chucks standing in my line of sight. I know them. Slowly, I move my boot until the toes of our shoes are touching.

"Hey," Ollie murmurs. He doesn't sound scared, which is weird because I know I scared him. His hands are bleeding. One has dirt stuck to it, and the other got a streak of blood on his jeans. He brushes the dirt away, hissing in pain.

"I hurt you." My head's starting to ache. I can see a little more, but I can't remember everything that just happened.

The corner of his mouth tips up. "The ground hurt me. It happens sometimes. Embarrassingly often, if I'm being honest."

I just stare at him.

I loved my brother and my sister. I gave everything I had for them. Now one of them hates me, gone into a world where I can't follow her. And the other one's not normal. He doesn't care about anything. I failed both of them and lost eight years of my life.

Oliver sits down on the bench next to me. He puts a hand flat on the bench seat, halfway between us.

"Shouldn't you be going home with Jonah and Gray?"

"I had to practically pay them to give us some space, but they're checking out the garden now."

I turn my head and frown at him, confused.

His bright eyes focus on mine. "Thank you for protecting me, Jackson. I was scared, and you came and defended me. I wouldn't mind if you didn't try to kill someone next time, but it made me feel safe and cared for."

"Oh." My ears aren't ringing so much now. I'm starting to remember where we are, and the red is fading to the edges of my vision.

The way he looks at me.

In the truck the other night, he acted like my life story didn't bother him. Like he still saw me as a person worthy of respect and love.

I didn't believe him.

My hand moves to rest on top of his on the bench, and he flips his hand over and laces his fingers with mine. "You okay?"

"I don't know." I pull in air. "You don't want me around Megan anymore, right? I'm not a safe person. I could go off at any time. I'm sorry."

Scooting closer, he tips his head and studies my face intently. He reaches up and brushes his thumb along the tired skin under my eyes. "You're really bad at being a bad boy, Jackson Moreno. Like, the worst."

I let my eyes drift closed. "I never wanted to be."

"I know," he hums quietly. He cradles my head in his hands and lets me lean into him.

I didn't believe him. But the way he looks at me, he doesn't give me much of a choice.

Chapter 27

JACKSON

Blue and red lights flash behind us in the rain, followed by the single, slow *whoop* of a warning siren. "Fuck," Garrett's right-hand man hisses, gripping the wheel as he decides between slamming on the brakes or the accelerator. The car is silent except for the thrumming of rain on the roof as he does the smart thing and pulls onto the shoulder of the country road about five miles outside Byrock. Behind my spot in the passenger seat, I can feel the pressure of two more tense, armed men and enough drugs to land fifty guys in jail, let alone four.

I can't make out anything in the rearview mirror through the blur of heavy rain. When we hear the sound of a car door shutting, the driver reaches down next to his seat where he keeps his gun.

"Wait." They all stare at me when I speak, because I haven't opened my mouth since I started except to grunt. Now I can see a dark figure picking his way carefully along the side of the road with his coat held over his head. He's coming to my window so he doesn't have to stand on the road with zero visibility.

"Shut up," the leader snaps. "You have no say here." There's a click behind my shoulder as someone checks his magazine.

"He's probably already called in the license plate. If you kill him, they'll look for the car. We should see what he wants." I'm on a fast track to getting both of us shot, our bodies piled in the trunk and chucked into the river. *Oliver.*

"As soon as he sees us and smells the car, he'll radio in and we'll be fucked."

"I–"

We all jump when the policeman knocks on the side of the car. "Shut up and roll down the window," the driver growls. My body braces for shots right next to my head, a spray of blood. No one realizes how loud guns are until one goes off by your ear.

Before I know what I'm doing, I tear the glove box open and pull out all the paperwork crammed inside. When I roll down the window, I lean out so my body blocks the view between the cop and the people in the car. "Hi, officer. Is there a problem? I've got my registration and insurance in here somewhere." I seriously doubt this car has insurance, but I can pretend I lost it.

My body ticks over into fight or flight at the sight of his uniform–I've been chased down, handcuffed, yelled at, and hit by officers on a power trip. I try to focus on the sensation of rain hitting my arms. Something shifts behind me, and my skin crawls, ready for a bullet through my back any second now.

"You've got a headlight out. That's very dangerous in the rain. I'm going to write you a warning, and if you get stopped again, there'll be a fine." He tries to scribble something on a wet piece of paper. "Do you mind if I—"

I lean back a little as he slides his pad far enough through the window to shelter it from the rain and sticks his head in after it. My lungs have stopped working; the heavy silence behind me crawling along my skin. Any man in the gang I grew up around would have gone off by now and killed everyone in the area who pissed them off. Probably would have driven over the bodies on the way out, just to make a point.

The cop tears off the citation slip and holds it out to me. "Can I see a valid driver's license from someone in the car, please?"

As I dig into my wallet and pull out my ID, I almost laugh at the thought that, if he decides to run it, I'm probably the person of *least* interest to the police out of everyone here. Fucking irony. He just shines his light on it, turns it over, then hands it back. I grab it fast enough that he won't see my hands are shaking.

"Thank you, sir. Please get that fixed as soon as possible."

"I will." The words only kind of come out because my mouth is so dry. When the officer sloshes away, I slowly roll up the window. There's water all over the inside of the door and my legs. When I get a better look at the "registration and insurance" I grabbed, it's just a pile of fast food receipts on top of a porn magazine. I tip my head back against the seat and take a deep breath, closing my eyes, not even caring that there are three thugs staring at me.

When I open my eyes again, expecting them to throw me out of the car or worse, the driver nods at me with something like respect in his eyes. "I'll tell Garrett what you did," he promises.

Please don't.

"I need to pee." Before they can say anything, I scramble out of the car and walk down the shoulder in the downpour. I bend over the ditch and puke, then gag on stomach acid and spit until I'm dizzy.

As I ride out from the trailer park at four in the morning, every part of me craves Ollie's house. He doesn't even need to be there. I'll just break open the window, pile all his clothes in his bed, and curl up in them. But I can only show up so many times at this time of night stinking of filth and drugs he's never smelled before. He's not fucking stupid.

So I go back to the garage and pass out on my face with my clothes and boots still on. At god knows what time of the day, the ring of my phone drags me back to consciousness. It can only be Ollie or Garrett, my two best friends. What a joke. "Huh?" I grunt, barely bothering to lift my face from the torn faux leather.

"Hey, handsome." Ollie sounds so proud of himself, but nervous too, awkward and pleased. Like he sat around for a while thinking of endearments, picked one he liked, and worked himself up to try it. This man will fucking kill me someday.

I sit up, trying to sound more human. "Hi, uh, sweet...cute...I dunno, Ollie."

He laughs, the goofy one that gets startled out of him. "It's fine. Enjoying your day off?"

I touch my cheek. "Tristan's couch is imprinted on my face."

"That bad, huh?" He sighs. "I wish I could come hang out with you, but the bank's getting audited today and it's a shitshow. I was actually calling to see if you could do me a favor."

"Thank God." I lean over to grab my boots. My socks are threadbare, and I'm starting to get calluses on my feet. I decide to steal a handful of Ollie's socks next time I'm over; his are all puffy and gray and soft.

"Megan had to go to school this morning for some kind of Saturday sports day thing. I'm supposed to pick her up at one, but I can't leave, and Tris is stuck here too. Could you get her? You can just drive her home and drop her off; she'll be fine doing homework until I get home."

"Are they gonna just hand her over to a biker?"

He snorts. "They're terrible about watching the kids once they hit middle school. If you park across the street, she'll come find you."

"Sure thing."

Ollie takes a deep breath. "Sorry I called you handsome. I mean, you are, but I've never used a pet name or anything before and it sounded a lot weirder coming out than—"

"Rules, Ollie."

He makes an aggravated sound

"Try again."

"I hope you fucking liked being called handsome because I'm not sorry and I'd do it again. Screw you. Better?"

"Better." Oliver likes to pretend he doesn't know where Megan got her attitude, but it's painfully obvious. "Text me the address of her school."

"Thank you, Jax. I—" He lowers his voice so whoever's at the bank can't hear. "I'm gonna start saying 'I love you' casually, when we talk. Because I think you need to hear it about fifty times a day. But I know it's a big deal to you, and you don't need to say it back. I know how you feel."

I nod, forgetting he can't see me.

"Love you, Jax. Drive safe."

And suddenly there's something thick and hot in my throat, a pressure behind my eyes. Because Ollie was my first *I love you*, but now he's the first *love you, drive safe*. They're two completely different things, and the second one hits like a freight train. My sister's boyfriend told her he loved her while he abused her. But the quick, tender *love you*? I don't think the darkness can touch that one. I realize he's still waiting for an answer. "I will. And..." I search for something I can offer back. "You're my reason."

"I know." I can hear that smile, the one like the sunrise.

The middle school is a run-down '60s building with pastel-colored playground equipment that, based on the trash underneath, is used to trade contraband ranging from peanut butter cups to cigarettes. I hang back on the far side of the street as the students filter out the doors, trying not to look like a kidnapper. Megan's one of the last, struggling to carry her backpack and put on her jacket at the same time, her hair tumbling everywhere. She tugs on the light windbreaker, made of some weird holographic fabric, and adjusts her gym shorts before looking around. Her t-shirt has a woman with snakes for hair on it—I'm guessing because the snakes look like Mars.

When she spots me, she grins and sprints across the street, ignoring the honks of the van she cuts off. Oliver would die. "Holy shit," she breathes, ogling every inch of my bike. "I saw the picture of Dad sitting on it. He said that you invited him to ride it because you thought he looked like a natural."

She grins when I bark a laugh, and we share a look of understanding between two people who can't help but worship the ground that man walks on. "Don't say *shit*." I hand her my helmet, gesturing for her to get her hair under control first.

"Not you, too." She scrunches up her freckled nose. The turned-up snub must have come from her mom, but most of her face is pure Ollie. "I thought you were cool."

"I'm gonna drive you on a motorcycle to get ice cream even though your dad said to go straight home. Does that not make me cool?"

Her face lights up. "Dad told me I should go straight back and do homework because he wants you to like us, so we're not allowed to annoy you every single day."

"Is that so?" I'm sure Oliver will be thrilled to hear that she's spilling his secrets.

She huffs in frustration and yanks a hairband off her wrist, holding it out to me. "Can you braid it real quick?" Crossing her arms, she turns her back and waits.

"I don't know how." I turn the pink, fluffy hairband around on my fingers.

"You just make three parts and go out-in, out-in, out-in." She waves her hands unhelpfully.

"You're speaking nonsense right now." I expect her to give up, but that was stupid of me. She spins around and pulls her hair over her shoulder to demonstrate on a small section. I'm supposed to be watching her hands, but I'm looking at her face as she animatedly explains. Most people wouldn't think it, but I love kids. They're hilarious, and mostly cooler than adults. Before I realized that people like me don't get to choose what their lives look like, I wanted to be a middle school teacher that helped students from bad neighborhoods get life skills. As if I'd ever be allowed within ten miles of a school job with a record like mine.

"See? It's just in-out, in-out." she repeats. "I can't believe you can play 'Highway to Hell' with no music, but you can't braid hair."

I gesture to my buzzed head. "Does it look like I get much practice?" That makes her giggle. I did know how to braid once. I'd do my sister's, so the kids at school wouldn't make fun of her for having messy hair. But it's been twenty years, and I've tried to forget everything to do with her.

After making Megan show me two more times, I turn her around and do my best. The whole thing turns out lumpy and kinks back and forth, but at least it's done. "Hurry up." I drop the helmet on her head. "I wanted ice cream thirty minutes ago." It's too big for her, but I don't have another one, so I help her cinch it as tight as it will go. "You ready?"

She hops up and down, clapping her hands. "Can we go really fast? Can we go off a jump?" It's the first time I've doubted if she's her father's daughter; Oliver crushes my ribs with his grip when we're barely going twenty miles an hour.

"Listen up." She calms down and goes all serious as I brace the bike and help her climb on. "Reach around and hold the sides of my belt in a death grip. Don't let go. And don't wiggle around. Pinch me if you get scared and want to slow down or stop."

She makes a farting sound with her mouth behind me, and I'm glad she can't see my smile. Making sure she's holding on tight and there's no one else around, I give her a faster acceleration than I should, just to hear her scream of delight. The kid's actually a much better passenger than Ollie. He rides like a stiff board, but Megan gets a feel for the movement and leans with me on the turns.

We have all afternoon, so I take the longest of long ways to the ice cream shop, miles out into the country, over bridges and past collapsing barns and rustling cornfields and flower farms. We ride alongside a train on the same tracks I walked the other day, then past some dogs that bark and give chase. Megan jabs me hard in the ribs to make sure I see the horses that gallop along the fence, trying to keep up with us.

After almost an hour, I pull into a retro-style diner I looked up before I left. The sun's beating down now, and I strip off my jacket as Megan takes wobbling steps across the asphalt, trying to get her balance back. When she pulls off the helmet, I see that she's flying high, her eyes shining and her gap-toothed smile blinding. The helmet massacred my sad attempt at a braid. "That was the most fun thing I've ever done in my whole life! How old do you have to be to drive a motorcycle?"

"I don't know. Sixteen, maybe?"

Her eyes go huge. "Only three years? Do you think I can make enough money mowing lawns in three years to buy one?"

"I guess so." I've never checked how much a bike costs. I didn't steal this one, but I'm pretty sure my dad did. I just pulled it out of his stuff after he died and drove it away before anyone else could scavenge it.

"Can I take a picture of yours so that I can ask the motorcycle store for the exact same one?" She asks a lot of questions that should be annoying but somehow manage to be cute instead, like her dad. When I start to climb off, she waves for me to stay for the photo. "What's your favorite ice cream?" she rambles, stuffing the phone back in her pocket. "I like cookies and cream. Or strawberry."

My steps stutter when she throws her arm around my waist, but I catch myself and keep walking. It's awkward not to, so I carefully put my arm over her shoulders.

She hasn't stopped for breath. "Have you ever wished they invented a way for snakes to go on motorcycle rides? If I put Mars in a box on the back, he couldn't see out and he might get cold. Do you think they make helmets where you could put the snake inside, by your ear?" I don't have to come up with an answer to any of these things, because she just keeps going until we get to the front counter.

Hooking her elbows on the edge, she boosts herself up to read the laminated menu taped to the greasy Formica. The cashier, an older woman, watches me like a hawk—a tatted thug with a child who doesn't look like him—and I'm genuinely scared she's going to call a human trafficking hotline. In the end she seems reassured by Megan's constant stream of questions about which flavors are her favorite, what type of cone she recommends, and whether she likes snakes. I can't remember the last time I had ice cream, let alone the flavor, so I order two cookies and cream cones.

Megan bounces in the direction of a plastic table outside, but veers immediately toward a field of long-haired cows across the road. "Can we visit them, please?"

"If you look both ways before you cross the street this time."

I follow a little ways behind her, licking drops off the edges of the cone before they can escape. It's good enough, but so sweet it makes my teeth hurt. I bet Ollie loves ice cream, the more sugary the better. I want to see him sitting outside this summer, in a tank top, with sunburned shoulders and his dumb red plastic sunglasses, eating an ice cream cone. I want it more than I've wanted almost anything in my life. I want to still be here in the height of summer. I want all the days in the world to just unfold a new layer of him every day. But I don't know what's going to happen.

Megan's hanging over the fence, cooing at the cows to come over so she can pet them. "Don't feed them ice cream," I warn when one of them trots toward her, because I'm starting to get a bead on how she thinks.

"Why not?" Megan looks confused. "They make milk, and ice cream is just milk, right?"

She has a point, in my mind. But I know Ollie would say *it's bad for them* and I ought to stick to at least a couple of his rules today. "If I wanted the cow to eat ice cream, I would have bought it for him instead of you."

She cackles at the thought and holds her cone out of reach as the cow's wet nose snuffles her cheek.

Crunching up bites of my waffle cone, I stare at the clouds on the horizon—those strangely detailed, puffy ones like a painting—and let all the thoughts fall out of my head for the first time in days.

"Are you gonna be my other dad?"

My brain jolts back into my body and I stare at her as she climbs down from the fence, squinting at me in the harsh sunlight. "What?"

"You and my dad are a thing, right? I saw you kissing the other day. You're not very sneaky." She buries her tongue in her cone to reach the last of the ice cream, but her eyes are serious. "Everyone says I need a mom, but I know people can have two dads because Eli does, and they're awesome. I wouldn't mind."

My chest hurts, though I'm not totally sure why. I open my mouth, but there's nothing to say.

Her voice gets quieter. "I had a mom, but she didn't want us. I don't know why." She chews on the inside of her cheek, looking at her feet. "If I'm annoying and you don't like me anymore, can you tell me instead of leaving? I don't want you to go. It would make Daddy really sad."

"Hey." Tossing the rest of my cone in the grass, I crouch down in front of her, looking up into her face. "You're not annoying. No one thinks that. Your mom was a bi—" I catch myself. "A really dumb person. Anyone who doesn't love you and your dad is missing out."

She rubs her mouth, sticky with ice cream. "Are you avoiding my question?"

"No." I stand up and put my hand on the tousle of her silky hair. "I just don't have an answer right now." I'm pretty sure I do. I was in a car full of drugs and guns less than twelve hours ago, about to get in a shootout with a cop. That's it. That's the answer. The one reason I'm here is the one reason I can't have this.

"Okay." She shoves her hands in her pockets and hunches up her shoulders, looking away. "Will you think about it? Dad said him and me always go together, though, so you have to like both of us."

"I do like you." I should let go and walk back to the bike, but instead I pull out her half-ruined braid and start over, combing it through with my fingers. It comes out straighter this time. "But I don't know if I'm a good enough person to be your dad, or Oliver's partner." Those words are a new kind of ache I've never felt before, because I've never let myself hope for anything I might lose. Today, I can't help it.

Turning around, she grabs my hand in both of hers and swings it back and forth. "We don't mind. Just think about it, please. And if you decide, let me know and maybe we can tell Dad together?"

"I will." I offer a fist bump. This time, we both make a firework noise and explode our fists. "Come on. What else can we do that's not homework?"

She skips alongside me back to the bike. "Can we watch a movie? Dad's tired of my favorites. Oh, and Mars can watch with us!"

"Sure thing."

When we get back to Ollie's house, Megan unlocks the front door, hangs Mars on her shoulder, and climbs the counter to make popcorn in the microwave. I should feel uncomfortable in this tidy little house that isn't mine, but I'm starting to learn the shape of it like I've always lived here–what floorboards creak, how to jiggle the bathroom door to make it stay shut. I still can't get over how many things they have out just because they look pretty, no other reason.

"These are my most favorites of all time." Megan fans two battered DVDs out in front of me as I collapse onto the couch, exhausted. She's holding *Alien* in one hand and *The Princess Diaries* in the other. I really fucking like this kid. When I shrug, she shoves *Princess Diaries* into the TV and beelines past all the open chairs and couch cushions to plop down next to me, propping her shoulder alongside mine. I stretch my arm across the back of the couch behind her, and she leans her head against it. Mars hangs out for a while, then starts exploring until he moves from her shoulder onto my chest. I'm not scared of snakes, so I just let him do his thing.

I've never seen anything like this movie—a dorky girl who starts taking princess lessons. She's supposed to be poor or something, but she lives in this huge place with all this fancy shit, even before she's a princess. Megan mouths along to every line, but still laughs at all the jokes like she's never heard them before. By the end, I'm mostly asleep, her weight on my arm and the snake curled on my belly. I'm vaguely aware of her changing the movie to *Alien*, but I don't remember anything that comes after.

I'm pulled out of the dark by a hand squeezing my shoulder. "Shhh," Ollie soothes, trying to keep me from jolting. I blink blearily up at him, standing there in his bank uniform with his keys still in his hand. Something about him coming back from work and finding me asleep in his house feels even more intimate than fucking.

As he nods toward the couch, his smile has something else behind it, complicated and wistful. When I look over, Megan's sprawled out asleep with her head against my hip, drooling. Mars is exploring my lap, and I'm glad he didn't fall. Taking pity on me, Ollie transfers Mars to his tank and sits down on the other side of Megan, tipping her over onto his lap so I can stretch and get blood back in my legs.

"I'm sorry we didn't do any homework," I whisper.

He shakes his head. "You didn't have to stay, Jax."

"I wanted to."

That complicated look comes back. He studies her sleeping face and strokes her hair.

"She knows all about us, Ollie. So if you're waiting for the right time to talk to her, it's back there somewhere." I point over my shoulder. Panic flickers in his eyes, so I press my knee against his. "You're good. She's happy about it."

"What did she say?"

I look down at my hands in my lap, the tattoos snaking up my bare forearms. It will be too hot to cover them up in the summer, and I won't be able to look respectable for him anymore.

"Jax?" Oliver slides Megan's limp form to the far end of the couch and sits down next to me, turning my face toward his. "You can tell me."

"She asked if I'm gonna be her second dad, like Gray and Jonah," I whisper, so we won't wake her up.

His eyes widen. "What did you say?"

Hesitating, I search his face, trying to find something, anything solid. An answer, a truth, a reassurance that neither of us have. "I–" Over his shoulder I can see Mr. Scalypants, sunning himself on a rock. He's been with this family longer than I have.

"What did you say?" Ollie repeats more gently. He holds up his hand, and I put my palm flat against his, our fingers lacing together.

"I told her I'd think about it." It was a mistake to say something like that without asking him first.

"You did?" When I look up from our joined hands, he doesn't even realize that his whole face has lit up, one horizon to the other, like a spring morning. I wish I hadn't told him. Sometimes I catch myself wondering if I could just reset everything and try again. If I walked away tonight, would some version of me find some version of him in a place where there's nothing keeping us apart? I'll never know, because I can't take the thought of missing a single second here, with them, until the end.

"Yeah. But Ollie, I don't..." I can't tell him what I'm trying to say without spilling the secret of what I've been doing at night.

"It's alright, Jackson. We've got time to figure it out." But he can't hide that hope in his eyes as he wraps his arms around me.

If only wanting were enough, I'd be the king of everything.

Chapter 28

OLIVER

"Guess what? I couldn't wait to tell you. I got an interview!" I cup my phone against my shoulder, typing rapidly on my computer. "It's a remote administration job for a marketing company from California."

"Hey." Jax's warm voice fills my ear. "Look at you go." I can hear exactly what kind of smile he has–the crooked one that crinkles the skin around his eyes.

"I'm looking at flights right now." I pull up the website and prop my chin in my hand, squinting at the numbers. "I'll have to check and see if Gray and Jonah can watch Megan for those dates."

"I thought this was a remote thing."

"It is! It totally is. They just, uh, *do an in-person interview.*" I cough the last part out as all one word, because I know what he's going to say next. It's the same thing I've been telling myself ever since I got the call this morning. If I say the words fast enough, maybe they won't stand between me and what I want as solidly as the Great Wall of China.

"You have to fly to California?" There's a warning note in his voice.

"Yeah. So?"

"So is that gonna be a problem?"

I spin my chair around and examine the fluorescent lights overhead. "No. There's lots of space in airports. And if I get stressed on the plane, I can just sleep. Flying isn't anything like driving or being stuck in a crowded room." That might be the most lies I've ever told in a row, but I don't fucking care anymore. If I want this enough, I can do anything. Isn't that what they teach you in school?

There's a long silence. Jax clears his throat. "Do you want me to come with?"

"Neither of us can afford that. The company will pay for me to fly, but not a plus one."

"Ollie..."

"Think about it this way. We can practice our sexting skills."

That makes him go quiet for a long time, like he's really thinking it through. I can picture him staring into space, his wheels turning as he processes all the possibilities.

I decide to get his mind off the flying thing before he digs any deeper. "See," I complain in my best innocent voice, "I don't know how I'll send you pictures. I don't think my whole dick will fit on the screen at once."

Just as Jax moans, Tristan walks out of the vault in time to catch the last half of my sentence. He claps his hands over his ears and walks back the way he came, chanting *la la la* as he disappears.

A second later, he's back. "Wait, who are you talking to?"

"Jax?"

He frowns in confusion and points from my phone to the back door and back to me. As if on cue, the door opens and Jax comes in with his phone to his ear. "Wanna get lunch?"

I hang up my phone and beam at him. "I'm ready."

"You guys are unbelievable," Tris complains. "He was twenty feet away."

"I couldn't leave my workstation, but I couldn't wait to tell him the news."

"I'm resigning." Tris grabs a blank sheet from the printer, writes *sexual harassment and a hostile work environment*, and signs his name. "Leave that on Stace's desk for me, please."

"Can you quit after I take my lunch? Remember who set you up on a date with Alice."

"You'll have to set me up on a date with ScarJo herself if you mention your dick in front of me again."

Jax can't stifle a snort at the mention of our favorite celebrity.

"Thank you, Tris." Swinging by my employee locker, I grab my extra-heavy lunch bag and lug it out the back door to where Jax waits near the cabinets he was refinishing while we talked on the phone. His eyes slide over me appreciatively, even though I'm just wearing the same rumpled work clothes as usual.

"Ready?"

Before I can climb on his bike behind him, he catches me around the waist and kisses me gently, then hungrily. He pulls back, his eyes so close to mine that they look all blurry. Even so, I can see the worry in them. "Are you sure you're going to be okay flying to California?"

I force myself to hold his stare instead of looking away. "I've got it." If my daughter's future isn't enough to make my brain cooperate for an afternoon, then I guess everyone was right about me.

"If you say so." He doesn't look convinced as he lets me go. Once I've got my arms around him, the lunch bag tucked between us, he pulls out fast enough to make me wail protestingly. "Sorry," he calls over his shoulder. "I forgot you weren't Megan." I flip him off.

We ride just a few minutes out of town, pulling off near the river and hiking down to the quiet banks. Megan and I found this place one Saturday when I took her, Eli, and Kenzie frog hunting.

As Jax drops onto a sunny patch of sand, I unzip my bag and pull out a heavy glass bottle of whiskey and two shot glasses. "I don't even like whiskey. I hope Tristan or Jonah will take the rest of this."

"It doesn't have a dog on the label," Jax deadpans. "So I don't think the little guy will be interested."

"Be nice," I scold.

"You know I'm right."

He probably is. I make him hold the shot glasses while I pour as carefully as I can. The heavy bottle keeps bobbing, dribbling whiskey over his hands. He hands me one of the sticky glasses and sucks his fingers clean. "Say something, Ollie."

I lift my glass. "To a happy six years—"

"That's not true," he interrupts critically.

"For not having any words, you're awfully picky about mine." I try again. "To not dying six years ago."

"Cheers." He taps his glass to mine, then tosses it back easily. I wrinkle my nose, then try to do it fast, like him. The burn leaves me doubled over, coughing and spluttering.

"Why'd you buy it if you can't even drink it, lightweight?" He rubs my back.

"I just asked the guy at the store what you're supposed to drink out of shot glasses." When he gives me an incredulous look, I shrug. "What? I'm a pint guy. I stole these from Megan's room; she keeps coins in them."

Jax fills his glass a couple more times to make up for my share as we lean against the loamy bank and watch the river bubble past, sparkling in the sun with every color in the world. The air feels vibrant and alive, grasshoppers springing over our legs and birds calling overhead. "What time is it?" he asks.

I check my phone. "One-fifteen."

"So right...now," he touches the earth between us, "you were being a little brat about conserving body heat."

"I don't know why you didn't just leave me to die." I slide over and rest my ear on his shoulder. He rubs his cheek against the top of my head.

"I thought about it, but there wasn't anywhere for me to leave you."

"Is this what a miracle is?" I ask suddenly, angling my face toward his. "Us here, now, like this?"

"No," he says without even stopping to think, his fingers playing with the bone at the top of my spine. "It might be fate, but I hope it's not. Fate always changes its mind and comes back for everything it gave you."

"So we don't let it." I let my eyes start to drift closed, watching the sunlight filter through my eyelashes. "When it comes back for us, we just say *no*."

He hums quietly. "That's not how it works."

"I can be really fucking stubborn."

"You can." His hand slips under my polo and spreads flat against my chest, feeling my heartbeat. "When I try, it spits in my face. But maybe you're stubborn enough. You tell fate to shove off, and it just unwinds. I'd like to see that."

We doze and drift for a while, drinking in all the sights and sounds and scents we almost lost under a million tons of rock. Then he sighs. "When's your flight?"

"Next Monday. Just for one day. I booked while we were on the phone."

His jaw works. "You sure, Ollie?"

"Stop. We're supposed to be celebrating." I get up on my knees. "One more. Let's close our eyes, for old times' sake."

He holds up the glasses to eye level and watches me spill again. "You're supposed to shut your eyes *after* you pour."

"Fuck you. Now close your eyes."

It's dark.

Not really, because the sun filters bright through my eyelids, but I pretend. This time I manage to get the alcohol down the right pipe, even though I gag after. "That's awful."

"Try this." I hear the bottle slosh, then he wraps his hands around my head and kisses a mouthful of it onto my tongue. The sweet smokiness of his mouth already tastes like whiskey kisses, so it really does go down easier this way.

It's time for me to go relieve my friend for his lunch, but Jax rests his rough palm over my eyes and pushes me onto my back on the fresh, warm-smelling earth, pinning me with his bulk as he tastes every part of me he wants. I resolve to send Tris some apology flowers or something.

Chapter 29

Jackson

Garrett waits by the car, watching them load up. Something's different tonight; they're stacking long, hard cases into the back of the SUV. My heart sinks.

"Ready?" He puts a hand on my arm and I pull away. I'm too angry to keep my head down.

"What the fuck is this?"

"We're driving a couple of hours west to hand them off."

I step back, shaking my head. "I didn't sign up for this. I'm out." Drugs are one thing. Guns? I have zero doubts that this man doesn't know what he's getting into.

"I'm pretty sure I remember you signing up for anything I wanted you to do, fucker. So unless you want to reneg our deal, hurry up and help." He slaps the back of my head and walks away.

Oliver's not in bed when I wake up. I lie there for a minute, trying to get my breath back and remind myself I'm not still on that fucking gun run last night. Everything seemed to go smoothly at the handoff, but I have such a bad feeling brewing in my gut.

Ollie's spot on the mattress feels cool to the touch. His flight takes off at three, but I can't for the life of me remember all the fiddly math that adds up to what time he needed to leave the house. When I sit up, his little black suitcase is gone from the foot of the bed and my flannel isn't on the back of the door.

I stagger down the hall, expecting to search an empty house until I find Ollie packing his shampoo and laptop charger. Instead there's a fucking mob of people in the living room–Tristan, Megan, Eli, and Kenzie–but no Oliver. Tris and Eli are playing video games, while Megan and Kenzie hang out with Mars on the floor. They all gawk at me wearing nothing but tattoos and boxers. "Fuck," I say, squinting at them, then walk back into the bedroom to try again. A couple of minutes later, I come out with clothes on and my teeth brushed.

"The fuck is everyone doing here?" Something's not right, and I've had about three hours of sleep, and I'm over it. Tristan looks pointedly from me to the littlest girl and mouths *shut up*.

"You shut up," I grumble, deciding to search for Oliver in the kitchen, where there's black coffee. By the time I have a full mug in my hands, I'm almost certain he's not in the house. "Where's Ollie?"

Tristan looks confused. "The airport? Where else would he be?"

"How did he *get* to the airport?" I close my eyes and make an effort to sound nicer, but all the warning signals in my brain are going off like a fucking fireworks display and I'm feeling borderline feral.

"Papa took him," the littlest girl pipes up.

I open my eyes. "Gray?"

"I assumed he told you." Tristan gives me another *what are you on this morning* look.

Why? I stare back at him, my brain going over the word again and again. Then I know. *Because he can convince Gray to drop him off at the curb instead of going inside.*

Without another word, I pour my coffee into the nearest potted plant and make for the door. "Bye?" Tristan snarks behind me. I just wave over my shoulder as I jog for my bike, fighting back the wave of hot anger trying to short-circuit my brain. The man literally just told me how stubborn he can be, tough enough to reverse the tide of fate, and I forgot. He knows that I would insist on going in with him, but he doesn't want anyone to see him struggle.

Maybe he has the right idea. Maybe he needs space. I don't give a fuck. All I know is that he's alone, and he shouldn't be.

It takes about ninety minutes to ride to the airport. The wind blows the cobwebs out of my head, but my brain's still prowling in endless circles like an agitated tiger stuck in a zoo exhibit. Five minutes out, I check my phone—no calls or texts, and his flight left a few minutes ago. He did it. Calming down a little, I pull into a cell phone lot outside the airport and buy a Coke from the convenience store. The sun warms my shoulders as I sit on the curb and drink it slowly, savoring the feeling of having nowhere to be for five minutes. Just as I sling my leg over the bike to head home, my phone rings.

"Ollie?"

Crying isn't a strong enough word for what I hear. It's gut-wrenching, wretched, terrified sobs that go on and on without a breath. He makes a weak sound, like he's trying to say something, then breaks again. Turning on the engine, I walk the bike backward out of my parking spot. "Oliver, baby, I need you to tell me where you are. That's it. Give me one word."

"B-b-baggage," he chokes out. He fights for breath, then gives up with a strangled wail.

"Don't hang up. I'm right here, outside the airport. You're okay." I can only hear him faintly over the engine as I gun it up to the terminal, driving with one hand.

Someone in the distance hollers at me not to leave my bike on the sidewalk, but I gesture to the completely empty pickup area and yell something about a medical emergency before abandoning it. The baggage claim stretches out in either direction from the doors. The right side is lit up and full of people waiting around the conveyor belts, so I turn the opposite direction and make for the dim lounge at the far end.

It takes a minute to spot the small figure huddled against the wall in the unlit corner, like a terrified animal that finds the darkest place to crawl into. Hanging up my phone, I drop to my knees next to him. He doesn't even react to me, just keeps coughing weak, painful sobs into his arms, his flushed face drenched in snot and tears. His body feels limp when I pull him against me, trembling as I rock him slowly back and forth. "You're okay, Ollie. I'm here."

"I can't." He almost retches from crying, then tries weakly to shove me away. "I can't. Please, I can't."

"You don't have to. But I need you to try and breathe for me, baby. You're going to pass out." I press a hand to his chest. "Take a breath in."

He tries, a series of short, shallow inhalations he can barely control. "They have my bag. Your flannel's in there. They took it." The word *took* trails into more sobs, dry and weak, and he buries his face in my shoulder. "I need my stuff back. They have my stuff. *Please* get my stuff back."

"We'll get all your stuff, Ollie. It's okay. They'll send it right back to you." I don't actually know how airports work, but I take a guess.

"Jackson..." He's still spasming and coughing more than breathing. "I'm so sorry. I can't. I'm sorry. I'm sorry." If I didn't step in, I'm pretty sure he'd keep chanting those two words over and over until his voice gave out for good.

"Oliver, please stop." I pull him as tight to me as I can, lacing my fingers in his sweaty hair. I've seen a lot of fucked-up things, but almost none of them scared me as much as I'm scared for him right now. I guess I thought I'd already seen a panic attack—when he felt scared to drive, or maybe in the cave-in, when he cried on my chest. I had no idea. He's so gone, stripped of everything except primal desperation and shame. And there's nothing I can fight.

Getting my legs out from under me, I lean against the wall and gather him up as tight as I can. He's finally stopped sobbing and started breathing, but his body stays limp and lifeless. After a few minutes, I kiss the top of his head and brush his hair back, using the sleeve of my shirt to gently wipe his cheeks. His eyes are open, but fixed on nothing. When he feels me cleaning him, he blinks a few times and starts to tense. So abruptly it scares me, he sits up and turns his face away, scrubbing roughly at it with his hands, wiping his nose on the interview shirt he picked out last night. "Fuck," he croaks, his voice wrecked. "*Fucking* hell." He smacks himself in the forehead, less like he's trying to snap out of it and more like he wants to hurt.

"Oliver." I put my hand on his arm. "Don't."

"Don't look at me." He twists away. "I just want to go home."

"Please, Ollie." I'm wrecked and wrung out; I can't imagine how he feels right now. The slump of his shoulders looks broken as he shivers on his hands and knees on the dated airport carpet. "Please look at me. I need to know that you're okay."

"Fine." Jaw tight, he turns around. His skin looks patchy and pale, his eyes swollen. There's snot in his beard. "This is it, Jax. You finally get to meet the real Oliver." His lip quivers. "Sorry to disappoint."

"Why would you say that?" I try to squeeze his shoulder, but he pulls back angrily.

"I don't know what's worse, that I can't even pull myself together when the future of my child is at stake, or that standing in a fucking line, something people do every day of their lives, can turn me into this." His breathing starts to get ragged again. "I'm *broken*, Jax. My head is broken, and apparently there's no love or want or reason that can fix me. I'm never gonna be normal, and I'm so scared."

"I know."

He doesn't really hear me, just keeps talking. "I can't let you pretend to be okay with this. You don't know what you're signing up for, Jax. Sometimes this happens every single day, twice a day, three times, and I can't stop myself, even when I know it will fuck everything up."

"I know."

Confused, he blinks at me. "You're not listening. I'm not just anxious or high-maintenance. This isn't some quirk. Love's not gonna cure me. I'm *sick*. This is every day of my life, and even if I get help, it will always be there."

"I know."

"*Why do you keep saying that?*" He looks like he can't decide between crying again, running, or punching me.

I'm not a writer like him.

I don't have words.

But I have stories, too.

Oliver

Jax sits up and pushes the sleeves of his flannel past his elbows, revealing his powerful forearms, dusted with hair and marked with chains and barbed wire. He watches my face as he takes my hand and places it on the inside of his arm. It's invisible to the eye, but the skin isn't smooth. I can feel two raised scars, not scattered like an experiment but intentionally placed. My other hand finds two more on the left arm. "These weren't here in the tunnel. I would have felt them."

"That's right."

I'm still dizzy from crying, and my stomach almost brings up the breakfast I forced down before I left. "God, Jackson." I can't cry anymore, so I just look out the window at the shady pillars of the pickup area, and the wide, tranquil land beyond. A family is piling into a shuttle with all their suitcases, arguing excitedly. I wonder where they're going. Who the hell comes to Iowa for a vacation?

"I've tried more than once in my life," he says. "And there were times I didn't get out of bed for weeks, didn't shower or eat, pissed in empty bottles and left them everywhere. It's a dark animal that catches up and consumes me sometimes, so I can't feel anything. I'm safe now, but if we stay together, you'll see me in bad shape. You'll wonder what you did, why you can't snap me out of it. You'll waste time trying to make sure I take care of myself. And the answer is that you didn't do anything, because that's just how it is sometimes. Love can't cure that, either."

Pulling his sleeves down, he cradles my face in his hands, drinking in every ugly part of me, and kisses me softly through all the snot and tears. "But I can still love you, right? And you can still love me. It can't cure us, but we fight so fucking hard, and maybe that's the thing we're fighting for."

"Jackson…" My voice fragments. "I tried to fight, but I lost. And I don't know what to do now."

His face when he studies me is full of honesty, which is more than most people give me. "I don't know either. But I'm here. We can start by getting out of this fucking airport."

"I can't go home right now." I pull my knees up and rest my aching head against them, the comforting, childish position that always helps me feel a little safer. "I can't face Megan or Tris; I can't explain why I'm not on the plane. Not now. Please don't make me do that."

We're both broke, so all we can manage is a crummy dive hotel with dark-paneled walls from the seventies and broken air conditioning. I just collapse face-first on the bed and stop moving. *I'll be here for the rest of the day, thanks. Preferably the rest of time.*

I listen to Jax pee, then his conversation with Tristan as he makes sure Megan's taken care of until tomorrow morning. He leaves for a few minutes, then comes back and presses a cold, wet bottle of orange juice against my neck. I just flinch away with a groan and go still again. My dry throat begs for the drink, but I ignore it. I'm not allowed to cheer up too fast after a panic attack; I need to stay miserable for long enough to justify the misery I just put everyone else through.

After a moment, his fingers start unlacing my shoes and pulling them off my tired feet. He grabs the back of my jeans and drags them down my legs. When my briefs almost slide right off with them, I catch the waistband just in time. "What are you doing?"

"Getting comfortable. Why not?" I hear him stripping off his jeans. The crappy mattress bounces as he sits next to me. He pushes up my shirt and rubs my back, working his thumbs into the tight knots of muscle. "You said this has happened to you for years. What do you do after, to feel better?"

I snort into the comforter.

"What's that supposed to mean?"

"You really want to know? I play a shitty mobile farming game and jerk off."

He's quiet for a minute. "At the same time?"

"*No*, you goof." Rolling onto my back, I sit up and grab the juice, chug it down. Jackson scuffles around on the floor until he finds my jeans, then extracts my phone and starts messing with it. "Wait." I guess there's no point in hoping he won't notice my lock screen wallpaper—a photo of him and Megs sleeping that I took the other night.

"Better show me this farm game before I find all your old dating app chat logs."

"Jax," I whine, crawling across the bed and trying to grab it away. "Stop. I'm trying to be miserable."

But it's too late. I'm up, I'm hydrating, and now I'm in his arms as he strips us both the rest of the way naked and leans on the headboard, pulling me to lie against his chest. The man's too good at getting his way.

JACKSON

"This is how I got into growing vegetables in real life," he mumbles sleepily into my chest, holding the phone up. He's got a fucking empire going on, hundreds of fields, ten dogs, a garage full of souped-up tractors. There's a town of smug cartoon bastards who don't do anything but ask him for favors. Reminds me of Byrock.

He can only lie with his hip on my dick for so long before it starts to wake up. I ignore it and wait to follow his lead, trying not to push him anywhere he doesn't want to go. When he feels me get hard, he rolls over a little and spreads his thighs to give his own cock room to grow. Playing the game with one hand, he absently runs his fingers up and down his length. The movement starts to get hungrier, his breathing faster, and he twists against me. I brush his hair back and kiss his forehead. "So you do jerk off and play at the same time. Like a little slut, huh?"

Throwing the phone aside, he peers hopefully up at me, a spark coming back into his eyes. "Come on, Jax."

"You do it." I tease my fingers up and down his spine as he does his best to jerk both of us in unison, which is impossible given our different sizes. "Wait," I order when he's getting close, precum thick and glistening under his foreskin and his other hand sticky with mine.

Ollie shoots me a distressed stare as I sit up and hand him a tissue to wipe his hands. "Let's watch some TV or something."

"The fuck?" He crosses his arms, looking exhausted and sulky like one of those hedgehogs that gets plopped in measuring cups and shit for cute photos.

"Being hard for you feels even better than coming." My body gets excited as I watch realization dawn on his face. It likes this game. Oliver's expression makes it clear he's not so sure.

I watch his cock while we cuddle in front of some home improvement show where a bunch of idiots do pointless things to a perfectly nice house. When it's half soft, I reach around and start playing with it. He immediately arches his back with a needy sound. I know his body well enough that I can get him so, so close before I let go and pull his hands out of the way. "*Jackson*," he moans. "I hate this."

"Do it to me now. But use your mouth, and stop before I come. Then tell me how you hate it."

Just like I thought, he becomes a fan real quick. A long evening of scattered hand jobs and blowjobs fades into a sweaty, confusing night without air conditioning where sex dreams fade into waking up to find Oliver teasing my dick. I hold him down and tug his foreskin, licking the most sensitive areas underneath until he bucks and squeals.

Somewhere around three in the morning, he rolls over and moves my hand from his dick to his ass, so I spend the rest of the night fucking him open with my fingers, a little more each time. By the time the sun creeps between the curtains, my cock hasn't been fully soft in so long I feel like I'm losing my mind. When I look down, I realize Ollie's rubbing off on the bed in his sleep. "Hey, wake up." I tug his hair gently.

I'm pretty sure he expected to face the morning by beating himself up about his parents, his job, all these things he can't do anything about right now. But he's too distracted to do much but groan. "Help me, Jackson. I'm dying."

"Let's take a shower."

He can barely walk, limping into the dingy bathroom, and I'm not much better. I turn on the hot water and push him underneath, kissing him eagerly. Then I turn him around, spread his legs, and push into the ass that's still wide open and begging for me. I get in exactly two thrusts before he comes so hard he's practically climbing the wall. It's the frantic noises he makes that send me over the edge, gasping for breath as I grip the shower curtain rod to keep from falling over and breaking my leg in the cramped tub.

The banging of car doors and muffled voices drift up through the open window as I scrub Oliver's ass and soft cock and he hums against my shoulder, the whole world clean and sharp. We've looked into the depths of each other, no more secrets. Something tells me that if I open my mouth now, I'll spill everything about Garrett and the fucking mess I'm in. If I did, maybe he could help me see the answer I've been missing this whole time.

"Jax?" he asks softly, as I lean against the wall and let him shampoo my scalp.

"Yeah?"

"My parents are coming to Megan's birthday party next week, you know. I want you to meet them. Like *meet* meet them. As my partner."

The moment snaps and I wipe the shampoo away so I can open my eyes and stare at him. "Are you sure?"

He nods, his face peaceful at the thought of not facing this family drama alone. Of having a strong, reliable person at his side, someone who makes him proud and shows his parents that he has everything together.

Hugging his slippery body to mine until he laughs and squirms, I let my unsaid words wash down the drain.

Chapter 30

JACKSON

I don't see the man at first, the one standing at the end of Tristan's driveway. I'm focused on checking the address on my phone, where Oliver asked me to go pick up a case of sparkling cider and some champagne on the way to Megan's party. The saddlebags on my bike aren't the greatest, so I have a backpack over my arm to carry the extra bottles.

Fumbling for my keys, I rehearse my fiftieth attempt of what to say to Oliver's parents tonight. "Hello" seems like a solid start, but beyond that I'm lost. Ollie told me I didn't need to hide my tattoos, but I went with long sleeves anyway. There's no reason to make this any more awkward.

My footsteps slow when I notice the dark silhouette under the streetlight. In the corner of my vision, another one crosses the sidewalk toward where a third waits at the edge of the lawn, hemming me in. I drop the pack on the ground and take a step backward. When the guy on the driveway moves closer, I recognize his mohawk from the gun deal last week.

"I didn't do anything." I hold my hands up, backing away. "I'm dumb muscle. I just stand there. If someone crossed you, it wasn't me."

I used to think the guys who wouldn't go quietly, who sniveled and begged and struggled, were pathetic. I didn't understand why they even bothered.

Oliver.

What have I done?

"Please. I don't know—*fuck*." The closest guy flicks open a knife and comes at me. I scramble backward so fast I trip, trying to get my own knife out of my pocket. I haven't had to pull it in so long that my reflexes are all shitty and I can't get it free.

Oliver.

My back hits the garage door and I kick out with both feet as the guy lunges at me. Someone grabs my arm and I throw myself into the center of his mass, trying to get past so I can run. I've got my knife now, but I can't work the mechanism open because my hands are numb. A body hits me from behind and I slam face-first into the dewy grass, the knife slipping away and tumbling across the lawn. I can feel hands all over me, someone kicking my shoulder, and I'm thrashing desperately just like that other day, just waiting for a gun in my mouth.

Oliver.
Oliver.
Oliver.

Excruciating pain blooms across my abdomen and I scream silently into the dirt. But my body won't stop fighting. I kick someone in the face hard enough to feel their skull fracture, and make a pretty good try at ripping the other guy's balls out of his nutsack. Throwing off the third attacker, I stagger across the grass, clutching the agony in my gut. I can't run, and all three of them are getting up, angry and ready for another go.

Oliver.

I'm so, so sorry.

Like some kind of joke, God pretending he cares about me for the first time in my life, one of the guys hisses something and they make a break for it, disappearing across the street just before a patrol car cruises past. In a fucking movie, it would be the same cop I saved the other night. We'd hug and do a song and dance number. What a joke. I curl up in the shadow of the fence, gripping the pain in my belly as my hands start shaking, followed by my whole body. I can feel shock slipping in around the edges as I stare at the blood streaked across Tristan's lawn, too much to come only from me.

I fought and drew blood like a good dog, a trained dog, because that's what I am. Even when it hurts, even when I can't take any more. Even if I just want to lie on Oliver's front porch in the sun while he strokes my back until my last breath.

Oliver

"You're stressing out Mars," Megan whispers as I pace another circuit of the living room. "What's wrong?"

"Nothing. Jax is just late." Trying to calm down, I lean over and kiss her forehead. "Put him away and hang out with everyone on the patio." I've given her bad habits, hiding from her grandparents. I want her to have a good relationship with them. "As soon as Jax gets here, we'll come out and join you."

Returning Mars to his tank, she runs over and hugs my waist. "I love you, Dad." It's supposed to be her birthday weekend, but here I am making her worry because it's impossible for me to hide things from her.

"I love you to the moon and back. Always and forever." I tug her messy braid. "Now go on, Skip."

As she slides the porch door shut behind her, I drop onto the couch and check my phone again. No message. He's only twenty minutes late, but I wish I hadn't sent him to go buy the stupid drinks. Him being here is more important.

The motorcycle purrs outside and I close my eyes in relief. After a long silence, the front door pushes open, the first time that Jackson hasn't knocked. I shoot to my feet. "Hey! Could you not find the drinks?"

He stops in the unlit entry without answering. When I flick on the light, I take in his pale skin, the glassy, desperate look in his eyes, his new orange shirt wrinkled and grass-stained.

"Did something happen?" I take a step closer when he sways a little. "Jax?"

"I...uh..." He swallows, blinking rapidly. We both look down at his hands. They're dirtied with something I can't make out, clutched to his stomach like he's cradling a small animal. When he unfolds them, dark blood slides between his fingers, his shirt dark and stiff with it. Drops start to fall on the entry floor, and he stares at them like he can't figure out where they came from.

"*Christ.*" I sprint to the kitchen and grab a roll of paper towels. Tearing off huge handfuls, I press them to his stomach and push his hands on top of them to hold them in place. "Oh, love, what happened?" My voice is shaking so much I can hardly speak. "I don't know what to do. I'm gonna call 911."

He grabs for my arm with one blood-smeared hand. "No. Please don't. It's not..." He tries to rally. "It's not as bad as it looks."

"What the fuck is that supposed to mean?" I pull him through the living room and into the bathroom, slamming and locking the door. "Get in the tub. I've got you." He's gripping my arm so tightly I'm scared he's going to break something.

"Oliver," he groans. "I shouldn't be here."

"Shh." Making sure the water runs warm, I pull the shower head off the hook and use it to rinse blood off his body. He whimpers pained sounds in his throat as I carefully unstick his shirt from his wound and lift it out of the way. "Hold that for me." The hand that's not clinging to me manages to hold on to the ruined fabric.

I stare helplessly at the deep gash across his abdomen. I guess he's right that it's not so bad, in that his guts aren't going to fall out, but it's sure as hell not good. "Why did you come here instead of going to the hospital?"

His grip tightens around my wrist, my bones protesting, and his wide eyes find me. "I thought I was gonna die," he whispers. "I needed to see you."

"But what *happened* Jax? Who did this to you? Did you get mugged?" Grabbing towels from the linen closet, too frantic to stop and work out which are the nice ones and which are the old ones, I work on cleaning the wound and applying pressure. "Does this have anything to do with why you're always out all night?"

My heart sinks when he doesn't say anything, just closes his eyes. Working in silence, I manage to wrap a few thick towels around the wound and secure them in place with all the old ace bandages I used to buy for my sore back and tweaked knee.

"I'm going to drive you to the hospital now, okay?"

"Your parents are here," he moans. Now that he's not bleeding out, he seems clearer-headed and stronger.

"Yeah, believe me, I'm very aware of that." I press my messy hands to my forehead, breathing hard. He stares back at me with dark eyes that tell me everything and nothing, until I climb into the massacred-looking tub, slipping on blood, and hug him to me. Shuddering, he buries his face in my ruined sweater. "I've got you, love. You're not going to die. Can you wait on the porch while I change?"

"Oliver..." I have to forcibly pry myself out of his grip.

"Go sit on the front step and hold down the towels. I'll be right there. I just need to rinse the tub and say goodbye. You can do that, right?"

Jackson nods. He doesn't make any more sounds as I help him to the front door, but I can feel the pain racking his body when he moves. "I love you, Jax. I'll be right there."

I start to jog down the hall, but his hoarse voice drags my feet to a stop. "Ollie." He's standing in the light of the living room lamp, shivering a little, his gaze fixed on me. The hand that isn't holding the towels in place starts to reach out, then drops back to his side, his fingers flexing. He takes a deep, unsteady breath. "I promise everything's gonna be okay."

"I know. They'll get you patched up right away at the hospital." I force a weak smile. "Just let me clean up." An expression I don't understand crosses his face, then he nods and turns away.

Tearing off my clothes, I throw them in my closet. I jump into the shower and use it to rinse myself and the walls and floor of the tub off at the same time, then spend a couple of minutes swiping blood off the floor so my parents won't have a heart attack if they need to use the toilet. I can't do anything about the trail of droplets across the living room floor, so I just pray no one will notice them. Ten minutes after I sent

Jax outside, I pull on fresh clothes and stick my head onto the porch, where everyone's playing Jenga on the patio table. "Hey Tris, could I borrow your car?" Mine hasn't been out of the garage in so many weeks I'm not sure the battery's still good. My parents don't notice the stilted cheer in my voice, but Megan and Tristan glance up in concern.

"Where's Jax?" Megan asks.

Where's Jax?

Where is Jackson?

I feel all the blood drain from my head, my vision blurring. I'm so fucking stupid. When I turn around and sprint through the house to the front lawn, neither Jax nor his bike are anywhere in sight. "Fuck!"

I almost crash into Tristan when I run back inside. "Ollie, what's wrong?" His eyes go huge when he sees the trail of droplets across the floor.

"*Please* give me your keys. Jax is gone. I think he's at your house, but I need to get there now."

"I'll drive you."

I don't have time to come up with an excuse for my parents, so I just beg them to watch Megan until I get back. She stares at me with teary eyes, ignoring my reassurances that Jax is fine, but I don't have time to be a good dad right now. Tristan hauls ass back to his house, forcing his shitty car to work harder than it has in a long time. When we pull up his driveway, Jax's bike isn't there. "No," I slide down in my seat and bury my face in my hands. "No, no, no. Please tell me this isn't happening."

"Do you think he's inside?" Tristan gently but insistently pulls me out of my seat, interrupting my panic spiral, and drags me up to the side door.

No backpack, no jacket, no spare clothes piled on the dusty chest freezer. Like he was never here. But the air still smells like him, mixed with a thick tang of blood.

"Ollie..." Tristan grabs a scrap of folded paper from the arm of the couch and holds it out to me. My brain struggles to do math as he drops it in my hand. Jax had maybe a fifteen-minute head start. Enough time for someone with a knife wound to pack up their stuff, write a letter, and leave? Apparently so. Especially if they're a stubborn, desperate fuck like Jackson Moreno when he gets an idea in his head. Especially if he's had the contents of the letter rehearsed in his mind since the first time he set eyes on me.

I spent six years waiting for a letter from this man. As I unfold the paper, I realize through a blur of tears that I finally got one.

Oliver,

I'm sorry. I don't want to go. But I've dug myself a deep hole, and I can't keep you safe until I dig myself out again.
Ollie.
Oliver.
Please don't be sad. I'm not. You're it for me, Ollie. My everything. That means we'll always find each other again. If I didn't truly believe that, I don't think I could make myself go. When I'm free, I'll search for you until someone that used to be Ollie stumbles across someone who used to be Jax, and the rest will be history. I'm looking forward to our third first kiss. It's gonna be okay. I love you.

Jackson

IV

Us

Chapter 31

Two months

Oliver,

I wish I could tell you where I am, but I don't trust you not to come after me. And I deleted your number because I don't trust myself not to come after you. I found out that my sister's boyfriend, the guy who had it out for me, is dead. The man who replaced him doesn't give a shit about me, as long as I pay the debt I ran out on. Then I'll be free, actually free, for the first time in my life.
My cut's healing up fine, but it's going to be an ugly scar. I hate that I scared you, and I hope you got the blood out of the floor. I don't know what I should say

sorry for first—the things I did, the danger I could have put you in, or the way I lied to you. I tried so hard to do the right thing, Ollie. But I wasn't strong enough. This time, I'm not going to stop until I can face you honestly.

I hope your anxiety isn't too bad. Please take care of yourself, and do everything you know I'd tell you to do. I promise to do my best if you promise to do yours. I love you.

Jackson

Twelve months

Oliver,

I had to sell my bike, and it fucking kills me. You always looked so ridiculous and sweet sitting on that thing. The way you yelped and crushed my ribs every time I accelerated too fast. I'm running out of things you touched, Ollie.
I knew it would be long, but not this long. Sometimes I regret everything I've done, all the way down to meeting you. If you're hurting even half as much as I am right now, you'll get why. I wouldn't have fought so hard my whole life if I'd known it was for this. That's not true. Of course I would. But I miss you so much I can't breathe. I feel like I haven't breathed a single time in the last year.
I love you so much.

Jackson

A year and a half

Oliver,

I'm writing this letter in my notebook, because I need to get the words out, but I guess I'm not sending it. Last week, the mail delivered back my last letter. I took it to the post office, and the woman told me that you aren't at this address anymore. She said mail only forwards automatically for a year, because by then a person has given their new address to everyone that matters. Now I realize how I made you feel when I didn't answer your letters. Helpless. Second-guessing every little thing. I'm sorry.
Now that I'm free, I could go back to Byrock and hunt down Tristan or Gray. They might tell me why you left instead of waiting for me. But I've been thinking, Ollie. Maybe forgetting is the key to finding you again. That's how it worked the first time. Maybe I should let you move on and make myself the kind of person you want when you meet him again for the first time. Because that's the kind of game fate likes to play, right?
I love you.

Jackson

Chapter 32

Jackson

"First time going north?"

I twitch awake, shivering. The cold has gotten up under my jacket and through my gloves. *That's what you get for falling asleep in the snow, dumbass.* Only my head is warm, under a gray knit cap with a rust-colored stripe around it. "Uh-huh."

A bulky guy with a beard sits down next to me and pulls out a box of cigarettes, lights one up. When he offers me the box, I shake my head. Every guy here is bulky and has a beard. I let my hair grow out because I didn't have the energy to buzz it anymore, but I try to shave my facial hair off every three weeks or so, just to keep myself from disappearing completely in the crowd.

"Did they tell you about the dark?" the guy muses, blowing out smoke.

"Not really." I just joined this year's crew to fly north to the Alaskan oil fields, and I'm already known as the guy who doesn't talk much. People mostly leave me be.

"When the sun goes down in November, it can stay dark until January."

Do I look like I give a shit about darkness? Breaking a stick off the bush next to me and flicking pieces of it into the show, I stare at him. "How does that work?" It sounds like a curse from one of Ollie's fantasy stories.

"It's the equator, and the way the earth tilts." He waves a hand vaguely. I'm not sure I understand exactly what the equator is, but I nod. "Just get your head ready, because living in the dark all the time can fuck with you."

"I know."

"Did you get your free breakfast?" the guy asks, distracted. I shake my head, and he gestures impatiently. "Go on. What's the matter with you? Passing up a free meal."

I used to be hungry all the time; lately, I've gone full days without food and hardly noticed. It's like the dark animal, but bigger and heavier, longer and longer stretches of time where I don't feel or care about anything. When I got this job with the oil company, I was excited. I could finally make enough money to take care of Oliver when I found him again. At least, I think that's why I was excited. It's getting harder to remember.

"Fine." Standing up, I nod to him and wade carefully through the snow until I reach the path to the main building. The crew that's about to fly from Bozeman, Montana to Alaska's North Slope spent the night at the company's facility. They're feeding us breakfast today, like a big sendoff to nowhere, before putting us on charter buses to the airport.

The buffet offers coffee, eggs, and the kind of overcooked bacon that turns to dust when you look at it wrong. Thad, the guy I bunked with last night, waves me over to his table in the cafeteria. Everyone is showing off pictures of their wives and kids, or girlfriends, and talking about how long it will be until we come back to the lower forty-eight and see them again.

Keeping my phone in my lap, I pull up the photo I look at every day. If it were printed, it would have holes worn through it by now. I took it on the only morning I can remember where I woke up before Ollie. He's sleeping, his naked body curled up in a tumble of blankets. The sun pours across his skin and peaceful face like liquid gold, making his messy hair look more ginger than usual. In the next picture, his blue eyes are cracked open as he smiles sleepily, reaching out an arm to grab the camera away. I'm supposed to get rid of everything, so I can forget. So I can hurry up the day where we don't recognize each other and we can start over. I've let go of everything but his old letters, the hat, and these two photos. I just can't make myself do it.

The other guys are griping about spending a few months apart from their loved ones. I don't think any of them have already waited two years. I don't think they've lain awake at night thinking about how much longer the next two years are going to feel, and the two after that.

"Who's he?" Thad asks quietly, looking over my shoulder.

"No one." I stuff the phone in my pocket, but he watches me with sympathetic eyes.

"It's alright, man. I'm not homophobic. It's always hard, the first time you go up, to leave people behind."

I shrug, my breakfast sitting like a brick in my chest, and Thad pats my shoulder and stands up. "We're leaving in forty minutes."

After I eat a few more eggs and drink a lot of coffee, I head to the room I slept in and gather my backpack. Besides a few jackets, some toiletries, and the bundle of letters, there's nothing to pack. When I'm ready, I go over to where Thad and the others are waiting and smoking. The cold air here bites like a motherfucker, making my eyes water and my lungs sting, but I know it will be worse up north. With my hands deep in my pockets, I loiter near the guys and inhale secondhand smoke while I watch bits of snow drop off the evergreen branches as birds flit back and forth.

I should be happy, I guess. I'm free from my past–for real this time. Pretty soon, the new blood at my old haunts won't remember I existed at all. I'm sure Garrett and the others don't remember me either, if they even survived whatever turf war was starting when I left. Now I'm going somewhere I've never seen before, to do good, honest work. But I'm edgy and tense because I've never flown before, and I don't know what to expect when the plane takes off. My body wants Oliver. He'd...well, I think he'd distract me by bumping my shoulder and smiling at me, saying something that makes me smile back, but I'm starting to lose pieces of him, my recollections flaking around the edges.

"Buses are here," someone calls, so we pick up our bags and migrate toward the two old vehicles idling near the gate, caked in dirty snow thrown up from the tires. My heart starts pounding as I get into line. Maybe I've made a mistake, going so far away. Maybe forgetting isn't the key after all, and I'll just end up alone in a place with no light and no memory of why I came. But all I can do is try to follow the path that might lead me back to him.

Nodding to the driver, I climb the steps and pick a window seat two-thirds of the way back. The engines are running to keep the heat on, and the bus gets loud as men and women shuffle into every open seat. Thad slides in next to me, raising his eyebrows. "Excited, Jax?"

"Sure." I'm lacing and unlacing my fingers in my lap, trying to stay calm and convince myself this isn't forever. He just chuckles and turns to talk to someone else.

"Commotion at the gate again," the person in front of us comments as he sits down. "Someone harassing security."

"Environmentalists like to come protest when new buses of workers get shipped out," Thad explains. I just nod, sliding down and staring at my fingerless gloves. My hands look fucked up, the knuckles dry and cracked, scraped up from work. The two fingers I broke badly last year before I got out of the gang healed crooked and lumpy as hell. I'll be forty in less than a year now, and my body doesn't recover from things like it should. I feel like one of Megan's snakes, shedding away layer after ugly layer of myself, trying desperately to find the man underneath who has whatever it is I'm lacking, who can break this cycle and get back everything I've lost.

I push in an old pair of earbuds and flip through the music on my phone. I keep making new rules, until there's more shit I can't listen to than things I can—no Beach Boys, no "Highway to Hell" or other beginner guitar songs, no folk music like the kind that gets played in little bars in Iowa for people to dance to. I wonder what kind of music the next Oliver and the next Jackson will share. At this rate, it will probably be fucking classical records in an old folks' home. But I'd be okay with that, too.

Engines snarl to life, and we start rolling toward the open gate, another full bus of people behind us. Everyone cranes their necks out the windows to see the commotion, but it seems to be over. There's no protest signs or yelling, just a guy in a parka and hat, arguing with a guard. Throwing up his hands, he turns away and starts to walk toward a public parking lot down the hill.

As the bus revs and spins its tires in the slush, he yanks off his hat with a frustrated gesture. A flash of ginger-blond hair like autumn leaves.

A second later, a breath, less than the space of a thought, I'm lunging over Thad and sprinting down the aisle with sixty startled pairs of eyes on my back. I almost fall into the driver's lap. "Open the door, please. Stop. Let me out," I beg, fighting not to throw myself straight through the closed doors. He hits the brakes, jolting everyone and making the bus behind us honk. There's nothing for him to do but obey me—he's busy trying to figure out if there's some kind of emergency going on in the back.

Someone yells *hey* behind me as I take a flying jump down the steps, my backpack slamming my shoulder, and take off running along the road. I keep slipping and skidding, not fast enough, never fast enough. For all I know, he's already getting into a car and driving away. Abandoning the road, I lurch into the deeper snow, stumbling over hidden rocks and bushes. As the hill drops away into an unplowed slope, I finally see his back far below me, most of the way to the parking lot. I cup my hands to my mouth. "Ollie!" He doesn't react, and for a second I think it might not be him after all, just a terrible misunderstanding.

My whole body protests as I take off down the hill, some steps dropping me up to my knees in snow. My boots are packed with it, my jeans drenched, my hands wet and aching. I dropped my bag somewhere along the way. "Oliver!" He just keeps walking.

Someone lays on the bus horn behind me, and the man finally turns around, startled. He takes a step back at the sight of someone running toward him, but when he sees me, really sees me, his legs give out and he drops to his knees in the snow.

I hit Oliver at a hundred miles an hour, tackling him like a linebacker because my body refuses to slow down. We fly backward onto the shoveled path, skidding and rolling, and I realize I probably just killed my boyfriend. After all that.

I end up on top of him, cradling his head as he clings to me with his arms and legs and gasps into my neck. I can't tell if he's crying or struggling to breathe with the air knocked out of him, but he won't let go of me so I can check. Watery mud smears on his skin and hair and streaks my drenched clothes.

A voice up the hill yells "What the fuck?" and the bus honks again. Ollie grabs my face in his hands, rough, pressing his forehead to mine.

"I'm so sorry, Jackson. I promised I'd find you, but it took me such a long time." He's breathing like he's the one who just sprinted a quarter of a mile in the snow.

I sit up and help him out of the mud, holding him in my lap. "You said you'd never apologize to me."

He pulls back and drinks me in. I know my face looks thinner and more worn. He has a few more lines around his eyes, and his hair's a bit shorter and his beard a little thicker, but otherwise he's the same. He reaches up and tugs off my hat, staring. "You have hair," he murmurs.

"I told you it was a boring color. Dishwater." I close my eyes when he pulls off his gloves and runs his fingers through it. The bus honks a few more times; I hear someone yelling, and then the rumble of engines driving away before they miss the flight. I'm absolutely getting fired for this. It's probably already done.

"It's so thick." He keeps stroking the wiry strands off my forehead. Then he fists my hair in both hands and pulls our foreheads back together, rocking slowly back and forth. "I can't believe it's you." His voice keeps catching. "I've looked so many places."

"How did you get here?" I look around at the trees and the wilderness and bad roads. The nearest airport, the one we were headed to, is an hour away.

He presses his nose under my ear, hugging me tight again. "I've been following your trail for a long time. I tried to find you in California, where you were doing construction. But you left just before I got there. I flew home, then here, and found out where the facility was, rented a car..."

I pry him off of me and stare into his eyes, my hand on his cheek. "You came by yourself? All this way?"

He nods, fighting not to tear up, his narrow jaw firm. There are so many stories in his eyes now, and I hate that I don't know them all. "Jax, I got help. Because I needed to keep my promise and come find you. We moved back with my parents, I got meds, and I've been doing therapy for over a year." He rubs a sleeve across his eyes. "Shit, I'm sorry I made you wait so long. I did my best."

I tip my head back and look at the endless sky, blowing out a slow breath. "Fuck." He did that for me. My mind can't even begin to process it. "I'm so proud of you, Ollie."

I can feel all his muscles relax, and he smiles weakly. "I've waited so long to hear you say that." His thumb brushes my lower lip. "You look as tired as I feel. We're both old now."

"I am. You're still cute as hell." His small grin widens, just like I knew it would, because I was wrong—I didn't forget a single thing about him.

"Close your eyes, Jax."

It's dark.

The curve of his neck still, still smells like tea and houseplants, sweat and tears and want. He kisses me hard, then harder, tongue finding my piercing like he needs one last piece of proof that it's me. My hands come up under his shirt; I can't help it. They need to feel the shape of his body in the dark. He doesn't seem to mind that they're wet or dirty or torn up.

"Why were you going where I couldn't follow you?" he whispers when we break apart.

I open my eyes. "I was getting ready for next time." I force a smile, trying to chase the pain off his face. "I had it figured out. You'd meet a hot guy who made tons of money on oil rigs. He'd take care of you so you could write, and—"

"*No.*" He looks gutted. "I want Jackson, you fucking idiot. He's the one I made a promise to, and I went through so much to keep it. If you took him from me, I'd hate you forever." He grabs the front of my jacket hard. "I kept my promise. Now it's your turn. Tell me you'll never walk away from me again."

I shake my head. "It's okay. I'm free now. I don't have to run anymore."

Ollie growls in his throat, his eyes burning on mine as he grips my jacket tighter. "That's great, Jax, but I don't give a shit right now. Even if the entire world is coming for you, if the literal sky is falling on your head in a ball of fire, you don't walk away." He gestures to the scene around us, the long way he's come. "Have I earned that or not?"

I close my eyes again, let the world shrink to a size I can handle, and rest my face against his chest. "Yeah. Yeah, you did."

Chapter 33

OLIVER

We don't even bother to talk through what happens next. It's inevitable—it always has been, and we just walk straight into it because we're ready. We've been ready for so long.

Jax has to leave me outside the gate while he goes into the front office. I stand there, shifting back and forth with my filthy jacket pulled up around my face, pretending not to notice the security guards glaring daggers at me. I haven't gotten any less terrified of making people mad at me than the day I first kicked Jax over and offered to take him to the hospital. All my therapy exercises are keeping me stable, but I'm getting more and more frayed after the flight and the drive, starting to come apart at the edges, and part of me wants to melt down just because Jackson isn't next to me right this second, because his hand isn't in mine.

He must feel the same way, because he runs out of the gate twenty minutes later and swallows me in one of his best hugs, the ones where his big body engulfs me and lifts my feet off the ground. "I stole a jacket from the lost and found on the way out." He holds it up, looking proud. "Change into this."

"*Jackson*. You can't just–here." I grab the jacket, kiss him, then carry it over to the guards. "Hi. Sorry, this goes in the lost and found. We picked it up by accident." When Jax sulks, I shake my head. "Some poor, shivering guy is looking for his coat right now because of you."

"Yeah, well I don't give a shit about him, and you're cold."

As we head down the hill, I pull my hand out of his and crowd into his side until he puts his arm around me. "Could you drive us? I'm a little...I mean, I–"

He cups the side of my head and presses his lips to my forehead. "You can drive whenever you want, and when you don't feel like it, I'll always be here, okay?"

When we get to my rental car, Jax pulls off both our wet jackets. He pulls down my pants, too, without any warning or hesitation. "Did you bring dry clothes?"

I grip the side of the car, looking frantically around. "Suitcase is in the trunk. You could have asked that before you stripped me."

The freezing air burns my exposed skin as he comes back with a pair of sweats. He makes me stand on my shoes and slide one foot in, then the other. It makes me feel like a kid, but I know this part, taking care of me, is the part his soul has missed. Halfway up, he pauses and stares at my briefs.

I laugh, wiping my nose, which is dripping like a faucet. "Megan found them at some teenage novelty store at the mall."

He brushes his thumb across the pink fabric, dotted with robot unicorns shooting rainbow beams out of their horns. "The fuck?" His dark eyes lift to mine. "Did you seriously pick these hoping they'd be the first underwear of yours I see in two years?"

My grin widens, breaks into a smile I haven't felt since the day he left. "It might have crossed my mind. Now please pull my pants up."

He doesn't. He straightens and pulls me into a soft kiss, licking gently into my mouth while his hand strokes and explores my ass in the stupid underwear.

"I still saved it for you." I tell him when he pulls back.

His brow furrows, but I can see the light in his eyes. "I wouldn't have been mad if you played with it. You didn't know how long it would be."

"I guess it'll be really extra tight, then."

"Jesus." He yanks up the sweats. "I'll need to check on that later."

Suddenly there are tears coming out of my eyes, not crying exactly, just a silent rush. When he notices, he starts wiping them away with his thumb, then pulls me into the warm cave of his hoodie. His fingers find their old place, caressing my hair. "Oh, Ollie."

My fists curl tight into the back of his shirt. "I thought I might never see you again."

"Guess what?" he murmurs.

"What?"

"Fate came back for us, and you said *no*. You did it."

I nuzzle his collarbone, surrounding myself in his smell. "There were a lot of boxes of tissues and medication side effects and meltdowns somewhere in there, too."

It was meant to be a joke, but he groans quietly. "Fuck, Ollie. I don't know what I did to deserve you."

On the hour drive to the airport, I confirm two seats on the next flight to New York. After seeing how he changed my life, my parents went all in on the *search for Jackson* project, including helping pay for flights. A raw, difficult two years together has stripped us all down and built us back up, and I finally got the apologies from them that I needed to hear.

We have until one in the morning to kill time at the airport, so we duck into gift shops until we find warm, clean, dry hoodies. Jackson grabs a black one with a white deer skull on it. The corner of his mouth tips up when I choose a light pink one that says *Big Sky* across the front. They cost a small fortune, but we're both shivering, even after blasting the heat most of the way here, and it's bliss to pull them on. Next we hit the food court, where I eat one fast food burger and Jackson downs seven, like he hasn't eaten since the day he left.

When we're full and warm, we find an empty, secluded hallway behind an internet cafe. Jax drops his backpack on the floor to use as a pillow, and our bodies settle into the position that's come most naturally to us from the very beginning, slotted together with one of Jackson's arms around my chest and the other stretched out under my head. Today he hooks one of his legs around mine too, and kisses my neck and ear until he drifts off, his chilly nose buried in the nape of my neck. I want to stay awake and just savor him there for hours. But I'm too exhausted.

When I wake up, he's sleeping on top of me, all of his limbs tangled around me and fingers wrapped in my hair, like he was trying to climb inside me.

I wriggle out and shake his shoulder. "Jax, we need to catch our flight."

"Don't." He struggles, protesting, and my heart breaks at the fear in his eyes when he opens them. His tense body eases as he reaches out, brushing his fingertips along my sweatshirt. "You never stay after I wake up," he breathes.

"I'm here. I'll be here so long you'll be wishing for any way to get rid of me."

I can feel my body and mind acting up as we get in line to board. That would be an incredible ending—I find my man, but I can't bring him home because I can't get on a plane. Jackson's hand around my shoulders anchors me, rubbing slowly up and down my sleeve. "Have you finished your book yet?"

I snort. "What do you think? It took me seven years to do the first half."

"Tell me where Samvir's at now."

I start reluctantly, distracted and edgy, but it does help. Then it's Jackson's turn to stress out as we board and I remember he's never flown before. The flight isn't too full, so we claim a row for ourselves and he makes me sit next to the window so he doesn't have to see out. As we take off, he props his shoulder on mine, death-gripping my hand, and has me describe everything I see on the ground below.

Once we're underway, I take out my knitting. He studies the purple and black beanie, which is going to have the mother of all pompoms on the top. "Megs' old hat is falling apart," I explain, so focused on my work that I almost don't notice his body go still. "What?" I push my glasses up and frown at him.

"Is she gonna be at the airport?"

"Yeah," I say slowly. "She and my parents are picking us up."

"Did you tell her that you found me?"

"Yes..."

He shifts uneasily. "What did she say? Does she even remember me?"

"Of course she does. We talk about you all the time."

He swallows. "She can't still want me to be her dad. I don't want to fuck up her life by barging in."

"Look at me, love." I smooth a hand through his hair, loving that I can do that now, loving the way the messy thatch of wiry, light brown hair softens his face. His gaze searches out mine. "Let her decide what she wants. She loved you, and she missed you, and she's old enough that she doesn't just forget someone and move on when they're not there."

"Fuck..." He rubs his eyes. "What if she doesn't want that?"

"Then you can be my partner and her friend. It doesn't change what we have, okay?"

He blows out a slow breath, his eyes roaming the cabin like he wants to break out and run. "Teach me how to knit."

"Really?" Figuring out how to shove the armrest between our seats up, he pushes me against the wall and lies back against my chest, making me reach around him. Swapping Megan's hat for my spare needles and yarn, I start a row and pass them over. His hands are so dexterous when he's fixing things, riding his bike, or playing with my body, but he keeps fumbling the needles, slipping the yarn off the end and mumbling profanities. "Now do you respect my art?" I tease. "It's harder than it looks."

I watch his hands as he tries again. He was wearing gloves the other day, but now I can see them clearly and they make my chest ache. They're torn to pieces by hard work, battered with swollen knuckles. There's some kind of burn scar on one palm, and two of his fingers look like they were fed through a rock crusher. I remember how they felt in the cave, rough but healthy and whole, and everything he's gone through since then. I don't yet know what he had to do to get free from his old life, but I know it wasn't easy.

"This is a fucking nightmare." He studies the half row of sloppy stitches he produced, then drops it on his chest and closes his eyes. I return to the hat while he dozes in and out. When the stewardess brings him a tiny cup of Coke instead of the can, he shoots me such a betrayed look I double up laughing.

"Six hundred fucking dollars and you can't even get a can of Coke?" I let him drink mine, too, then stroke his hair until he falls asleep for real. As I stare at his face, I try to imagine forgetting it, then meeting it again in some other place and time. I know his eyes would catch me first, just like they did when he walked into the bank in Byrock. Next would be his smile. I'd be a goner.

I rest my hand on his chest. It doesn't matter, because he's mine. Fate took him, and I took him back. I'll never let it happen again.

Jackson

Neither of us says anything as we walk through the Syracuse airport hand in hand, like we're a regular couple getting back from vacation. Only Oliver can feel me shaking.

They have these weird glass doors that block you from coming back into the airport. Part of me never wants to cross them and find out what's on the other side. But Ollie hops right through, little bastard, knowing I'll have to follow. I stop for a second, disoriented at all the people standing around with signs, pointing and cheering as their friends and families come out. We get pushed out of the way by a big group of shrieking, hugging people. Everything's chaotic and unfamiliar, and I feel like I'm about to break Oliver's hand.

He says my name louder, probably for the third time, and I follow his pointing hand to an older man and woman. If you mashed them together, they'd look kind of like him. For a second, I assume the girl next to them belongs to someone else. Then she turns around and I see Oliver's eyes looking back at me.

This girl has braces, with no gap between her front teeth. Her braid lies sleek on her shoulder, and she has on some eyeshadow and lip gloss. Her face has rounded out, she's at least three inches taller, and her body isn't a scrawny little stick anymore. A pained sound breaks in my chest. My little girl is gone, and I didn't get to watch her leave.

Oliver touches my arm, starts to whisper something, but Megan breaks into a run and throws her arms around me. "Jax, it's me. You remember me, right?" The familiarity of her mischievous voice calms me down, even though she lisps a little with the braces. She tips her face up to mine, her eyes anxious and hopeful. "I have so many things to show you. I got a boa, and her name is Medusa, and I got a new guitar and I can tune it by myself and play ten songs, and...I missed you, Jax. Did you miss me?" When she squeezes me and rests her forehead on my chest, I finally get my arms to close around her, to feel for myself that she's real.

"Yeah." I finger her smooth braid. I'm going to have to work on my skills. "I missed you, wild girl." Her cheeks dimple as she grins at me.

"Come meet Grandma and Grandpa."

I'm so overwhelmed that I just kind of hold out my hand and let them shake it. I didn't put on new deodorant or even check my hair since we woke up on an airport floor. I can't remember when I last shaved. On their previous visit, I was bleeding all over their son and his floor. I can see caution in their eyes, but they smile politely and say something welcoming. I guess watching your son overhaul his entire life just to find one person might make you take him seriously. I want to thank them for taking care of my Oliver, but that seems like a pretty weird thing to say to his parents, so I keep my mouth shut.

They keep asking us, as we drive home in the early dusk, if we want to stop for food, what food, if we want to go anywhere or do anything. My knee is bouncing hard enough to shake the seat, and I keep wiping sweat off my palm on my jeans before taking Oliver's hand again. One minute I'm about to go to a place where it's dark for two months straight, and now I'm in a car with noisy rich people who are basically my parents, even though I barely know their names.

Eventually, Ollie leans forward in his seat and whispers something to them, and they pipe down a little. We pull up to a huge house in a neighborhood of luxury homes and nice cars and perfect lawns. Oliver's father carries our stuff inside and disappears with it, leaving me to stare anxiously after him as I stand in the entry in my dirty clothes.

Oliver takes my arm. "Come on. We have a little apartment downstairs where we're living for now." I'm relieved I don't have to go into the part of the place where the ceilings are forty feet up like a fucking cathedral. He kicks off his shoes and leads me down a carpeted staircase to a door. His dad left the bags outside the door, all polite, like the space really is a separate house that doesn't belong to him. As soon as Ollie pushes it open, I hear a noise so familiar that it makes my whole body relax, a home-noise–the humming of heat lamps. The living room down here is smaller than the palace upstairs, but bigger than their living room in Iowa. Which is good, because they have the mother of all snake tanks down here. It makes Mars' habitat look like a shoebox. Maybe this is why Mr. Shaw doesn't come past the door.

"Look, did you see?" Megan pops out of a door that must be her room and grabs my hand, pulling me over to the tank. A huge snake, probably six feet long, with brown and dark red markings watches us, draped lazily across the carefully placed rocks and plants in its habitat. "Isn't she gorgeous?"

I can't help a snicker as I look over my shoulder at Oliver. "It's bigger than your dad."

"Don't remind me," he groans.

"You can hold Medusa tomorrow if you want," this little girl says casually, like she's offering for me to play with a kitten. "Dad said I'm in trouble if I take her out tonight."

"Let me see Mars. I missed my buddy. Is he okay?"

He still has a picture taped up behind his tank, and I realize it's the dashboard of the sports car that I hung up two years ago. There are little bits of tape stuck everywhere, like it fell down and got taped back up a million times. Mars is sunning himself with no interest in me at all. "He's gotten chubby."

"Has *not*!" Megan squeaks, but she keeps shooting anxious looks at him until she sees that I'm smiling. "Asshole."

"Oh, are you allowed to cuss now?"

"Yep!" she chirps at the same time Oliver says "No" from across the room where he's unpacking his bag.

I turn around and lean against the wall in this strange place I've never been before, my hands folded behind my back. I don't know where I'm supposed to be or what I'm supposed to do.

When Oliver notices me, he puts down the stack of jeans in his hands and comes over. "You okay, love?" He needs to stop calling me that, or my heart's going to give out. I shrug. He gestures toward the bedroom. "Are you tired? Do you want to go to bed?"

I shake my head and press myself more firmly against the wall. "I want everyone to stay in the same room." My eyes find his, willing him to understand. He smiles softly. "Hey, Megs? Why don't you put on a movie— something nice, please? No dismemberment?"

The couch in here is one of those massive things with a bed-looking part sticking off one end. Ten people could use it without touching each other. But that's not what we do.

I only have a couple of pieces of clothing in my bag—I was going to live in company gear when I got to Alaska. So I stay in my Montana hoodie and change into a pair of Ollie's biggest sweats. I wedge myself into the corner of the couch and watch Oliver come out of his room with a pillow under one arm and a blanket over the other, in a t-shirt and soft sleep shorts. It confuses my brain that he's bought clothes since I left that I don't recognize, and I run my hand over the shorts when he sits down, getting used to them.

He snuggles right down against my chest, throwing a leg over mine, and Megan sits on the other side of me. For a while she stays upright, like she's not quite sure what to do, but as the movie goes on I notice her scooting closer and closer. When I lift my arm and put it around her on the back of the couch, she immediately slides down and rests her head on my shoulder.

I don't want the movie to end, even though I'm not really watching it, but eventually it does. The room goes dark, but no one moves. Megan's actually asleep, and Oliver's just pretending, drawing slow shapes with his fingers across my body under my hoodie. Their weight pins me down, firm and safe and no longer the stuff of dreams, making sure that nothing can move me again.

Chapter 34

Six Months Later

OLIVER

Planting my knee on the bed, I launch myself across the mattress and land astride Jax's pert ass, sticking up under the sheets. "Happy birthday, happy birthday, happy birthday," I sing tunelessly, bouncing my hands on his black-inked back and rubbing my bulge against his crack, hoping the latter will make him forgive me for the former.

"Just leave me here to die," he mumbles face-first into his pillow. "Any minute now."

"Oh come on, it's not that bad." Balancing myself with my hands on his hips, I continue absently rubbing myself off on him. "Forty is the new twenty."

He rolls his head sideways and swats at me. "What would a thirty-nine-year-old know about it? You're practically a baby; you have no idea."

When I hear real hurt in his voice, I roll off and land next to him. "What's wrong, love?" I brush my fingers along his bicep until he looks at me again.

"Why couldn't we have met when we were twenty? I've missed twenty years with you, Ollie. And now I'm fucking geriatric." He plants his face in his pillow again, his messy hair sticking in every direction.

"If we'd met when we were twenty, we wouldn't have Megan." Pushing the sheet down, I rub his back slowly. "And neither of us would be who we are. The 'us' we have now wouldn't exist. Besides, we have so many years left. We can go so many places, and you can get us all the senior discounts." I break into embarrassing, squealing laughs as he rolls on top of me and I try to kick him off. "Wait, wait, I have a present for you."

"Is it ten inches long and attached to your body?" he growls into my neck, sneaking his hand down my shorts.

"No, no, help, fuck." I thrash around, laughing too hard to speak.

"Then I don't want it. We have to take advantage of this time before I'm too old to perform anymore."

"I'm serious," I gasp, twitching uselessly. "It's a serious present." Finally, he pulls his hand away and collapses next to me, peering at me past the fold of his elbow with one intent, dark eye. Stretching out, I grab a business card off my bedside table and hand it to him.

He frowns at it, tilting his head. "Does Marcel Leighman know he's my birthday present?"

"Read the top."

Rolling over, he pushes my shirt up under my armpits and kisses me deliberately all over as he reads the card. "First Chance House?"

"Jonah told me about it. He got asked to speak there, about his disability."

"What is it?"

I play with his hair. He's let it get completely out of control over the last six months, a cheekbone-length mop of thick, dark-blond hair that somehow manages to look sexy no matter what he's doing. "It's a center for at-risk youth that does mentorship, life skills classes, and some crisis intervention."

"Oh." He rests his chin on my ribs and frowns at the card like he's going to find all the answers written there. "But–"

"I went and had lunch with Marcel the other day. He said every single employee and volunteer at this place has some kind of record. They do it that way on purpose, so the kids feel understood."

His eyes flick up to mine. "Really?"

"He wants to meet you. I told him you were good with your hands, and he said they had some classes you could help with."

"Damn." He runs his fingers over the embossing on the card. "Thank you, Ollie." Then he buries his face in my stomach and squeezes my hand twice, which means *thank you* again.

The bedroom door flies back and hits the wall, making me very glad I didn't give Jackson the present he asked for. "Happy birthday to youuu," Megan sings obnoxiously loud, parading into the room with her guitar.

"Jesus Christ." Jackson rolls on his back and wraps his arms around his head as she continues the song, strumming violently at the end of every line.

"Happy birthday, super ancient old maaan." She plops on the end of the bed and yodels out the last line. "Happy birthday to youuuu."

As I join in the final few notes, I study his shirtless body stretched out across the mattress, all the tattoos and old scars, joined by a thick, raised dark one across his abs and the thinner, ragged white one up the inside of his arm from the train window glass. I can't see the other scars, but I know where they are. Everything he's survived.

He lowers his arm far enough to look at her with one eye. "Sloppy as hell. What was that fingering supposed to be?" Her adoring grin gets wider. He's been giving her guitar lessons ever since he came back, and when they're not doing lessons, they jam together almost every night while I knit or work on my book.

After Jax had been back for a month, I went to my parents and told them I wanted to move back to Iowa. Megan and I missed our friends, and we love the pace of life in Byrock. I wanted to be back in time for Tristan and Alice's wedding. I promised that before we packed a single box, I'd line up a therapist and a doctor for medication management so that I didn't lose all my progress. To my surprise, my parents asked if they could move with us—not *with* us, I think Jax would have killed them—but to a town about thirty minutes away.

To my even greater surprise, my parents sat me down on a long, teary afternoon and apologized for Kay. It took them eight years and me breaking down for them to realize the damage that had been done. And they asked—begged—that I would allow them to help with our living expenses for one full year while I finish my book and give my deferred dream a try. I still fill in part-time at the bank, because I missed it that much, and Jax works at a hardware store. But I spend hours each day on my writing, and every weekend we go somewhere new, driving north to Minnesota or west to Wisconsin, south to Oklahoma, or west to Wyoming. I get to watch my partner and my daughter wander around all the sights, gaping at the things they've never seen or tried before. On the way home, they make me read my book out loud while Jax drives, in the minivan I always wanted.

"Dad, get up. We have a present for you." Megan shakes Jax's leg.

"I don't think I want any more of your presents," he grumbles.

"Pretty sure you want this one," I butt in, and he rolls his eyes over to glare at me suspiciously. He doesn't say *not unless it's ten inches long* in front of our kid, but his face does.

"Come on, Daddy." Grabbing my bathrobe off the door and handing it to me, Megan drags me to the kitchen. The birthday decorations we hung up last night after Jax fell asleep are still standing, including the ones adorning the reptile tanks—most of the streamers and balloons are orange and gold, but we threw in a few black ones because we just can't help ourselves.

Smelling the coffee I pour myself, Jax staggers out a few minutes later in a faded t-shirt and ripped shorts, his hair mashed under a backward ball cap. "It's my birthday," he points out in his throaty morning voice when I side-eye his outfit.

"Come ooon." Megan's imploding with badly suppressed excitement; she would be dancing by the front door if she didn't have Mars on her shoulder.

Jax follows us onto the front porch of our little bungalow, then stops dead, staring at the driveway. "Shit," he says quietly.

Heading down the steps in bare feet, he circles the motorcycle–or skeleton of a motorcycle–sitting next to the van. It's an Indian model, like the one he had to sell, but nowhere near as beautiful. The parts that aren't missing completely are in questionable shape. "You guys..." His brown eyes flash light in the sun as he rests his hand on the flaking saddle and looks up at us.

"Daddy wanted me to say that it's a special project for you and me to fix up together so I can learn about bikes, not that we couldn't afford a nice one," Megan offers helpfully.

His faint smile widens as he squints over at me. "Is that so?"

"You're fired, Skip."

I can tell Megan's itching to run across the lawn to Jackson, so I take Mars and carry him back inside. Instead of slithering into one of his hides, he pauses after I put him down, like he's looking at me. "What do you think, buddy?" I prop my arms on the edge of the tank and rest my head on them. "I think we finally made it." He just flicks his tongue impassively.

Pouring another coffee, I cross to the window and watch the bulky, tattooed man and the spindly girl examine their new bike. He hooks an arm over her shoulder and leans his head close to hers, pointing to different pieces and explaining what they'll do. When Jackson glances up and sees me, he smiles crookedly at me over her head, still talking her through whatever repair they're planning. The hand on her shoulder lifts up and he extends his thumb, index finger, and little finger, the rest folded over. *I love you.*

And that's how I fell in love and lost it again. How my heart never stopped searching. They say a story is only as good as its ending. Some heroes look death in the face for one chance at love. Others stand up to fate and win. But I like the ones no one bothers to write down, where the hero flaunts the demands of fate and says *fuck it.* He just goes home, opens his front door, and walks into the arms of the ones he loves. Because in the end, that's all he was ever fighting for.

Thank you so much for reading *Show Me Wonders*! If you loved Ollie and Jax, please consider leaving a review!
If you'd like to explore Jonah and Gray's story, pick up *Make Me Fall* and the sequel novella, *And All Their Stars*!
For release date announcements, follow @rileynashbooks on Instagram, join Riley Nash's Underdogs on Facebook, or subscribe to my newsletter at www.rileynashbooks.com

To read a **free short story** about the whole gang—Ethan, Victor, Gray, Jonah, Jackson, and Oliver—getting together for Christmas, subscribe to my newsletter at www.rileynashbooks.com or join Riley Nash's Underdogs on Facebook!

Water, Air, Earth, Fire Series

Hold Me Under – Victor and Ethan

Make Me Fall – Gray and Jonah

And All Their Stars – Gray and Jonah novella

Show Me Wonders – Oliver and Jackson

Standalones

Christmas Special

About the Author

Riley Nash, based in the rainy PNW, writes emotional M/M romances about boys who fall hard, face the darkness, and never give up on each other.

Fueled by cute dogs, those weird Coke With Coffee drinks, and projecting my personal issues onto handsome men and making them fall in love.

Visit www.rileynashbooks.com to subscribe to their newsletter, join Riley Nash's Underdogs on Facebook, or follow @rileynashbooks on Instagram.

Made in the USA
Middletown, DE
24 December 2022